Bray d

MW00916404

REZ BALL

REZ

BALL

BYRON GRAVES

Heartdrum
An Imprint of HarperCollinsPublishers

Heartdrum is an imprint of HarperCollins Publishers.

Rez Ball

www.epicreads.com

Library of Congress Control Number: 2023932495

ISBN 978-0-06-316037-8

Typography by Kathy H. Lam

24 25 26 27 28 LBC 9 8 7 6 5

First Edition

In loving memory of my father—
"Shoot it like you're at home."

CHAPTER 1

MARCH 10

REZ BALL—IT'S BEAUTIFUL chaos. Sometimes it feels like that's what *we* are: beautiful, chaos. And right now, it's all we've got. We were getting our asses kicked all game; then in desperation, we started playing wild, run-and-gun, flashy basketball, like we do back home on the Red Lake Nation. Only minutes ago, this game looked like it was over. Like we were toast.

Now?

Now the walls and floor of the Bemidji State basketball gym are shaking like a small earthquake just rumbled across northern Minnesota.

I glance up at the scoreboard and take a much-needed deep breath.

Two minutes remain in the regional championship game.

1

We've never made it this far before. If our team wins, we go to the state tournament, which our school has never done, ever. If we lose, well, we go home, like usual.

This is, legit, the biggest basketball game in the history of our school.

The buzzer sounds, signaling the end of a time-out. I wipe a little bit of sweat from my brow, cup my hands together, and shout to the rafters. I take a sip of my bottled water. I've got cotton mouth real bad from how much I've been yelling.

My best friends, Wes and Nate, are in shock, a mix of disbelief and straight-up joy. We exchange high fives.

"Tre, can you imagine if Jaxon was out there? They'd be doing even better than they are right now," Dad says with pure certainty. Mom runs her hand along his shoulder, nodding at Dad in agreement.

For a second there I thought Dad was going to say something about me being out there, hooping, helping this team. Me and Nate play basketball, too, but we're only freshmen and play on the JV team. It's not nearly as dope as playing on varsity. We don't hear loud cheers when we make a basket. No one arrives early to our games to see us. They come to get a good seat, buy popcorn and candy, and settle in for the *real* game after ours.

My dad nudges me with his elbow. We smile at each other, but they're broken smiles, the kind that look happy and sad at the same time. It is too damn loud to say anything, but our eyes say enough. My mom reaches across my dad. She takes my hand and squeezes it. The mixed emotions are intense.

Jaxon should be here. This was his team, his friends, his fans. It's been a surreal, strange, awful nightmare these last couple of months without him. Not just for me and my parents, but for our entire community. He was like a superhero on our rez.

My parents are wearing matching shirts with images of him soaring in for a dunk, with the caption *Gone but never forgotten*. Hell, half of our crowd is wearing the same shirts. As I look around, I spot my uncles, teachers from our school, the super-sweet lady who works at the post office. Even our tribal chairman is rocking the same memorial shirt.

The referee blows his whistle and hands the ball to Kevin, our center. He towers over almost everyone else on the court. He looks frantic waiting for his teammates as they fight to get open. Our point guard, Mason, the scariest dude at our school, shakes his defender and catches the pass at half-court, then races to the basket. A cloud of defenders surrounds him. He comes spinning out of the group and banks in a layup.

The crowd erupts—cheering, whistling, holding cell phones in the air.

I look at Wes's phone screen. He's recording our players as they throw their arms into the air like boisterous preachers, summoning the crowd support.

The Bemidji High School players cup their hands to their ears, hoping it's going to help them hear better. Their coach is yelling, but the players are shaking their heads in confusion. The inbounding player panics and throws a long pass that flies out of bounds.

3

My dad grabs me by the shoulders and shakes me like a rag doll. This is by far the happiest he has been since we lost Jaxon. It warms my heart seeing him feel this good again. Seeing him happy, his pain forgotten, even for a little while.

While we're still celebrating, one of our guards is already pulling up from way beyond the three-point line with two defenders draped all over him.

The sound disappears from the arena, like pressing mute on the TV.

The basketball, flung with a perfect release, spins toward the basket.

Swish!

We're only down six points, 96–90, with one minute to go in the game.

On our side of the gym, our fans are all wearing red-and-black shirts and jumping up and down, high-fiving, whistling, and screaming. The Bemidji team's inbounding player calls to his team, but our crowd overpowers his voice.

"Come on, guys. Win this one for Jaxon," I say through clenched teeth.

Nate hears me and pats me on the back.

Bemidji's inbounding player throws a high, desperate pass across the court, but it flies out of bounds. A referee signals that it's our ball.

Me and my boys exchange overly excited high fives that leave a sting.

Someone behind me war-whoops. The singers from our local drum group pound on their hand drums.

Bemidji's players look to our side of the gym. They shake their heads. One of them looks pissed, his face scrunched in disgust.

But our crowd eats it up.

A bunch of our fans in the front row give the middle finger to the Bemidji student section across the court. They're wearing fake war bonnets that they probably got off of Amazon or some shit. They decorated their faces like they're wearing war paint, but in their school colors of blue and white.

"Where's that tomahawk chop at now?" Nate asks through cupped hands. A bunch of people from our rez look back at him and laugh. Bemidji was doing that shit all game, throwing it in our faces until we made our comeback.

Some of the older white fans have their hands clasped in nervous prayer as they stare up at the scoreboard.

"Jesus was Black," Nate says, and again cracks up everyone around us. And the fact that he's a Black Ojibwe is by no means a coincidence.

Mike, one of our forwards, catches an inbound pass from Mason, and in one smooth motion, he sets his feet to shoot a three from the wing as the outstretched arms of two defenders fly at him.

Swish.

Nothing. But. Net.

96–93.

Bemidji's players spread out across the court, passing the ball to each other. They're not trying to score. Or make a mistake. They are trying to run the time out until the game ends. Desperate to stop the clock, Mason fouls one of the Bemidji players on purpose. He knocks down his first free throw. 97–93. We are down by four with twenty seconds to go.

Warriors players gesture to the crowd to amp it up.

We stomp our feet into the stands, scream at the sky. Right as the Bemidji player is releasing his second shot, I yell out, "Miss it!"

He barely draws iron on his free throw. It misses, dropping down from the front of the rim fast and hard, like an icicle from a roof on the first day of spring. Mason blazes down the court and, without the slightest hesitation, launches a three from NBA range; it sinks right through the net. Bemidji calls their last time-out with seven seconds left on the clock and the score at 97–96.

I glance over at Nate and Wes. They're both shaking their heads in utter disbelief.

Our school has never beaten Bemidji before. Ever. I think until right now we all assumed it was impossible. But we are down by one point.

Bemidji inbounds the ball to their point guard, who races away from everyone else and gets over half-court. The clock is ticking down. Five seconds. Four seconds. Three seconds.

Mason fouls him to stop him from running out the clock, forcing him to the free-throw line. Mason is jawing at him. The Bemidji player shakes his head, then turns his attention back to the ball in his hand. Mason is like a rap diss track come to life in a basketball jersey. He's forever fearless and walks with an *I don't give a fuck* swagger. Even under these bright lights, he's still a G hooping at the park.

Their point guard takes his sweet time at the free-throw line. Mason's hands push into his knees from exhaustion, but he's still talking. The crowd is too loud for any of us to hear what he's saying, though. It's a one-and-one free throw, meaning if he misses the first, it becomes a live ball. Mason winks at their point guard as he sets himself into his shooting position. The shot goes up, rattles around the rim, sneaks down toward the net, and then bounces back out.

Mason grabs the rebound and jets down the court. Only seconds remain. We are down by one point, and almost every Bemidji player swarms at Mason like a cloud of wasps, but somehow, he weaves his way out of them unscathed and heaves a shot from beyond half-court.

The crowd goes as silent as a graveyard.

The shot is a prayer—an impossible miracle.

But tonight, miracles have been happening.

The buzzer cuts into the silence as we all watch the ball float toward the basket. Players from both teams stare helplessly.

It ricochets hard off the rim.

We. Were. So. Close.

My eyes get teary, and my chest feels like a trash compactor closing in on itself.

Everyone from our rez is quiet now. The gym is filled with the cheering and whistling of the Bemidji fans. But not a single Red Lake fan has walked away yet. We are all still staring at the court, like the game isn't over. Like it can't be over. Or like we're all collectively in a state of shock.

Then our team motions to the crowd, waving like orchestra conductors. And suddenly it sounds like we *won* the game, and our crowd cheers one last time, as loud as we did for every flashy play.

As we leave our seats and make our way to the exit, I stop walking, dead in my tracks. Jaxon. I take a deep breath.

Jaxon hated riding the bus home after games. He'd always complain that the bus was cold, and that the bumps along the country dirt roads were painful, so he'd get his coach's permission to ride home with us.

My parents and I would sit in the stands as the gym emptied out, finishing what remained of our bags of popcorn. We'd debate which of Jaxon's plays was our favorite as we waited for him to come out of the locker room with that big, cheesy smile of his. Always asking if we saw that one play, or that one dunk, like we'd somehow missed it.

But he's not here. We don't need to wait.

And the thought feels like another gut punch, the same kind I feel every time I remember he's gone. And it breaks me into pieces for the millionth time. Wes puts his hand on my shoulder like he knows exactly what I'm thinking. He gives the same *I'm here for you* nod that he always gives me when I freeze up.

We walk carefully across the icy parking lot to our rusted-out minivan. Even in the dark parking lot, it's easy to spot—the white garbage bag and duct tape covering the passenger-side window kind of stands out.

"Nobody lost that one," Dad says as he puts his jacket on and fishes a cigarette out of his inner coat pocket. "Jaxon would have been proud of his teammates. . . . He would have been so proud."

CHAPTER 2

JULY 11

SUMMER IS MY favorite time of year. No school. No blizzards. Just lots of sunlight and free time to hang with friends and work on my game. The sun is bright, and the air feels like a sauna. But I love it. A gym will never be as hot as an outdoor basketball court in the summer. If I can get conditioned in this setting, I'll be in shape for anything. I dribble the ball and imagine a packed gymnasium of fans, and the state championship on the line. Out of the corner of my eye I see Wes rolling up on his bike. I show off by throwing a crossover followed by a sharp dribble behind my back.

"Seven seconds left on the clock . . . Red Lake down by one point, state championship on the line," Wes says as he leans his bike against the fence of the basketball court. It's right across from the

10

cemetery where my brother is buried. It looks like it's been freshly mowed and the old flowers have been cleaned out. Makes me feel a little better that it looks nice over there. It's about a mile down the road from where I live—the one and only paved road that connects our entire reservation from end to end. Not passing by the cemetery is basically impossible. I wish it wasn't across from the basketball court where I hoop on the regular. Sometimes I use that as motivation when I'm too tired. It pushes me to work a little more in honor of Jaxon. And other days I try not to think about it at all.

I take a hard dribble to what I like to call my sweet spot, the elbow of the free-throw line. I never miss it from here. Well, pretty much never. But damn, if it's a point game and I can't get to the basket, this is where I love to shoot from. I've ended a lot of pickup games with a final shot from right here.

Wes says, "Three, two . . ."

I square my shoulders up with the basket and rise for the shot. "One!"

I know it's good as soon as it leaves my hands.

Swish.

"Oh my God! The crowd goes wild. Tre Brun wins Red Lake its first-ever state championship!" Wes says in his best announcer impersonation. "Indian Country is going ballistic." He's holding his iPhone up, recording me. He wants to be a filmmaker and has decided I'm going to be the subject of his first documentary. A Native hooper, trying to make it to the NBA, no matter the odds stacked against him. He promises it won't be poverty porn. I trust him. He's been my best friend since we were in kindergarten.

Even though we're only pretending, and it's muggy as hell out, I still feel chills run down my arms. Also, it's weird having someone record your workouts.

Wes steps out wearing a black cheetah print short-sleeved shirt with a red flannel wrapped around his waist and distressed skinny jeans. He has vampire-red eyes this morning, either from staying up until sunrise playing video games or from just smoking a bowl or both. His mop of sandy-blond hair falls to his shoulders. Wes's mom is white, and glancing at him, you'd think he inherited more of her genes. At our school, his part-rock-star, part-skateboarder white-boy look makes him a space alien. The rest of us wear baggy Nike or Adidas gear, with loose jeans. It's pretty much our unofficial school uniform. And he's the only one who doesn't have black hair or brown eyes.

Wes digs out a couple of bottles of Gatorade from his backpack and hands me one. "You still cool with this?" He gestures to his phone. "You don't think it's weird or going to get annoying over the next three years?"

"Nah, bro, it's cool," I say between breathless gulps. "But I'll feel bad if I don't end up going anywhere and you waste your time shooting a ton of footage for nothing. Hell, who knows, I might not even make varsity."

"Dude, don't worry about me. No matter what, I'm getting a chance to shoot and edit. And stop being stupid. Of course you're going to make varsity this year."

"I hope so," I say, twisting the cap back onto my Gatorade.

"I spent the night watching that classic Allen Iverson documentary over and over, taking notes. Got a ton of ideas. I'm thinking we should do a couple of interviews before the season starts; I've got questions already written. You cool with that?"

I nod.

"Sweet. Let's get footage of you getting shots up. I'll rebound for you. Go around the world," Wes says, meaning for me to shoot from the corner, the wing, the top of the key, until I make my way around the entire three-point line.

Wes likes basketball. He plays for fun and for exercise. He's nowhere near as obsessed as I am about it, plus he's always been super supportive of my hoop dreams. I hit my first five from the corner and jog to the wing. Wes passes me the rock with one hand, holding his cam in the other. "Okay, Steph Curry."

As I'm shooting jumpers, Dallas pulls up to the park in his beat-up old Grand Prix. A cloud of dust rises from the dirt road. Dallas is one of the starters on the varsity team and the only player on the team who has ever acknowledged my existence.

"Aye, what's up, niij?" Dallas shows me his palm, which is like basketball sign language for asking for the ball. His long hair is tied into braids, and he's rocking a white tank top and black basketball shorts that have an eagle feather design running down the side. "What's the deal with the recording?" Dallas asks, launching a jumper that swishes through the net.

"We're shooting a—"

"Just messing around. It's nothing," I say, interrupting Wes. I'm too embarrassed for any of the varsity players to find out (a) my best friend thinks I'm going to the NBA and (b) we're shooting my origin story documentary. I'm still nobody. They'd clown the fuck out of me. Dallas's eyebrows rise like he doesn't quite believe us, then he swishes a smooth jump shot.

Wes passes the ball back to Dallas. He takes a couple of dribbles and hits another jumper.

"Best sound in the world right there," Dallas says.

Wes passes the ball to me this time.

"Joining us on varsity this year, bro?" Dallas asks, wiping sweat from his brow.

"I hope so," I say, and take a shot, nervous to brick it now that Dallas is here. I'm as good as the starters on the team but don't want to sound cocky. No one on our rez likes people who brag. Even if you're the dopest at something, people will only like you around here if you're humble about it.

The ball bounces over to me and I pass it to Dallas.

Dallas asks, "Dang, bro, how tall are you now?"

"Six foot four."

"Same height as your brother," he replies. "Same skinny, lanky arms. You know you shoot just like him? Same form and everything. If it wasn't for your shaggy hair hanging in your eyes, I'd think it was him out here."

This weird mixture of happiness and pain percolates in my stomach.

Dallas adds, "You know, back in the day I was the shortest one in my grade. Always got picked last in gym class. I sucked at basketball. So bad. Always getting my shots swatted. People loved clowning on me. Then one day when I was feeling sorry for myself after getting my butt kicked, your brother asked me if I wanted a couple of tips." Dallas stops talking and examines the basketball in his hand. He spins it and looks hypnotized for a moment, then swallows and clears his throat. "For the next month Jaxon didn't play pickup basketball with our classmates. He showed me how to head fake and how to do a crossover, and showed me dribbling drills. He said I might be small, but I could still be great, and that I just needed to adapt my game for being a shorter player. After that, I started balling on people. Jaxon always made sure to hype me up when I made a good play." The look on Dallas's face is happy and sad at the same time as he stares across the road at the cemetery.

"I didn't know that. That's pretty cool. He was a good guy," I say, and it seems to bring Dallas back.

"He was. For sure. One of the best. . . . But hey, work hard this summer. We could use you this year. I see how hard you've been working. Your game has come a long way." Dallas dribbles to the hoop and makes a reverse layup. "Fuck, it's hot out. I'm going to head home. If you guys want, you're welcome to come over later. We're having a little party tonight. Come through."

I give him a fist bump and nod, then slightly squint my eyes, trying my best to play it cool like I go to parties all the time.

CHAPTER 3

JULY 11

THE BASS OF a hip-hop song blares as we walk up to the party. Cars stretch from Dallas's parents' house all the way down the dirt road, reaching out to the highway. Their house looks like a lot of the homes on my rez—vinyl siding, faded paint job, a floppy front door hanging by the hinges, and a boarded-up window.

I say to Wes, "I don't know, man. Maybe we should walk back to your place." I've never been to a party before, and I worry that I shouldn't drink at all until I'm a lot older, if ever.

"You know they party like this over here all the time and nothing ever happens, right?" Wes says. "You've seen the pics they post."

"Yeah, but that would be my luck. The one party I go to would be the one that would get busted."

"Let's just pop in for a minute, see what all the hype is about."

"Why do you want to party here so bad?"

"You're the one who got invited. Look, we're going to be sopho-mores when school starts. It's time for us to start doing high school shit."

"For what, though?" I want to know.

"For what? For the experience. For the stories. For the—"

"Okay. Okay. But let's not stay too long."

A group of juniors and seniors from school are piled onto a couch playing a football video game and passing around a blunt. The girls' basketball team is standing in a circle, with red Solo cups in their hands. Decked out in their red-and-black Lady Warriors basketball tracksuits like they've got a game in a few minutes.

Along the living room walls are framed pictures of Dallas and a bunch of Warriors team photos and trophy celebrations. One of Jaxon holding the district championship trophy in the air—his teammates' arms wrapped around him—stares out at me from the middle.

Wes taps my arm, bringing me back to the present. He points through the cloud of weed smoke and nods at Dallas, who's in the kitchen.

"What's up, niij?" Dallas asks over the music.

"Nada," I say, and my body unclenches now that I'm with the person who invited me over. Like I have my ticket to be here.

"Never seen you out at a party before, bro. Didn't even know you drank," says Mike, one of the starting forwards on the team,

17

exaggerating the accent of our rez, holding on to the vowels extra long and mashing words together. He and Mason are brothers. They have the same mom but different dads. Mason's dad is known around our rez for being the guy who brings the drugs in. He's been in and out of prison a few times. And Mike's dad is a cop on our rez. Go figure.

"I do. Just not all the time," I lie.

"Want a drink?" He points toward the kitchen with his lips and a nod. He's wearing a backward Minnesota Twins baseball cap, a baggy Nike hoodie, and loose-fitting jeans.

I nod, like I've been dying for one.

Dallas grabs a plastic McDonald's cup off the counter, tosses in ice, and fills vodka almost to the brim, followed by a splash of Sprite. "Here you go, niij."

One sip and I almost die coughing it up.

Mike laughs and slaps my shoulder. "Rookie." But he says it with a smile.

I pass the drink to Wes.

A Tupac song comes on. Mike says, "Really the old-school jam, eh? Red Lakers still be bumping Tupac like it just came out."

I feel a slap on my back so hard that it stings.

"Out on bail, fresh out of jail, reservation dreaming, soon as I step on the court, I'm hearing all the chicks screaming." Mason is doing a pretty spot-on Tupac impersonation with a remix to the lyrics. He's wearing a baggy white T-shirt, loose-fitting blue jeans, and a fresh pair of Kobes. Specks of hair cover his usually clean-shaven bald head.

"Thought this was a varsity-only party?" Mason asks Dallas.

I dig my phone out of my pocket and scroll through social media, trying to act like I didn't hear him. My phone is my security blanket in any social setting. If I feel awkward, I start scrolling and hope everyone around me forgets about my existence.

"We've got to show him how us varsity players drink," Dallas says, throwing a soft punch into my shoulder. "I mean, you know dude is going to play varsity this year."

Mason says, "Shit, we been the same squad since we started hooping together in sixth grade. Only one we're missing is Jaxon." He looks at me. "And I'm sorry, but you're no Jaxon."

His words make me feel like I'm suffocating. Everyone checks to see my reaction. Even if I was brave enough to say some shit to him, I wouldn't have the air to share it. Plus, who knows, maybe he's right. Maybe I'll never be as good as Jaxon was. I nod like a chickenshit, like I'm agreeing with him, and it kills me a little on the inside.

Okay. A lot on the inside.

Mason adds, "But other than Jaxon, this is the same team we've been running with. Ain't no one coming in and breaking that up our last season. And you only recently started hooping. You don't have the experience that's needed. Packed gyms, the noise, the pressure, every team you go against giving you their fucking best every night." Mason swipes Mike's cup out of his hand and takes a drink. "All of us on this team earned our stripes; we been balling since we were in diapers."

Dallas isn't having it. "Psshh, stop acting like you don't think Tre can hoop. We've seen him on JV getting buckets."

Mason replies, "Shit don't count if it happened during a JV game."

Back to scrolling on my phone. I wish they never would have brought up my possibly playing on varsity. Like Mason needs another reason to hate me. A text from Wes pops up even though he's standing right next to me.

Well that was awkward AF

You think? Smdh

Should we bounce?

Yeah

"Where you guys going?" Dallas asks, speed walking after us. "You just got here."

Me and Wes look at each other with blank faces, each waiting for the other to have the answer. Dallas looks at me, then Wes, then back at me. He takes a sip of his drink, then nods, with a look in his eyes like he's just figured it out. Dallas holds up a finger, asking for one second. He goes back into the kitchen, says something to the huddled-up varsity players. My stomach churns, hoping they're not making fun of us for leaving the second someone said something mean. Dallas takes a big drink, then sets his cup down on the table and nods at us before walking over. Dallas throws an arm around us both. "I get it, man. I'd feel the same way if I was you. Let me walk you out real quick." He guides us out the front door. We walk outside, down the front porch, and onto the dirt road. After we pass by several parked cars, Dallas stops walking.

"Aye, bro, don't let that dude rattle you. Mason had a real tough childhood. I mean, we all did in some way, right? But he had it especially bad. I've known him since kindergarten. He's confessed a lot to me over the years that I won't ever repeat." Dallas folds his arm and looks off into the trees that run right alongside the road.

I think about telling him that Mason has been my favorite player since I can remember, other than my brother, of course. I always loved how Mason played with so much courage. And he was never afraid to take a big shot, even though he was on a team with my brother. And that it extra hurts when a hero of yours acts like they hate you. But as I say it in my head it's too embarrassing to say out loud.

"It's okay, man," I reply. "I appreciate you being cool with us."

"Anytime. Jaxon was like a brother to me, too; I was close with him my entire life. Having you as a friend and teammate this year will feel like I have a little part of him back."

Even though it's pretty dark, and the lone light bulb from the porch is barely stretching over to us, I worry that Dallas can see my eyes getting teary, so I nod and look away. "I got your back. Okay?"

"Right on. I appreciate that," I say, breathless.

"Oh, and just so you know, I'm not making excuses for the way Mason acts, but I just wanted to let you know that he doesn't hate you. And that he's kind of that way because of everything that happened to him. He acts mean, tough, and says fucked-up stuff to people. It's kind of his shield from the world. But don't take it personal, okay, Tre? That was my bad in there; I should have stepped in more. This is my place, and I invited you. We cool?"

"Yeah, of course."

"Cool, cool. Well, I'm going to get back in there before someone gets into a fight or sets my parents' place on fire. You know how rez parties get." Dallas gives us both a fist bump, winks, and jogs back.

Wes puts his hand on my shoulder, and we turn to walk back to his place.

"Aye," Dallas yells from the front porch. "Just hoop on his ass, Tre. That'll bring him around."

"Okay," I squeak back. Dallas throws a fist in the air, then goes inside.

"Nice one," Wes says, slapping my arm.

"Fuck you," I reply, but we both laugh.

"Pizza rolls," he suggests. "Doritos and video games? Be like the old days, before you decided you were going to become a future NBA MVP."

CHAPTER 4

JULY 12

MY **PHONE VIBRATES,** waking me up. Through blurry, tired eyes I squint to focus. It's a text from Wes.

Hungover?

Nah. You?

A little. Can't believe we stayed up until the sunrise

Yeah, man. I could go for an energy drink lol

Feel up to doing our first on-camera interview?

TBH I'm a lil nervous, but yeah

Don't be. We'll go over the questions and can start over if you mess up or whatever

Okay

The cold, damp air in the basement of Wes's place is a welcome relief from the hot summer day. I can feel the cold from the concrete floor through my basketball shoes. Spiderwebs hang in the corners, and the lone broken window was replaced with a wooden board. Movie posters cover the zigzag cracks that run along the concrete walls. In the corner are lights on makeshift stands made of sticks, a white sheet as a backdrop, a stool, and a tripod for his iPhone.

Wes adjusts one of the lights and takes another look into his phone. "Since this is an interview video, I thought we would do introductions. You mind sitting in that stool there so I can make sure I've got these lights in the right place?"

Wes moves the lights around, looks through his camera, turns off a light only to turn it right back on. I shift in the chair, but no matter how I sit, I feel awkward.

Wes stares at his phone screen and gives me a thumbs-up. "Perfect. We're ready."

I cough to clear my throat.

"You good?" Wes asks.

"Yeah."

"Don't be nervous. We can shoot any of your answers again if you don't like how they sound. It's not like we're live."

"Cool," I say, shifting on the hard metal stool again.

Wes tucks his hair behind his ears, still staring at his phone screen. "Say your name, age, year of high school."

"My name is Tre Brun. I'm fifteen and going into my sophomore year."

"Tre, what are your goals for this coming season?"

"Making the varsity team. . . ." I look down at my shoes and laugh.

"Don't be shy, dude. Be bold, be proud. Your truth will look dope as fuck when we're all done and you're in the league. Keep it one hundred."

I agree and get back at it. "I plan on making the varsity team and helping them win our school's first-ever regional championship, and then, hopefully, our first-ever state championship."

Wes gives me another thumbs-up, his focus on the phone screen. "And what are your long-term goals for your basketball career?"

"I want to win multiple state championships for my school, for my reservation. I know it would mean a lot to the people here, especially the younger kids. I want to pave the way for them, and sort of, I don't know, show them that they can do whatever they set their minds to, even if it seems impossible."

"What about after high school?"

"I want to be the first player from our reservation to play

Division One basketball. And then, as wild as this sounds"—I fight a frog in my throat—"I want to . . . make it to the NBA."

"What do you think getting into the NBA would mean to you, your family, your reservation?"

Before I can answer, there's a knock followed by loud stomps coming down the stairs. "Yoooo . . . whatcha all up to down here? Shooting a porn or what?" Nate asks.

"Fuck you," Wes says, and we all laugh.

"You promise not to say anything to anyone?" I ask Nate.

"You *are* shooting a porn," Nate says.

"No, you fucker. This was Wes's idea, but we're shooting, like, kind of like a little documentary on me. In case, you know, if I ever do anything with basketball."

"Shit, what about me? Where's my documentary?" Nate points at me. "You know half the time I get the best of this dude here, right?"

"Psshh . . . I let you have a couple," I jokingly say. Not going to lie, Nate is getting pretty legit, and I hope someday me and him will be the ones running the varsity team.

"Yeah, right," Nate says. "Anyway, I was going to see if y'all wanted to hit up the Bemidji mall. I scored a twenty spot for mowing my aunt's lawn."

We abandon the documentary for now and hop in Nate's dad's van. The doors cry like dying robots as we open them. Inside the van, empty soda bottles and junk food wrappers are scattered everywhere. "Been meaning to clean this shit, keep forgetting,"

Nate says. "Begged my pops to let me take his new van. Never seen him laugh so hard in his whole life. Least he lets me borrow this one, though. He said if I make the honor roll this year, I can have it."

"Good thing you failed sixth grade, otherwise we wouldn't have a friend in our class already able to legally drive," Wes says with a chuckle.

"Shut up. I was sick as hell that year. Missed too many days." Nate stares at Wes.

"I was just saying I was grateful for a friend that could already drive," Wes says.

"Better be." Nate punches Wes in the leg. "Ain't too late to leave your ass."

"Holy. Just touchy, this guy," Wes says in a rez accent, and we all laugh.

Nate starts up the van and we take off, passing through the heart of the rez first. Little kids play with sticks on dirt roads; unleashed dogs run wild. In a few of the yards are the skeletons of forgotten rez bombs. Some of the homes look beat-up, tired, and sad, like they could use a hug and a face-lift. But others look fresh, with new paint jobs, updated windows and roofs, and nice, newer cars in the driveways.

That's kind of how our rez is. A mix of rugged and pretty. Ten minutes of driving through the rez and we pass by the casino that sits right on the rez line. After that it's a half hour ride through dense forest, then flat farmland and past smelly cows as we get closer to the city of Bemidji.

• • •

We bum around the shopping mall. It's pretty much where we always go when we want to do something besides driving around, playing video games, or messing on the internet. You can only fuck around watching goofy videos and drooling over online models for so long.

Bemidji is so big that it has two McDonald's, two Burger Kings, three Subways, a ton of other fast-food spots, a big movie theater, bars, restaurants, a Target, a Walmart, small local shops, hotels, a university and a technical college, and an airport.

Basically, it's the complete opposite of the rez.

There's not a ton for us to do here, but it's somewhere to be. You can totally see from one end of the mall to the other. There's a shoe store, a jewelry store, a couple of clothing stores for old white women, an ice cream joint, an arcade with outdated games, and a bookstore.

"Aye, fam," Nate begins. "Remember the last time we were down here and that white girl in the shoe store kept looking at us like we were all sus? And then next thing we knew that security was low-key following us around? Shit was bogus."

"Yeah, man. Not the first time. Not the last time," I say.

"Yeah, dude," Wes puts in. "I guarantee you they wouldn't have all that if it wasn't for all the Natives that come and shop here. Our rez, White Earth, Cass Lake."

"And they still always be acting like we're trying to steal some shit," Nate says. "Always be like that. At least you look white,

Wes. Shit. I bet you can come here and not get security called on your ass."

"Not if I'm with you guys. Guilty by association."

"Man, shut the fuck up." Nate playfully shoves Wes.

"Hey, you know I always step in and turn on my white guy voice anytime people try to bother us. Like that last time we got followed around Target by that security guard. I smiled at him and asked him if everything was cool and he got all awkward, mumbled something, bumped into a customer's shopping cart?" Wes says.

"Yeah, bro, you got like Jedi mind trick type shit," Nate says.

We stop in front of the bookstore. In between displays of books, I spot Sam ringing up a customer at the front register. She has worked here as a cashier for about a year now. I've had a crush on her since the first time I saw her. Embarrassing. I know.

Her black hair is short and messy with shaved lines along the sides. She has a nose ring and bold purple lipstick. At a glance, I'd assume she'd be too cool to talk to someone like me. Not only does she have style, but she's way out of my league. But Sam is actually cool as hell. One of my favorite things about her is when she does these super-fast mini claps and lets out a squeak of excitement any-time we talk about new Marvel comics, especially *Spider-Gwen*, which is her favorite. Plus, she always puts me at ease. I don't like a lot of eye contact, and she must have picked up on that, because now she only glances over, smiles, and then we go back to flipping through the new paperbacks.

Wes asks, "You finally going to ask her for her number, or her social media?"

"It's now or never," Nate says, fighting back a laugh.

When her customer leaves, she catches us studying her.

Wes pushes me inside. I push him back.

"Hey, guys, come in," Sam says in a soft, smoky voice.

"Hey." I quickly walk to the back of the store, to where they keep the comic books and graphic novels. Wes and Nate hang near the front of the store, moving to the magazine rack.

I grab the *Umbrella Academy, Volume One* graphic novel even though I own it already.

I *have* to talk to her. Otherwise, Wes and Nate will give me shit the entire ride back. I think of a bunch of things to say, ways to ask for her number, but they all sound awkward as hell. I reach for this month's *The Amazing Spider-Man* even though I've already read Wes's copy.

Sam peeks around a corner, holding a stack of books. "Anything I can help you find?"

"No. Just looking."

Standing on her tiptoes, she fights to place a book back onto the top shelf. Her Bemidji Lumberjacks T-shirt rises up, revealing the edge of her panties. She notices me looking.

Shit.

She blushes and lowers back down from her tiptoes. "Ugh, this shirt always does that."

"Want help?" I ask, reaching for the book.

She hands it to me, and I easily place it into the opening on the top shelf.

"Thanks. I appreciate it. Must be nice being so tall." Sam's eyebrows furrow. "Tre, right?"

I'm in shock that she knows my name. "Yeah. Tre."

"Phew. *So* glad I was right. I'm always terrified of getting people's names wrong. I've heard your friends say your name a few times when you've been in here."

"You've got a good memory."

"Thanks." Sam smiles and runs a hand through her hair. "Oh, the latest *Spider-Gwen* just dropped." She grabs a copy off the shelf and holds it up. "Check out the artwork on this cover!"

"Sold," I say.

A moment later, Sam rings me up at the counter. "Anything else you were looking for?"

"Nope. That was it." I nod at Nate and Wes, who are sitting on a bench out in the mall concourse. Nate throws up his hands, shrugging. After paying, I say to Sam, "Thanks for always being so helpful and nice."

"I hope you love the new *Spider-Gwen*. You'll have to let me know what you think."

I grab the bag from the counter. "I will. Thanks."

"Any fun plans for the rest of your summer? Any trips, parties?"

"I play basketball, so I do that a lot."

"I'm not into sports. But that's cool. I guess with your height that makes sense."

"Yeah, I got lucky."

"Doing anything cool this weekend?"

"Just hooping. What about you?"

"Getting together with friends. We're going to do a little make-shift picnic at the beach, then go see the latest Marvel movie. But we've got an odd number; my friends are all dating someone, so I'm like the third wheel."

"That sucks. That's usually me," I lie. None of my close friends have dated anyone yet. "But I bet you'll still have fun."

We stay looking at each other for a second. Now is the time. Give her your number. Or ask for hers. Anything.

A couple of customers walk in. "Welcome to Abigail's Books." Sam nods at me and turns her full attention to the customers. I nod back and walk out.

I'm barely out of the store when Nate prompts, "Well?"

"Well what?" I reply in an annoyed whisper.

"Did you get her number?"

I shake my head.

"What the fuck? Today was your day. I heard her recommending a book to you and everything. You had small talk. Totally missed your chance."

"She's out of my league. Plus, she goes to Bemidji High."

Wes chuckles softly. He doesn't even glance up from the latest issue of *Slam* magazine.

It's still early in the afternoon when we bounce from the mall, so we go for a drive along the shore side of Lake Bemidji. It's this single-lane, secluded road outside of the city. Sometimes we come down this way to daydream. We call it *the rich white man road*.

Through the car speakers, we listen to rap lyrics about fancy wheels, tons of money, and big mansions. And it gives me the chills. The first home along rich white man road is probably one of the biggest. It has a large black gate at the entrance, a sign that reads *Private Property*, security cameras, and a speaker alongside the driveway like you sometimes see in movies where you have to press a button and explain who you are and why you're there.

"That's straight-up goals right there," I say, mainly to myself.

As we continue slowly, Nate asks, "Damn, can you imagine living in one of these houses someday? I mean, for real, look at these places. They're like mansions or something."

"Yeah, man. There ain't even *one* house like this back on the rez. Yo, check out that one down there." Wes points with his lips. "It has a gate, like the president or a celebrity lives there."

A moment later, Nate turns down the music and announces, "Hey, hey, hey. There's a cop behind us, fam."

Me and Wes sit up a little straighter, like startled kids who just got yelled at by their parents. "Drive normal, keep going the speed limit; we'll be okay," Wes insists.

"Yeah, man, but we got the reservation license plates on this car. They're going to pull us over any second for some bullshit. I know it."

My heart speeds up super fast. Nate's as scared as I am. I want to check on Wes in the back seat, but I don't want to look suspicious. "How long has he been following us?"

33

"Shit, I don't know, man." Nate grips the steering wheel like he's choking it. "I noticed him a few seconds ago."

We're all afraid. We've heard stories about white cops from our cousins or uncles or aunts, our parents. Everyone has a horror story about a white cop messing with Natives. It's like they hate us. Breathe, I think. Breathe.

"Goddamn!" Nate exclaims. "His lights are on. He's pulling us over." Nate slows down and drives off the two-lane highway onto a dirt road, stopping the van on the side of the road.

Nate stares straight ahead, putting his hands on the dash. "Fuck. Everyone, stay calm. Keep your hands in plain sight. No quick movements. Say *yes, sir, no, sir.* You got me?"

"Yeah," Wes and I reply at the same time.

"Here he comes," Nate says before exhaling a deep breath.

The cop taps hard on the window a couple of times. He's an older white dude, with a beer belly that's fighting the buttons of his uniform, salt-and-pepper brown hair, stubble on his chin, and baggy, tired eyes.

Nate rolls down his window.

"Do you know why I pulled you over?" the cop asks.

Because we have rez plates, I want to say.

"No, officer, I don't," Nate replies.

"You went over the lines a couple of times."

"I'm sorry. I didn't know that I did. I try to drive carefully." Nate's voice is shaky. The way I talk after running sprints.

"Have you been drinking? Or using any illicit substances?"

"No, sir."

"You seem fidgety. Nervous. Is there something you aren't telling me?"

"No, sir. I haven't been drinking or doing any drugs."

"Don't lie to me. I know how you Red Lakers are."

"I haven't been drinking or doing drugs. And I'm only nervous because I don't know if I'm in trouble or not. I've never been pulled over before."

"What about your friends here?" The cop peeks into the vehicle before turning his attention back to Nate. "Let me see your license and registration."

"Okay. I'm going to reach into my back pocket for my wallet, then the glove compartment for the registration. Is that okay?"

"Yeah, just no quick movements. Whose vehicle is this?"

"It's my dad's." Nate hands over his license and registration.

"Take the keys out of the ignition and set them on the dash," the cop says, and then walks back to his car.

"You don't have anything on you, do you?" Nate asks Wes in a whisper.

"No, I don't. I never dare to leave the rez with anything because these cops down here will pull over every damn car that has Red Lake plates."

Nate checks his rearview mirror. "Fuck, man. Worst fear right here. Makes me never want to leave the rez for nothing. My dad's been training me on how to deal with getting pulled over ever since I can remember. He tells me the rules every time I'm leaving

35

the house. He'll be pissed if he finds out I drove down to Bemidji. I lied and told him we were just going to be on the rez. Oh shit. What the fuck, man?"

"What's going on?" I ask.

"Another cop car pulled up," Nate says. "Here comes that cop and his buddy."

The officer that pulled us over walks up to the driver's-side window.

The other one strolls along the passenger side of the van, glares at me, surveys the garbage-strewn floors, then stops and stands. He's a young white dude. Clean cut, with short blond hair and body-builder arms and shoulders. His aviators reflect our nervous faces.

"I'm going to need you to get out of the van," the cop tells Nate.

"Yes, sir. I'm going to get out slowly. Do you want to open the door, or do you want me to?"

"Go ahead and open it, but keep your hands where I can see them."

"Yes, sir." Nate gets out of the van slowly.

"Come this way with me." The cop gestures to the back of the van.

"What do you think they're doing, Wes?" I whisper.

"I don't know. And I'm afraid to look back." He pauses. "Wait, I can see them in the passenger mirror. They've got Nate doing one of those tests they give drunk people."

"Like walking a straight line and stuff?" I ask.

"Yeah. He just walked a straight line. Now they've got him standing on one foot."

"What the fuck?"

"Yeah, man. This shit is stupid. I didn't see him driving over the lines. That cop is full of shit. Nate had both hands on the wheel. He doesn't text and drive. He drives like an old lady."

"Yeah, he does, doesn't he?"

"Oh shit," Wes says. "That other cop is coming over here."

"I'm going to need you both to step out of this van. We are going to search it for drugs, paraphernalia, and alcohol."

"Okay," I say. "Should we get out one at a time?"

The cop shrugs. "Sure."

We walk to the back of the van. The cop who pulled us over is shining a light into Nate's eyes. He's rattling off a bunch of questions. Nate does his best to stay calm, answering, "Yes, sir," or "No, sir."

"Are you guys one hundred percent certain that there aren't any drugs in the vehicle? You know lying to a police officer is a crime, so your best bet is to be honest with us. We'll call in a drug dog if we need to." The younger cop stares at us long and hard.

"No, sir. We don't have any drugs on us. You also have zero reason to believe that we would have any drugs on us, other than racially profiling us for being from the reservation," Wes says, real smooth and calm, almost like he rehearsed it. Sounding just like a lawyer would. A part of me is proud of my smart and badass friend, and the other part of me is terrified that he might have just riled up this guy.

"We have training in these sorts of things. If my partner had reason to believe that you or your friend over there were using illicit substances or were possibly in possession of them, then he had every right to question and investigate," the younger cop says, adjusting his aviators.

Wes clears his throat. I want to tell him to let it go.

The older cop walks up. "All right, I'm all done with the field sobriety test. But I know if we search this van, we'll find something. What jail do you guys want to go to?"

Nate jogs over to us. His chest is heaving like we just ran a game of five on five.

I put a hand on his shoulder. "You okay?"

Nate eventually nods. We watch as the cops dig around inside the van, then around the tires, underneath the hood, and in the undercarriage. Fighting tears, Nate whispers, "Fuckers better not plant shit on us."

"You guys are free to go." The older officer is sad-faced that he didn't even find a single empty cartridge of THC. Not a single skinny joint. Nothing.

We get back into the van and sit in silence. Nate doesn't put the key in the ignition for a good five minutes. When he does start the van, he takes his time putting on his seat belt and turning on the headlights. We leave the music off for the longest, quietest drive of our lives back to the rez.

CHAPTER 5

AUGUST 1

IT'S STILL DAMN near dark out as I rub sleep crust from my eyelashes and let out a yawn. I am not a morning person. Not. At. All.

I stretch my legs, then sync my phone with my Bluetooth headphones, turn on music, and stuff my phone into my armband. Everyone else my age probably sleeps in during the summer. I mean, why wouldn't they? But here I am, up before the sun, getting ready to put myself through hell. I shake my head and start the run from my parents' house down the long, winding dirt road, keeping a close eye out to avoid rocks and the dips and holes along the way.

Drake blares through my headphones as I hit the one paved highway that courses through the reservation. I run across it and down into a little path alongside the road, carved by years of people riding bikes and four-wheelers.

It's a quiet morning; only a couple of cars pass along the highway. No rez dogs are running up and barking at me this morning. They must all still be sleeping. Lucky fuckers.

I jog past a small church that looks like it was originally a log cabin, then past the post office, the tackle and bait shop my uncle Ricky works at, and then the fisheries, before finally hitting the park where I've spent most of my summers. There's a softball field with bleachers, a skateboard ramp that serves as a perch for the teenage cigarette smokers, and an old clay basketball court with cracks that spiderweb all across it with faded lines from the one week it must have been a tennis court. I don't think I've ever met a Red Laker who plays tennis.

When I get to the basketball court, I pause to catch my breath and wipe sweat from my brow. I drop down and do push-ups until my arms quiver. I fight for one more but fail and collapse to the court. I stay on the cold, hard clay for a few seconds, enjoying the rest. Then I pop up and hit squats and lunges until my legs wobble. Another quick rest. One minute.

Basketball is a game of intense stress, fast action, and then short breaks. I train to copy that cycle. I walk over to one of the basketball rims, remove my headphones, and pull off my armband and set it aside. I take time to catch my breath. I want to make sure I run these sprints as hard and as fast as I can.

Running sprints always reminds me of when me and Jaxon were kids and we used to play silly games in our yard, like tag.

Even he couldn't catch me. He used to get so mad about that. The older we got, the more it bothered him. He'd beg me to race him once a week during the summer. Jaxon would pop into my room, sit down next to me, and watch me play video games for a couple of minutes like he was there to hang out, then he would go on a rant, telling me how much faster he'd gotten from his training.

Jaxon legit wouldn't shut up about it. Once I got annoyed enough, I'd pause my video games and go outside to race him. He'd sometimes even bet me one dollar over the race. Easiest money of my life. I used to always tell him that the Flash was faster than Superman, since Superman was his all-time favorite. And when I was feeling extra cocky and really wanted to push his buttons, I'd throw on my Flash T-shirt before we ran. I wish I could race him right now. I'd even lose one just to see his wild smile.

The thought makes me laugh to myself and my eyes get teary. At the same time. Now I'm ready to run. Steadying myself, I look down at my feet, at one knee pushed forward while my other leg reaches back, heel off the court, ball of my foot pressed down. My legs are in the right position. The basketball court in front of me is clear, empty.

And . . . go! I explode into a sprint, racing down the length of the court. My arms and legs become blurs. I'm the fastest runner in the entire high school.

I run the length of the court and back. Sprint to the opposite free-throw line, reach to tag it, and run back. Then a dash to half-court and back, then the closer free-throw line and back. People call them "ladders" or "crushers" or "man makers," which sounds kind of sexist now that I think about it, but I call them "basketball hell."

With my hands on my hips, I gasp in air that feels like breathing in fire. My lungs burn. When I can breathe again, I go to the line and do it all over again. I run sprints until I almost puke, until I feel dizzy. I lose count, to be honest. I never have a number in mind. I go until I literally can't. I'm too tired to jog home, so I walk. Feels like it takes forever. I'm dying for a drink of water and my stomach is growling.

Half an hour later, before I even walk in, I can smell breakfast. Bacon, toast, eggs.

I walk through the front door and through the living room toward the smells from the kitchen. Our living room walls are covered floor to ceiling with family photos, paintings of jingle dancers and powwows by a local Ojibwe artist, and of course antlers from Dad's hunting trips. If it weren't so clean it would look cluttered.

In our kitchen, I see the breakfast Mom made, still hot in the pan. I dish some up. Mom is typing up a storm on her laptop. The wooden table where we eat and where she is working is only a couple of feet away from the living room, which comes in handy when the Timberwolves are playing at dinnertime because we can see the TV.

"I made scrambled eggs, bacon, and toast for you, Tre," Mom says, never looking up to see my heaping plate. She taps a single key a little harder than she typed the rest. "There we go." With a final click, Mom shuts the computer and smiles at me. Her long black hair is tied neatly into fresh braids, and she's got a mud mask drying on her face.

"What are you up to?" I ask, setting my plate down on the table before returning to the kitchen to grab a fork and a glass of water.

"Just finished enrolling for the fall semester. I'm going to get my master's in social work, finally. I've wanted to for so long but was busy with . . . everything."

"Get it, Ma. You going to keep working at the same time?"

Mom sighs. "It's going to be so hard. But I've been stuck in my same position for too long. I'm ready to move up. It will be worth the long days once I'm done. I stopped school once I got pregnant with Jaxon. I was able to get back in and finish my bachelor's degree, but it was the most exhausting time of my life. I was working part-time, going to school full-time, and taking care of you guys."

I put a hand on her shoulder. "I'm proud of you, Mom. You got this." Mom pats my hand and looks up at me. I grab her fork and almost empty plate and coffee mug from the table. She snatches her final half strip of bacon off the plate.

"You want me to dish you up more?" I ask.

"No. I'm full. I just couldn't resist that last piece."

"Want more coffee?"

"Yup."

I fill up Mom's coffee mug, then sit down next to her and dig into my breakfast. Mom takes a small sip. She stares at her coffee mug as she cradles it in her hands. Like a baby holding a teddy bear. Silver and turquoise rings—Dad always gets them for her at powwows—cover her fingers. "How was your workout?" Mom asks.

"Sucked. But, you know, in a good way. Was exhausting. But I can tell it's paying off." I dig into some scrambled eggs covered with melted cheese. "Thanks for making breakfast. This smells good. I'm starving."

Dad walks in and adjusts a picture of Jaxon, even though I don't think it was even crooked. In the picture, Jaxon is hoisting up his trophy for becoming our basketball team's all-time highest-scoring player.

Even with as many family photos as we have framed around the house, it feels like at least half of them are of my brother. It's like a never-ending memorial. You can't go anywhere in our house without a basketball photo of Jaxon.

I'm serious. They stretch all the way down the hall, past the bathroom that we used to fight over, to our bedrooms. Across the hall from mine is Jaxon's old room, which has been kept just as he had it, like he never left. Like he could still come walking back in the front door any moment and have it waiting for him.

Even down the stairs, in the den, and in my parents' bedroom, Jaxon's basketball pics are on all the walls. Okay, I'm being a little dramatic. I just hate that most of my pics are of me looking like a pimply faced nerd, with awful haircuts and Jaxon's hand-me-down clothes, while Jaxon looks like Superman in his Warriors jersey on the court, throwing down a dunk or pulling up for a three-pointer. He grows from a skinny freshman to a muscular junior as your eyes move from one side of the hall to the other. Every time I walk to my bedroom, I feel both motivated to match what he did and a heavy burden on my shoulders.

"I remember that night," Dad says, still looking at the picture he adjusted. "Jaxon was so excited to break my record. I didn't think anyone ever would."

Chowing down my breakfast, I wait for him to say something about me maybe someday breaking Jaxon's record. Or something about me. Really, anything about me.

I mean, even if I didn't play basketball, I never get in trouble at school, earn pretty good grades, always help around the house. But it doesn't matter. Sometimes I feel like I'm the ghost here.

When Jaxon started playing basketball, which seems like it must have been as soon as he could toddle, Dad couldn't wait to take him to basketball tourneys on the weekends, watch basketball games with him on TV. They'd talk basketball over every breakfast and every dinner.

It was so annoying. No one ever wanted to talk about video games or comic books with me. Mom would be tired from work. Jaxon would be busy on his phone. Even when my uncles stopped by, all I would get was a quick pat on the head, and then it was time to brag about Jaxon's most recent game. Jaxon was the only one who'd chill with me and ask about what comics I'd been reading or how my classes were going. But then he got super busy with basketball. But whatever. I'll show them all soon enough.

I shovel down breakfast and scroll through social media.

I get a text from Nate.

What are you up to?

Listening to my dad drone on about his scoring record for the millionth time

WBU?

Wanna see if we can go find some fives? I heard there's a bunch of people up at the basketball courts

Man. I already got in a long workout this AM. Still kinda recovering

Bro. Quit being soft. I bet Kobe or Bron worked out in the AM AND in the PM. All day. You want to be as great as you say you wanna be this season, best put that work in

Okay. You're right. I'll guzzle Gatorade and stretch out this soreness

Cool. My dad let me borrow the rez bomb van for a couple of hours. I'll come pick you up. I texted Wes. He's going to roll with

Ten minutes later Nate is honking the horn as a rap song blares out of the windows of the van. When we get to the basketball courts a couple of five-on-five games are going on. The girls' basketball team is on one of the courts. On the other is a mix of our high school varsity team, junior varsity team, and dudes who used to hoop in high school.

Basketball has been a popular sport on our rez since I can remember. But lately, it's on a whole new level. People are almost always running games up here.

"What's up, Tre?" Dallas asks as he jogs up, his gaze never leaving the game.

"You wanna run with us?" I gesture to Wes and Nate. We probably look more like we'd be in the math club, if our school even had one, than a legit basketball team.

After a moment of deliberation, Dallas says, "Sure." He sets down his bag and digs out a basketball, which he dribbles between his legs and around his back. We watch the game in front of us, waiting our turn.

Kevin, the center for our high school team, runs down the court, points up to the sky, asking for an alley-oop. His teammate throws the ball way too high. But somehow Kevin flies up to grab it and slams it home. "Game," Kevin says, mean mugging the shit out of the thirtysomething dude he just whammed on.

Everyone secretly is always annoyed at how cocky Kevin is. It's not about what he says, it's more about *how*. The way he says *game* like he's rubbing it in. Probably doesn't help that he's the jock type from any teen movie ever. Zero self-awareness. Jaxon used to say that Kevin was one part Captain America, one part Jar Jar Binks. Someone who means well, wants to do good, but is a bumbling goof. Kevin nods at me with that super-cool tough-guy look he tries to pull off, then trips on his own shoelaces. He's the least graceful basketball player I've ever seen. Good thing he is so tall and scary strong. I pretend not to see him fall.

When the four of us—me, Dallas, Wes, and Nate—step onto the court, we squeeze in a couple of jump shots while the team that just played guzzles water. We ask another hooper to hang with us to bring us to five players.

"Check it up, then," Kevin says. "Winner's ball."

"I'll guard the nerdy version of Jaxon," Mason says, pointing at me.

They throw the ball to Mason, and he tries to cross me over, but that's his go-to move. I'm glued to him. He gets mad, slaps at my arms with his free arm, then fires up a quick pull-up jumper. I get a hand in his face. His shot bricks off the rim.

"Fuck!" Mason screams, punching the air.

Dallas grabs the board and we run down the court. I go to the basket, but Mason is nudging, pushing, elbowing. Nate gives me a look. When you play enough basketball with someone, especially a friend, the two of you get psychic abilities, like Jean Grey and Professor X of the X-Men. Nate wants me to run toward him, and he will set a pick on Mason, freeing me up.

Nate isn't all that tall, maybe right about six feet, but he has broad shoulders and is strong as hell. He sets a screen that stops Mason dead in his tracks.

Dallas gets me the ball, and I drive to the basket. Both Nate's defender and Kevin come at me. I hit Nate with a quick bounce pass as he rolls to the basket for an easy layup.

"That was a moving screen," Mason cries out as we run back down the court.

After a flash of jumpers, layups, blocks, and dunks, suddenly, the score is 10–10.

Next basket wins.

"Let's get a good look!" I yell to my team.

I dribble downcourt with Mason swiping at the ball, moving like he's my shadow. Instead of picturing my next move, I'm imagining the worst, like Mason stealing the ball or swatting my shot and then talking shit about it. I picture people laughing. My heart thumps like a flea-ridden rez dog scratching itself. *Come on, Tre. Focus. If we get this bucket, we win, and we'll have bested a team with three starters from arguably the best team in the state.*

Crossing half-court, players blur into moving colors, sneaker squeaks, and shouts. Mason slaps the court in front of him. He growls at me like a UFC fighter at a weigh-in, then waves, daring me to bring it on. Fuck it. I need to show these guys that I can hold my own, that I deserve to wear the same jersey, that I'm not just Jaxon's nerdy little brother. I'm going to be just as good as he was. Dribble. Dribble. Left, right, left. The ball is like a yo-yo. Confidence shoots through me. I dip my shoulder and fake hard to the left. Mason cuts me off, or so he thinks. He did *exactly* what I wanted him to do. I cross the ball to my right before he can recover.

I release a jumper over his fingertips. I watch the ball spin in the air.

Please go in.

Please.

The ball swings down, spins around, flips out and right into Kevin's hands. Mason is already down the court. He catches the pass and makes a layup. "Game!"

"We got next!" a guy shouts from the sidelines.

Just like that. One shot, one miss, one second in time, and I'm no longer like my older brother, hitting game-winners for breakfast, being clutch AF. More importantly, I missed my chance to earn respect from these guys, especially Mason. And after what he said at that party about the varsity being fine without me.

As we head to the van, Nate says, "Shake it off, fam. We'll get 'em next time."

After Nate drops me off, I take a shower, throw on basketball trunks and a retro black Kevin Garnett jersey. I take a second to pick up the scattered comic books, graphic novels, and *Slam* magazines from my bedroom floor. I stack and scoot them next to my bed, but then a glance at the top magazine makes me pause.

I grab the issue of *Slam* with Steph Curry on the cover. LeBron, Kevin Durant, Steph Curry . . . basically everyone who made it to the NBA came up in this magazine. I thumb past the NBA stories until I get to my favorite section, the one about the top high school players in the US. I stop on an article about a seven-foot-tall point guard from Crestview Christian Academy in southern Minnesota.

He has a head of curly blond hair and perfectly straight white teeth that could have only come from braces. His arms are long but ripple with muscles. The headline reads *God's Son: A Basketball Prodigy*.

From the kitchen, Mom hollers, "Tre, dinner is ready!"

I fold a corner of the page down to read for later. I hop up and quickly throw my clothes in the laundry basket, then make my bed. I don't mind it being messy, but if my room gets too gross, Mom will give me an ear beating.

In the kitchen, I'm glad to see my mom made mac and cheese with chunks of hot dogs and a pitcher of grape Kool-Aid. She jokingly calls it the Social Worker Special. She doesn't make enough money for fancy food, and her job leaves her too mentally and emotionally drained to spend time making a meal that requires a lot of steps and time. So, we should be happy to get the Social Worker Special. I dish up a big bowl and sit with my parents.

Mom's in the middle of a story. "Anyway, I had to have the police accompany me over to their house. The baby was screaming and crying. I could hear the poor thing from outside. When we went inside and found her in her crib, her little cheeks had sunken in." Mom tears up. "Her diaper hadn't been changed in a couple of days. The mother tried grabbing me and screamed in my face to not take her baby away. I can't wait to get my master's degree, hopefully move up, and make bigger changes to the system."

I set my fork down and finish chewing a bite of hot dog. This is a normal night for us. I sit here inhaling food and thinking about stuff. Used to be the most recent comic book I'd read, or a level of a video game I couldn't beat. But these last couple of years, it's been basketball. I sit, eat, and zone out while Mom and Dad talk about Jaxon or bitch about their jobs.

My dad works for the sanitation department, so for him, it's all about frozen water pipes and backed-up septic tanks. But at least tonight I get a break from hearing about Jaxon. I swear to the Creator, almost every dinner, he's all they talk about. Good memories, funny memories, and then the what-if-he-were-still-here conversations come up. How he would have led Red Lake to the state championship, and then gone to a D-1 school, and then the NBA. And how smart he was, and how funny he was, and how tragic the car accident was. Sometimes the stories make us laugh. Sometimes they make us get quiet. And every so often, we cry.

It hurts the worst when they blame themselves. I never know what to say, or if I should say anything at all. But it tears me up inside when I see them get that distant look in their eyes when their stories go that direction. Some nights they talk in circles, wondering if Jaxon would still be here if they had been stricter or if he'd had a curfew. On really bad nights, they slowly start blaming each other, pointing out who let him get away with what. Or they get caught up on the events of that day. How they should have put winter tires on Jaxon's car, or how they should have gotten him something better for winter driving, like a Jeep or a truck, instead of passing down their old car. Those nights their voices grow quieter with every sentence. Those nights rip the stitches off my heart. And the next morning, it feels like we each have to start healing all over again.

So, I guess I should be grateful to be hearing about their work-days tonight instead of all of that. Whenever I eat, I try to daydream instead of listening to how tough their jobs are. It messes with my head to think about what it's like being a grown-up, too. Working jobs all day that are super stressful, only to come home and complain about them until they go to sleep. And the bills they owe are always a little more than the money they make. I guess they have it better than a lot of other people on this rez, though. That's why I have to make it to a big college, and then the NBA. I know it's a long shot, and I know it's going to be a lot of work, but I don't care.

I have to make it.

CHAPTER 6

AUGUST 25

THE FIRST DAY of my sophomore year, and everything looks and feels the same way it did last year. The jocks and cheerleaders are hanging out in their spot—they call it the wall. It's right in the middle of the school, a short walk from the cafeteria and the gym, and equal distance to any classroom. It's kind of like an elite club; the coolest kids in school come here and stand against the wall, making small talk between classes and watching everyone else pass by. Pretty sure you need an invite.

Jaxon was always right in the middle, smiling and laughing, everyone hanging on to his every word. The wall itself is covered with this painting of a group of Ojibwe warriors riding horses over a hill against a purple-and-orange sunset. The painting reminds

54

me of who our ancestors were. Who they had to be. I think that's why we like that being our school's sports name. Warriors.

There are hints of weed in the air as I walk by a group of stoners who are huddled together and laughing their asses off against the white brick walls and red lockers. The girls' dance team passes by me in a mob. I never see any of them alone—not even going to the bathroom. No one waves or says hi. I used to at least be Jaxon's little brother, and now, I guess, I'm just me. The halls are packed, but I tower over the other students at school so I can easily see all the way down the hall.

I nod at Dallas, but he doesn't notice, and I hope no one else saw my failed nod. I scan the hall, hoping to spot Nate or Wes or, hell, anyone I know from my grade. Feeling alone and awkward, I walk to my locker, lean down to open it, and pretend to organize stuff to kill time until class starts. There's a tap on my shoulder. Before I know who it is, I'm smiling and spinning around. "Hey."

Liquid splashes into the air. A can of Red Bull hits the floor, spilling out the remaining liquid, creating a Rorschach puddle of caffeine. Other students navigate around the mess.

Holy shit. The victim of my spin move looks like a rock star. A rock star I've never seen before. The hottest girl I've ever seen. IRL. In person. OFC.

The girl is wearing black cat-eye-style sunglasses, a Nirvana T-shirt, and black distressed skinny jeans. Her curly black hair rests over her now-folded arms.

"Aww . . . shit. I'm sorry. I'm so clumsy. I can't believe I did that," I say.

"You're lucky that I was pretty much done with it."

"I'll bring you one tomor—"

"Don't sweat it; it was an accident. Anyway, I wanted to ask if you knew which way"—she digs her phone out of her pocket and holds the screen up—"Mrs. Anderson's room is. It's my first-hour class."

"I can walk you," I say.

"No, that's okay. This school is small, but the order of the classroom numbers makes zero sense. Can you just point me to the right hallway?"

"It's my first-hour class, too. I'm Tre." I reach my hand out to shake hers.

Her eyebrows rise above her sunglasses. "What are you, running for tribal chairman?"

I pull my hand back and stuff both hands into my pockets.

"Well?"

"Well what?" I ask.

"Are you going to your first hour during the first hour?"

"Oh, right. Yeah. Hold up." I scramble to put my backpack into my locker.

"It's right this way." I point down the hall and we start walking. "You must be new here, right? I've never seen you before, and I'm pretty sure I've seen everyone who lives on this rez." I'm awkward as all hell, because that's who I am, I guess.

"I'm from here . . . sort of. My mom was born here, but we

moved around a lot. We were living in the cities until she lost her job and we had to move up here to live with my grandma. Damn, this school is even smaller than I thought. How many students go here?"

"Depends on the month. Right now, I think we have about three hundred for the entire high school. But that usually drops in half by winter break."

"No shit?"

"Yeah. At least that's how last school year went. Some dropped out, some got expelled, and some switched to ALC—Alternative Learning Choice."

"That's wild. My mom said it was a super-small school, but I thought she was exaggerating. Tre, I have a serious question for you." She stops abruptly and turns toward me. "Truth or dare?"

"Huh?"

"You heard me. Truth or dare?"

"Umm . . . truth."

"If you could be any dinosaur, which one would you be and why?"

"We better get in there." I start to open the door to Mrs. Anderson's class, but the new girl pushes it shut.

"You have to answer my question before we can go in there. It's important."

"Any dinosaur?"

"Any."

"Alive or dead?"

She fights back a smile, but not enough to hide her dimples. "Dead."

"Hmmm . . ." I take her question way too seriously. "I'm going to go with a T. rex." I wait for her to clown on me about it for being so basic.

Instead, she nods slowly and takes her sunglasses off, tucking them into the front of her shirt. "Raptor."

The school bell signaling the start of first hour blares through the hallway. A couple of students weave past us into class.

"Truth or dare?" I ask.

"Dare." She stomps on the word, but her eyes look amused.

And I know what I want to ask her, but my mouth's stapled shut and my hands feel all clammy. I'm not cool enough to ask her that. I'm. Just. Me. Fuck it. What would Jaxon do? He'd be brave enough. Shoot your shot, Tre. "Would you dare to . . . hang out with me sometime? I promise not to spill any more of your drinks."

"You shouldn't make promises like that."

"Good point."

"I'll think about it," she says with a sly grin.

"Well, I suppose we should go in there, huh?" I ask, waiting for her to call me a nerd.

"Fuck, I suppose," she says. I open the door and hold it for her, and we finally walk in together.

"Nice of the two of you to grace us with your presence," Mrs. Anderson says. "Here's the syllabus for this semester. There are two open seats in the back. You haven't missed much. As I was saying, we'll be reading one of my favorite books, *Apple in the Middle* by Dawn Quigley."

I'm an idiot, getting all dizzy over this girl I met a couple minutes ago. I don't know what grade she's in. I don't know if she's seeing someone. Hell, I don't even know her name.

Chill, Tre, chill. Okay, the syllabus. Read the syllabus.

"And here is a copy for each of you," Mrs. Anderson says, setting a copy on each of our desks.

"This is one of my favorites, plus the author is Ojibwe," the new girl whispers to me behind a cupped hand.

"Looks cool," I whisper back.

Then inside I die. Looks cool? Ugh. Nice one, Tre. Real nice.

The rest of the hour, I spend my time doing what I usually do: staring out the window, daydreaming about playing basketball, thinking about what my mom is making for dinner. Plus, I sneak glances at the new girl's black nail polish, the way she pushes her hair behind her ears, her long lashes, her thick, kissable lips.

When the bell rings, I'm a nervous wreck. Do I say something to her? Do I ask her if she wants to hang out later? I've never asked a girl to hang out before; I have no idea how this is supposed to go. The classroom door becomes a logjam of students nudging their way out.

"Hey," she begins. "I have . . . Intro to Ojibwe Language for my second hour. Ms. Fasthorse. Where is her room?"

"It's down the end of the hallway, last room on the left, right before that exit."

She cups a note into my hand like we're in a prison yard and walks off before I can say anything else.

"Tre. Earth to Tre." Wes waves his hands in front of my face.

I bat them away. "What?" I ask with a laugh, knowing damn well what.

"You know that girl?"

"No," I say with a shrug.

"Nay," Nate replies with an elbow to my back.

"What?" I look back at him.

"I seen y'all walking down the hallway, looking like lovebirds and shit. You trying to sma—"

I cut Nate off by half-heartedly shoving him in the chest. I want to tell him how great I think she is. And how I feel like I'm already falling for her. Like love at first sight. But he would clown on me so hard. I fasten my backpack straps and close my locker.

As everyone hurries to their next class, I dig the note out of my pocket, check to make sure no one is nearby, then read it.

I changed my mind.
You totally owe me a Red Bull.
Want to buy me one after school?
PS Text me you clumsy bish
Oh and add me on social media
Khiana

It includes her phone number and social media handles, accompanied by bats and black hearts around it. Speaking of hearts, mine sinks from my chest into the floor. She drew hearts on the note. Suddenly, I'm in a new universe where Mystery Girl, I mean Khiana, is everything. It's a comforting thought. For once, I'm not trying to fill Jaxon's shoes. I'm not missing Jaxon or thinking about basketball. She's the only person I've ever met who didn't think of me as Jaxon's little brother first. I get to be me for once.

CHAPTER 7

AUGUST 25

THE FINAL BELL of the school day rings. I throw books into my locker, then grab my phone. I take a deep breath, then type in Khiana's number and shoot her a text.

> Do you want to hang out?

> Yeah. Meet me out front

As he hurls a basketball at me, Nate asks, "Aye, bro, you want to go hoop?"

I barely catch it with one hand. "I, umm." I shove my phone into my back pocket. If I tell him the truth, he'll tease me *and* ask a bunch of questions.

"Well?" Nate asks, still waiting.

Walking up, Wes asks, "What's going on?"

"Yeah, what's going on, Tre? You coming or what?" Nate adds.

"I forgot. I'm supposed to do a thing."

"Oh yeah, what's that?" Nate asks with a mischievous smile, like he knows I'm bullshitting him and wants to stretch out the moment.

"I'm going to hang out . . . with a girl that just started school here."

"Ah, shit. I knew it," Nate says. "I knew you were on some BS. What's her name?"

"Khiana."

"Howah, you talking about that girl that looks like a witch?" Kevin asks as he opens up his locker. "You trying to snag that?" He's wearing one of those letterman jackets you only see in older movies, crisp jeans, and a button-down dress shirt. I swear he has a different pair of shoes for each day of the month. His parents own The Other Store. They're probably one of the only *rich* families on our rez. He's always posting when he gets the latest pair of retro Jordans and the newest iPhone, and he drives a brand-new Jeep Compass. If he wasn't nearly seven feet tall and one of our best basketball players ever, I bet he'd be getting hated on for being a light-skinned rich boy.

I shrug at Kevin and kind of laugh. "I'll catch you guys later." I speed walk to the exit.

Khiana is leaning against a car, staring at her phone. She tells me she can't burn through her mom's gas. I offer to drive but tell her I only have my permit, not my license yet. She shrugs it off and we hop into my car. My parents and my uncles assured me as long as I stay on the rez and drive the speed limit I'll be fine. They said it's always been that way around here.

My car is an older Chevy Impala, a bit of a rez bomb. The AC is broken, the driver's-side window won't roll down, the engine sounds like Godzilla dying if you go over fifty, and it has this weird smell in it that I haven't been able to get rid of for the life of me.

The highway is lined by walls of pine trees and shoots off into winding dirt roads alongside creeks and a couple of small lakes. To an outsider, it's postcard-perfect beautiful. But living here, seeing it every day on the way to school, it's harder to feel that way.

We pass by the cemetery where Jaxon is buried. I wish I could talk to him about my hanging with Khiana and ask him for advice. Like what to say. How to act. When do you know if a girl *likes* you likes you?

We pass by the water tower, the basketball courts and softball field, and the commodity hall, which is a big redbrick building where people go each month to pick up their commodities. This is the government-rationed food for families who qualify for food stamps. We grew up eating commodity food until Dad got his recent job. Sometimes we still buy it from friends who need cash.

"What's Red Death Mafia?" Khiana asks, pointing at a bunch of gang graffiti that covers the walls of the commod hall.

"One of the main gangs here. They're a faction of the Bloods. Their rival gang around here is the West End Mob."

"I heard stories about gangs, but I guess I just didn't quite believe it. Like this place is all dirt roads, lakes, streams, and trees. It's kind of hard to imagine gangs in this setting, you know? The rez here looks like a country music video."

I shrug. "They're here. Once in a while something messed up happens. Someone will get stabbed or shot. But I think they mainly just sell drugs."

"Scary," Khiana says, her neck craned, still looking back at the graffiti.

We pass by the post office and then The Other Store. "Why's it called The Other Store?"

"Because it's the *other store?*"

"Huh?"

"Well, there are only two convenience stores on the rez, The Trading Post and, well, you know."

"The Other Store . . . *hilarious,*" Khiana says in a British accent. "How far is this place?"

"It's like another twenty minutes from here. But believe me, it's worth the drive."

We drive along quietly for a while, past rez dogs play fighting in the ditches, little kids riding bikes down dirt roads, over the bridge that crosses Shemagun Creek, past a burned-down church, a beaten-down, forgotten basketball court. Then it happens. I get that awful feeling. I haven't driven this far in this direction since Jaxon's accident.

"What happened here?" Khiana asks. Red and black ribbons, teddy bears, deflated basketballs, tipped-over candles, dried, rotten flowers all surround a giant tree that's busted and toppled over. "Oh no. Must be a memorial for a car accident."

Saying it out loud is going to hurt. It always does. "That's where my big brother crashed and died. Was a weird night. Last New Year's Eve. The roads were icy. He was driving home after dropping off a friend. Then, I don't know. The cops said he must have been driving a little too fast, hit this curve wrong, slid off the road . . ."

Khiana puts a hand on my shoulder. "I'm so sorry, Tre. I had no idea. That's terrible."

"I can't believe I forgot. I didn't even think about the fact that I was going to drive past it. I usually never drive this way. But the spot we are going to used to be our favorite summer hangout." I start to choke up and get embarrassed. Come on, Tre. Don't get all sad in front of Khiana. Worst first date ever. If this even is a date.

"I'm sorry, Tre. I can't even imagine. I've been lucky to never lose anyone close to me, yet. Well, except for my dad, but he passed away when I was still a newborn, so I don't remember him. Anyway, subject change?"

"Definitely."

"What do you like to do for fun?"

"Promise not to laugh?"

"I can't make promises like that. I swear I'll do my best."

We smile at each other and just like that, a little bit of the sadness leaves me.

"I love to read comic books. Jaxon actually got me into them. He'd let me read his comics if I did his chores for him. I had to hold them super carefully, and make sure to put them right back into their protective plastic sleeves with the cardboard backing. But I could legit spend an entire day reading comic books and graphic novels."

"That's dope. I love a guy who reads. Comic books are cool. I tried getting into them a couple of times because I liked comic-book movies and shows, but it got expensive. It's hard to keep up with a series."

"What about you?" I ask. "What do you like to do for fun?"

"Video games. Definitely video games. Anime. But outside of hobbies, I'm a loner usually. Don't get me wrong—a few good friends are cool, but I don't really go to parties or get-togethers. I get anxious and don't end up having any fun. I like low-key things. Like this."

"I feel you. I have a couple of close friends, Nate and Wes. We've been close forever. I mainly chill with them, especially since my brother passed away. Hey, we're almost there." I nod ahead. The tree line along the left side of the highway gives way to the lake and a beach that curves along the horizon as far as the eye can see.

I slow down and turn off onto an uneven road. The car bounces up and down as I try to smoothly cruise over all the bumps. We park right along the sand, and I turn off the ignition. Khiana hops out and speed walks to the edge of the shore. She sticks her arms out on both sides and tilts her head back.

"Dang, you really got a thing for beaches."

"Who doesn't?" Khiana lets herself fall back, landing softly on her butt. She runs her fingers through the sand before tossing some into the air. "Come on, sit, sit. We're hanging out here until we get to see the sunset. I've gotta get pictures. I bet it's insane. My social media game has been weak as hell lately. And everyone loves a good sunset pic."

"True." I sit next to Khiana, but not too close.

"Thanks for bringing me out here. This is so chill. What else is up with you? Besides being a comic geek. What else do you like to do?"

"I'm into video games, too, but I don't have as much time to play them anymore. I like all the usual stuff—movies, shows, social media—but to be honest, mainly basketball. I got really into basketball a couple of years ago."

"I figured."

"Really?"

"Well, I mean, look at you. You're tall as hell, and fit. Would be weird if you didn't play at least one sport."

"I am?" I look down at myself, like Pinocchio when he turns into a real boy.

"Oh, right? Like you don't do a thousand crunches and push-ups every single morning. You know you're ripped."

"I guess I didn't really think about it. I've just been obsessed with becoming the best basketball player I could be. So, I've been working out all the time, but didn't really think about how it was changing me."

"Okay," Khiana says, with a *yeah, right* tone in her voice.

"What about you? What else do you like to do besides movies and games?"

"Promise not to laugh?"

"I can't make those kind of promises. Or whatever you said."

"Shush. So, a couple of years ago my mom brought me to the Minneapolis Institute of Art, and they had a monster movie exhibit. It was so dope. Do you like Hellboy?"

"Love."

"Same. Anyway, they had props, costumes, masks, all kinds of stuff from real movies. I was so hyped about it that I got obsessed with wanting to do the same."

"What's that? Make movies?"

"Nah, I don't think I have the people skills or discipline to do all of that. But I do love making masks, crafting, painting, doing all kinds of makeup. I make really dope cosplay outfits, if I do say so myself. Want to see?"

"Of course."

Khiana scooches closer to me, swipes through her phone, pulls up the photos, and then taps an album titled *Cosplay.*

"Check this one out. I did like a gender flip of Link from The Legend of Zelda," Khiana says, bursting with energy that she hadn't shown before. Khiana swipes through photos of her dressed up as Link, with the hat, a shield, a sword—the entire outfit.

"You made all of that?"

"Mm-hmm. Sure did. Took me forever. But it was fun. Here's another. This is me as Samus, from Metroid."

69

"That's insane. You got serious skills. I could never even imagine doing something like that."

"I'll have to tell you sometime about all the road trips I made my mom go on with me as I hunted down everything I needed for this costume. It was months in the making."

"Worth it."

"Yeah, it's my passion. After high school, I want to get into working on movies and shows, doing costume designing and possibly becoming an on-set makeup artist. Still figuring out where to go to school for that, or how to break into that sort of thing. But all roads point me to Los Angeles."

"You'd for real move out to LA?"

"Hell, yeah. That's my dream. My passion. It's what I want to do. Gotta at least try. You know?"

"For sure. You're brave. Respect."

Khiana smiles a massive smile and sways back and forth, almost like there's a slow, soft song playing. But the only sounds are from the waves splashing ashore.

"Kind of reminds me of my brother. We used to spend nights chilling in his bedroom, talking about our lives someday. He was going to play basketball at a Division One college, and then someday go to the NBA and live in a big city."

"What about you? What's your wild dream?"

"Same thing. I just didn't know it back then. I was short, not athletic, and not really into sports like he was. Then the last couple of years I went from five foot nine to six foot four. I gave basketball a try and was surprisingly good at it. Now it's something I love, and what I'd like to do with my life. I know that's like a long shot, becoming a pro basketball player and whatever, but like you said, you gotta try, right?"

"For sure."

Khiana doesn't scoot back over. Our legs stay touching, and we lean against each other. We sit in a comfortable silence and listen to the waves.

CHAPTER 8

AUGUST 25

AFTER DROPPING KHIANA off back at her mom's car in the school parking lot, all I can think about while driving home is how this has been the best night I've had in forever and how mad my dad is going to be. He already blew up my phone with a bunch of texts reminding me of my 9:00 p.m. school night curfew. I'm so screwed. Shutting off the music, like that's going to help, I turn down the dirt road to home. Maybe Dad is asleep already. Maybe he and Mom are watching a movie and won't blow up at me for coming home late.

As soon as I come around the last corner of our road, I can see a campfire in our firepit and my uncle Liver's pickup truck in our driveway, his wooden hunting scaffold in the back. Uncle Liver's real name is Donovan, but they started calling him Liver as a joke because he could outdrink anyone.

When I park my car, I spot a freshly shot buck, gutted and hanging from a stand. Hopefully, Dad will be in a good mood since they got a deer.

I get out of the car and find Dad, Uncle Liver, and my uncle Ricky sitting around the fire, beers in hand. "Hey, Dad, hey, Liv, what's up, Ricky?"

Uncle Liver is kicked back in his chair, wearing the same denim jacket he's had since I can remember. The light from the fire pushes shadows on his face that make his crimson nose and bushy eyebrows bigger than normal. His black-and-gray hair is slicked back, held in place by a navy bandanna. His belly peeks out from his grease-stained white T-shirt.

"Hey, neph," Uncle Ricky says. The brim of his Minnesota Twins hat sits as low as it will go. That's how he wears his hats, and he is almost always looking down. His skinny frame is hidden by his baggy jeans and an oversized Red Lake Warriors basketball hoodie.

Everyone nods and I sit down with them. Feels like I interrupted something. Dad takes a sip of his beer. "You were out past your curfew."

"I know. I'm sorry. It won't happen again."

"Who is she?" Uncle Ricky asks, elbowing me and laughing. He's in his forties but likes to pretend that he's still in high school. Sometimes that's what's cool about him, and sometimes it's what is most annoying about him.

Dad squints at me and waits for my response.

"I got caught up hooping at the basketball courts out west. Lost track of time."

"Aye," Uncle Liver says. "You don't have to bullshit us, neph, we were your age once. We used to be up to no good, too."

"Still up to no good." Uncle Ricky crushes an empty can, dropping it by his feet, and digs into a cooler for a new beer.

"Your auntie Lisa said she saw you driving to the beach with a girl she didn't recognize," Dad says.

"Classic rez shit, eh, neph?" Ricky says. "Can't even be sneaky without someone spotting you somewhere."

Dad's not having it. "Ricky, shut up. Tre, don't break curfew, don't bullshit me, and reply to my texts when I'm checking in. Okay?"

"Yeah, Dad."

"I'm glad you're home. I get nervous when you're out on the roads. Lot of things can go wrong, even when the weather is nice. Never know if there's going to be a drunk driver coming at you, or any other type of accident. Nothing good happens after dark around here."

"Aye, that's when all the fun stuff starts, if you ask me," Uncle Ricky says.

"So fun you can't hold on to a job for more than two weeks at a time, eh?" Dad says.

"Holy, you didn't need to go there. Just ruthless, this guy," Uncle Ricky says, gesturing with his thumb.

A cold gust of wind comes in from the lake, which is only

about the distance of a basketball court from the edge of our back-yard. The campfire swirls. When the wind dies down, I push my chair closer and hold my open palms toward the fire. The heat feels good.

"Going to start on varsity this year?" Uncle Liver asks.

I shrug. "I hope so."

"Hope?" Ricky echoes. "Forget about hope. Hope isn't real. Got to go out there and take what's yours. You're the son of the greatest basketball player to ever wear the Warriors jersey."

"Don't listen to this guy, neph. The only time Coach White-feather ever let his scrubby ass in a game was when we were up by thirty," Uncle Liver says.

"Psshh. Baseball was my sport," Uncle Ricky replies. "You know I was recruited by University of Michigan? I was a hell of a pitcher. I'll have to show you one of my highlight tapes some-time, Tre."

"Yeah, unc, that would be cool."

Liver adds, "Your dad was the basketball player out of all of us. I liked football. Ricky was a good baseball player. But your pops, he could shoot the lights out. You should have seen him. He'd cross people over so bad they'd fall over, then hit a jump shot on them. Only one to ever be as good as him was your brother."

Light from the campfire dances around Dad, shining on his face. He folds his arms and sinks into his chair. When he's drink-ing, he has a hard time when anyone brings up Jaxon, even if it's for happy reasons.

Uncle Liver asks, "Can you dunk it now?"

Smoke from the campfire wafts toward me, and my eyes are burning.

I rub my eyes. "Yeah. Since last summer actually. But now I'm getting better at it. Throwing down different kinds of dunks."

"Hell yeah. Lucked out and had that growth spurt, eh? Thought for a second there that our basketball team was going to be trash for the next few years. Now they'll be in good hands. Working on that outside shot?"

"Yeah, it's coming along."

"Can you beat your dad in HORSE yet?"

"We haven't played yet. I don't know, maybe. He used to give—"

"Tre, you should probably go inside and get to sleep. You have to be up early tomorrow morning for your workout. Mom left walleye and wild rice in the fridge for you."

"Aww, come on, Ed. We never get to hang with our nephew. It's only ten."

"Good night, Tre," Dad says.

"Night, Dad. Good night, guys."

CHAPTER 9

AUGUST 26

I'**M WATCHING PEOPLE** hoop outside the school the next day, thinking about asking for the court next. Someone nudges me from behind. I turn to Khiana. She's wearing black skinny jeans, The Legend of Zelda Vans, and a T-shirt that reads *I'll sleep when I'm dead.*

I lean against the fence, no longer interested in playing basketball.

"Did you read any of *Apple in the Middle* last night?" she asks.

"No."

"What? You were supposed to read chapter one last night."

"Oops. Did you read it?"

"Want me to tell you what you missed?"

"Please. Wanna walk to class together?"

She nods and we move away from the basketball court.

"Aye, where you think you're going? Afraid to catch an ass whooping?" Nate calls as he spins the ball on his fingertip. I shrug and keep walking.

Khiana laughs. "You guys take your basketball fucking seriously around here."

"Yeah, we do. It's like a cult or something."

"I like cults," Khiana says, and then launches into this giddy explanation of the first chapter of *Apple in the Middle*.

After third hour, the hallway floods with students heading to lunch. As I stuff my book bag inside my locker, Khiana taps my shoulder. "Want to go for a ride during lunch?"

"Howah. Are you two banging now or what?" asks Kevin, who has the locker next to mine, as he digs out a plastic baggie full of peeled boiled eggs and proceeds to stuff one into his mouth. The smell of eggs poisons the entire hallway. Before either of us can answer, chunks of egg crumble and fall down his chin. Dallas, Mason, and Mike walk up.

"What's up with the eggs anyway?" Dallas asks Kevin, waving the smell away.

"I'm bulking up. Christ, don't you guys know anything?" Kevin asks. He looks like they just asked him who Michael Jordan is.

Mike laughs. "Christ, I'd rather stay all skinny than smell like farts all day."

Kevin fakes punching Mike. Mike gets into a pretend boxing

stance. "I'll bash you up, Kev. I ain't scared to fight a rich white guy. Even if it means you'll sue me."

Kevin rolls his eyes. "Fuck you." They start laughing and jokingly pushing each other.

Khiana is scrolling on her phone.

Mason shakes his head. "You guys aren't even funny."

The sound of a loud thud explodes from down the hallway. We all look over and see a couple of students grappling with each other against the lockers and throwing wild punches.

Fight, fight, fight!

Everyone quickly circles the fight, chanting, cell phones up in the air recording the action. I look at Khiana and jerk my head to the door, saying with my eyes, *Now's our chance.* She takes the hint, and we are off down the hallway.

"Does that happen often?" Khiana asks.

"Maybe like once or twice a month."

"Dang. What the fuck? I don't think I saw a single fistfight the entire time I was at my last high school."

We get into her car, and she blares melodic but heavy metal music as we drive down the road. We stop into The Trading Post and grab energy drinks, mini tacos, and an order of fries to share.

"Want to go and eat somewhere cool?"

"Duh," Khiana says.

I guide her to a spot that rests atop a cliff that overlooks the lake. We park and dig into our food. In between bites of fries, Khiana says, "This is definitely not athlete food."

I shrug. "It's not like the food at school is either. It's all tasteless canned food or gruel. It's like prison food. Other than pizza day. Those rectangular slices are heaven."

"My last school had so many options for lunch. They had a salad bar, fresh-baked goods, pasta, lean meats, all sorts of healthy food."

"Where'd you go to school?"

"In Edina." I've heard of Edina, but I must look confused, as Khiana continues: "It's this wealthy, mainly white school in the western suburbs of Minneapolis. My mom used to complain about how expensive it was for us to live in that district. But it's a great school, as far as graduation rates, college acceptance, and all of that."

"Do you miss it?"

"Yeah . . . and no. Kind of sucked that I had to move my last year of high school, though. Like starting all over, no friends, ugh, talk about bad timing. Thanks, Ma."

"So, you're a senior?"

"Yeah, and you are a . . . ?"

"Sophomore." I almost choke on the word. I watch Khiana's face, waiting to see if she shows any sign of disappointment in the huge gap between our grades. But she shrugs and chomps on a handful of fries.

"Lucky for us that our first-hour American Lit class is combined; otherwise you would have just been the dude who spilled my energy drink and not the guy who made me feel less alone on my first day at a new school," Khiana says.

"Lucky. For sure," I say, and reach for a mini taco.

I'm nervous eating in front of Khiana. I take small bites, making sure I'm chewing quietly with my mouth closed and constantly running a napkin across my chin to make sure there isn't food slobbered on it. Definitely not how I'd eat if I were alone or hanging with the guys.

"So . . . are you seeing anyone?" Khiana asks.

I can't believe she actually asked me that. This must be the part where I say no, and then she says no, and then we make out and fall in love or whatever. Either way, my heart is beating harder than it ever has during a basketball game. "No, I'm not." I leave out the part that I've never dated anyone. Or even kissed anyone, for that matter. But I want to give her a cool and mysterious vibe. "What about you?"

She grabs the last fry, rolls her window down, and holds it out to a mangy rez dog that is lingering nearby. He takes it from her hand and runs off.

Khiana wipes her hands clean with a napkin. "I was. Then she . . . cheated on me with the quarterback. Cliché as fuck, I know." For the first time, her invincible exterior melts a little.

"I'm . . . sorry," I say, regretting bringing up such a touchy subject. I think really hard about something better to say. But I'm stuck with *sorry*.

"Don't be. They deserve each other." She takes a drink of Red Bull. "And before you ask, because everyone does, yes, I said *she* broke my heart. I'm two-spirit, which among other things means I date boys and girls. And just so you know, my pronouns are *she, her*."

"That's cool," I say. Khiana shoots me a WTF look. "I mean, about the two-spirit thing, not about the cheating part. And mine are *he, him.*"

"Cool, cool. Well." She shrugs. "On the bright side, we are both friendable."

"Friendable?"

"Yeah, friendable. I made it up. I'm clever like that. It's like fuckable, but the friend version. We can be each other's friends without having to piss anyone off. If either of us was dating someone right now, they might not be cool with the two of us getting to know each other. At least, that's been my experience so far, and I could really use a friend right now."

CHAPTER 10

SEPTEMBER 25

IN MY CAR, parked outside her grandma's, I ask Khiana, "Are you sure you don't want to go to the homecoming dance for just a little while? We could go and make fun of how everyone stands around while music plays but no one dances."

"As exciting as you just made that sound, the last place on earth I'd want to be at is a school dance, or any sort of social gathering. I told you before that I get pretty bad social anxiety, but it's a million times worse at things like that. It's bad enough that I have to go to school when I'm forced to. I'm definitely not going when it's optional," Khiana says—quietly, like it's a secret—as she chews on her fingernails.

"Oh, I, right, my bad. I knew that. So, what do you want to do?"

"I don't know. We could drive down to Bemidji." Life comes

back into her voice. "There's a new horror movie that just came out last weekend."

"We could. But I'm broke until I get my allowance next week," I say.

"What happened to your birthday money?" Khiana slaps my arm. "Last week when you got us energy drinks you had a wad of cash."

I lift my leg up high enough to show her my new basketball shoes.

Khiana rolls her eyes. "You have more shoes than I do. Not fair."

"No, I don't," I say, but stop for a second to think about it.

Khiana gives me a *yeah, right* look, her right eyebrow rising sharply.

I shrug and set my leg back down.

"Anyway, I'm broke, too," Khiana says. "At least you're sixteen and have your license now. Your turn to drive us off the rez, finally. When we aren't broke, though."

My phone vibrates. It's a text from Wes.

Going to the wack ass homecoming dance?

Nah lol what are you up to?

Me and Nate are about to get down on a death brigade: bellum edition tournament. We could use your help. We're going up against other teams of up to four players. Come through. I bet we can dominate this shit like we used to.

"What's up?"

"Wes hit me up. Him and Nate are about to play in a video game tournament online."

"Yeah? Which game?"

"*Death Brigade*. The new one."

Khiana squeaks and claps her hands together. "*No* way. The bellum edition? Do they want company? It's up to four players on a team, right?"

"Yeah. I could ask."

"Already on it."

"Wait, what?"

"Oh, I added that nerd on all my social media like a week ago when I saw he had the guts to wear a Sailor Moon hoodie to school. I mean, fuck gender norms, am I right?"

"Yeah. For sure."

"You're not like jealous or anything stupid like that, are you?"

"No. Not at all. But maybe I should text and ask him. Since he invited me, and I didn't tell him I was with you."

"What's it matter? You said it was just those two, right? Them plus us equals a full squad. Have you played it yet?"

"No. But how hard can it be? I played the first two."

"Anyway, I already asked Wes. He said to come through."

"Okay, cool."

"You'll have to excuse the mess," I warn Khiana as we walk down the stairs to Wes's basement. I say it as quiet as I can, knowing how it has looked in the past.

"Psshh. I'm sure I've seen worse," Khiana says.

The smell of weed, old food, and body odor hits us as we walk down the last couple of steps into the dark, dank basement. The floor is cold concrete, with the only light streaming from the TV screen.

"You should have just said it would reek of nerd virgin male puberty. That would have been a more gracious warning," Khiana says as her nose wrinkles.

I was today years old when I realized just how goddamn bad it actually smelled down here. I guess this is the first time we've ever had a girl down here, though. Having a cute girl by your side makes all the gross boy smells magically more noticeable.

Noted.

"Hey, guys!" Khiana says, waving to Nate and Wes on the futon.

"Hey!" they both say, jumping up and turning toward us. Nate brushes off Cheetos dust from his shirt.

"Whoa, what is going on over here?" Khiana asks, venturing into the corner where Wes has the documentary interview spot constantly in place.

Khiana examines the lights, the chair, the white sheets hanging on the walls.

"It's for a documentary," I say, looking everywhere but at Khiana.

"A documentary? For what? Why would you guys never tell me about this?"

"It's about Tre. And his basketball . . . endeavors."

Nate snort laughs. "Nay. This guy. I love when Wes uses fancy words."

"Oh, it's a sportsball thing? Never mind. Just kidding. That's awesome. I didn't know you were a director." Khiana says *director* like it's the coolest, fanciest thing ever.

Wes scratches the back of his head. "I wouldn't go that far. This is my first one. But I'm learning as I go."

"Hey, Khiana, do you play video games?" Nate asks. "We got five more minutes until this campaign loads. We're going up against Team Weebgang. It's a sixty-four-team tourney. Single elimination. So, if we keep winning, we might be here awhile."

"Dope! You got four controllers?" Khiana replies.

"Yeah, well. I have two, and Nate brought two," Wes says.

"Sweet. Welcome to Team Meezy. You're one of us now." Nate walks up to Khiana and waves the controller overhead, tapping her shoulders like he's knighting her.

"Nate takes *Death Brigade* pretty serious," Wes says.

Nate hands the controller over to Khiana. "Aye, nothing wrong with wanting to win, at all costs."

"Okay, Cobra Kai. Mr. Sweep the Leg over here. Anyway, do you guys want an energy drink—Mountain Dew?" Wes says with a proud grin. "My dad is making us pizza rolls and cheese sticks."

"I'll take an energy drink," Khiana says. "What you got on hand?"

"All kinds. We play all night long on the weekends, so we load up. Want to come upstairs and pick one out?" Wes and Khiana walk up the stairs together, talking and laughing.

I squeeze in next to Nate on the futon and pick up a controller off the coffee table that's littered with empty soda cans, an ashtray overflowing with weed roaches, a rig for a dab, and a crap ton of forgotten candy and snack wrappers.

"What up, Tre? Did you make an appearance at the homecoming dance?" Nate laughs. "Everyone standing against the walls like usual?"

"Nah. Khiana wasn't feeling it, and I sure as hell wasn't going alone. You didn't want to go to the dance?"

"For what? And miss this *Death Brigade* tourney here? You know how long we've been waiting for this?" Nate asks like I just said I never heard of frybread.

"I don't know. How long?" I ask.

"I don't know. Like forty-eight hours, since they announced it on their social media accounts. But that's like six months in video game geek time. Get your headset on." Nate grabs a headset off the coffee table and drops it in my lap. "Wes! Get your skinny, flat Indian butt down here. We only have two minutes."

"Geez, chill. We're right here."

I turn to see Khiana and Wes taking careful steps down the stairs. Khiana is carrying a tray filled with pizza rolls and mozz sticks. Wes's arms are bear-hugging as many energy drinks and Mountain Dews as they can.

"Your dad is dope," Khiana tells Wes. "And super funny. And he's pretty hot. For a dad."

"Gross." Wes fakes puking.

"What? Just saying." Khiana laughs, pushing off the snack wrappers to make room for the snack tray. They set the food and drinks on the table in front of us and squeeze in on the futon. Our shoulders are pressed tightly together.

Nate snatches a couple of pizza rolls off the table. "One minute to go. Get your headsets on and controllers ready."

Khiana winks at me, then slides a headset on. She checks to make sure her controller is synced up, and then her eyes take on the same sharp focus I used to see on Jaxon's face when he was shooting free throws. Khiana grips her controller. "Let's do this."

The screen changes to a countdown with characters from the game popping up to count down each number. Nate joins in with the chant. "Seven, six." Wes joins in with a smile on his face, shifting more comfortably into the couch before leaning forward. That's when you know he's serious about a game. "Five, four." Khiana gets even louder than the guys. "Three, two." Khiana hits me with an elbow, and her eyes say *come on, join in*. "One, zero."

The demon on the screen grumbles, "Prepare to have your limbs ripped from their sockets, your eyes gouged and eaten, your heart ripped from your chest, and your soul . . . taken."

"Holy shit," Nate whispers. "No, they didn't." His mouth hangs open.

"What? *What?*" I ask.

Nate replies, "They've released the AI-controlled King Chaos demon into the mix. The geek forums said they might do this. If you see him, use an invisibility cloak and don't move."

"If you can find one." Wes chomps on a mozz stick. "They're supposed to be near impossible to find."

"Skoden," Khiana calls, running out of the base and into the forest. She starts firing off her machine gun.

"Go. Go. Cover her," Nate tells us as his character chases after hers.

Over our headsets, a kid we're playing against says, "You stupid clowns are going down in a new record. Less than one minute. Watch."

"What if I do this?" Khiana asks, before switching from her machine gun to a bazooka. She fires a missile at our opponents. It explodes, and two of them scream and disappear.

Wes asks, "How did you do that? I didn't know you could do that!"

The tip of Khiana's tongue hangs out as she bites down on it. One eye shut, she leans to the left, then back to the right, pressing into Wes. "Come on, go, go," she whispers as her character sprints behind a tree and ducks.

I go after her, but then my controller vibrates. "Player three has been summoned to the hell world. Enjoy eternity."

"Shit. I'm sorry."

"Ugh, you used to be so good at the older versions of this," Nate says through clenched teeth, leaning harder into me than I'm sure he realizes. "Thought you'd pick it right back up."

"We got you suckers now," an opponent tells us through their headset. Machine gun fire and missiles surround Wes, Khiana, and Nate. Their controllers shake and vibrate.

I set mine down on the table and grab a pizza roll.

"It's okay, guys. I got this," Khiana announces. "Nate, when I say go, throw a light grenade into the field. Wes, at the same time, run to the left, but make sure to barrel roll and get behind that rock. Ready?"

"Yeah," they reply like they're hypnotized.

"*And . . . go!*" Khiana says. On her command, they do exactly as she says. Khiana's character switches weapons to a bow and arrow, steps out from in back of the tree she was hiding behind, and clicks into a zoom mode.

Click.

Click.

Head shot.

Head shot.

A robotic voice in the game announces the victory. "Team Weebgang has been eliminated. Team Meezy advances to the next round."

"Goddamn. Where did you learn to play like that?" Nate asks.

"I watched a YouTube video on my way here. Plus, I received a beta copy of this months ago. Amateurs." Khiana fights back laughter and cracks open an energy drink.

Wes stares at her with starry eyes. "That. Was. Impressive."

"You a beast, Khi," Nate says. "I mean that in the best way possible. We were fucked right there until you pulled off those moves."

Khiana shrugs. "I'm all right."

"You should start a video game streaming channel. Hot girls always end up with a shit ton of followers. I mean . . . umm . . . you know what I'm saying." All of a sudden, Wes stares at the

91

screen very intently. He shifts his focus to the snacks. Bites into a mozz stick as marinara drips down his face.

Wes uses the cuff of his hoodie to wipe away cheese and sauce from the side of his mouth. "Probably get sponsored, too, I bet."

Khiana blushes. "You think so?"

Through a mouthful, Wes says, "Yeah. I could help, you know? I'm pretty good with video equipment and editing."

They're staring at each other so long it starts to get awkward. Khiana elbows Wes and nods at the screen. "Next round. Stoodis," she says.

CHAPTER 11

OCTOBER 3

THE TIMER ON my phone dings. I reach over and hit stop. Studying and homework are super hard for me. Not because I'm not smart. Once I buckle down and focus, I can breeze through most of my homework. It's just that studying and homework, well, they're always the last things I want to do. So, I have to force myself to sit down and read or do homework, and I'm the worst about waiting until the last minute to study or get schoolwork done. I set little timers on my phone for half an hour each because in my head, that doesn't sound so bad. And then I usually reward myself with a snack and a short social media break. I place a bookmark into my science book, making note that I'm about halfway through the chapter that I'm supposed to read before class on Monday.

I sit up on the edge of my bed and stretch my arms, then let out a big yawn. A car is rumbling down our dirt road. A few seconds later, I can hear the distinct rattle of the muffler of Uncle Ricky's rez bomb. I tuck my phone in my pocket, grab the empty bag of Doritos off my floor, and peek out the window. I look out my bedroom window and see my uncles Ricky and Liver walking up. Liver is carrying a small teal-colored cooler in one hand.

They knock on the door a few times; I wait for my mom or dad to yell for them to come in, but they don't. With a huff, I walk out of my bedroom and down the hall to the front door, and open it for them.

"Boozhoo, neph," Uncle Liver says.

"Boozhoo."

"Where's your dad?" Uncle Ricky asks. "We came bearing gifts. Aye."

"I don't know. Figured he was hanging out in the living room or at the kitchen table here." I glance at the sofa and over at the table even though I already know he isn't there.

"His truck is here, so he can't be too far. Maybe he's still passed out," Uncle Liver says with a chuckle.

"Nah, he never sleeps this late. He must be out back. I'll go with you. Could use a break from studying anyway," I say.

Uncle Ricky slaps my arm. "Were you really studying, or were you on that Xbox?"

"Psshh, I was studying. Come on," I say, slapping his arm back.

I wave them through the living room, to the kitchen door that leads to our porch, and spot my dad in the backyard, raking leaves.

My mom is following him around, stuffing the piles of leaves into big orange bags with pumpkin faces on them.

"You got company, with gifts or whatever," I say.

Dad wipes his brow with the cuff of his black Red Lake Warriors District Champions jacket from a couple of seasons ago. "What are you two losers up to?" he asks his brothers.

"Came by to have a couple cold ones with you."

"Suppose I could use a break," Dad says, setting the rake on a leaf pile.

As she ties a knot around a filled-to-the-brim pumpkin bag, Mom asks, "You boys hungry? I could warm up burgers and hot dogs that we grilled yesterday."

"No, that's okay. We're good."

Dad says, "Just say yeah; you guys know she won't stop trying to feed you."

Ricky laughs. "Okay, one hot dog."

"Two, please," Liver adds.

"Come on, neph, hang out with us a little while before you go back to being a brainiac."

We sit at the table on the back porch. My uncles dig into their cooler and pull out beers, handing one over to my dad. They light up cigarettes and kick back into their chairs.

"Getting all decorated for Halloween, eh?" Uncle Liver says, pointing at the clings of bats, witches, and pumpkins that cover the windows of the house, as well as the spiderwebs and fake spiders that hang from the edges of the porch.

"Getting there," Dad says. "We need to dig into the rest of the stuff in the garage."

Mom comes out with a platter of hot dogs and burgers with ketchup, mustard, and buns. Meat steams in the cold air.

Liver says, "You're the best cook on the whole rez, and the best host."

"I just like to make sure you two young bucks stay healthy."

Uncle Liver rubs his belly. "You don't have to worry about me."

"Miigwech." Uncle Ricky takes a bite of a hot dog.

Dad takes a couple of swigs of beer and looks over his yard-work. "Dressing up this year, Tre? Or too old for that stuff?"

"I don't know yet. Maybe."

"Still remember looking forward to seeing what you and your brother would come up with for Halloween costumes," Uncle Liver says. "Our favorite trick-or-treaters! You guys were Batman and Robin for a few years there when you were real young. Was perfect. Jaxon was so much taller than you back then—it made your outfits even more spot-on. Then your brother got all into Superman, down to that little squiggle of his bangs. Think I got a few pictures on my phone." Uncle Liver pulls his phone out of his pocket and starts scrolling. Uncle Ricky elbows Liver, gives him a WTF glare, shakes his head, peeks out from under the brim of his baseball cap just enough to glance at my parents, then over at me.

My dad stares down at his can of beer, his lips pursed. "Jaxon sure did love Halloween." Mom looks at her fingernails, her eyes welling up.

It's like a punch to the guts every time my parents get sad again. Especially my mom. I want to get up from my chair and wrap my arms around her and tell her it's okay. But I don't want to make a scene. I wish my uncle didn't bring that up. The smallest mention of Jaxon and my parents almost turn back into how they were the week of his wake and funeral.

"Did you find it?" Mom asks, still studying her chipped fingernail polish.

"Huh?" Liver asks.

"The picture. Of the boys on Halloween."

"Umm. Yeah. One sec." Uncle Liver scrolls through his phone again. "Here it is." He hands it over to me. The photo is from about ten years ago. Mom is leaning down between us with a big smile on her face, and her arms around our shoulders. Jaxon is wearing a Superman costume that looks straight from a film set. His hair is slicked back, his smile is perfect, his dimples pop from his cheeks. I remember his costume being legit, but I didn't remember it being this sick. And there I am, of course, goofy as usual. Half a foot shorter, dressed as the Flash, with my crooked smile and missing teeth. I'm holding up my bucket of candy.

"Well, let me see," Mom says.

I hand the phone over to her. And I'm a hot mess of fear and excitement.

Mom's face lights up. "I remember this. I spent a month, off and on, searching online for the materials to make their costumes. And then another month cutting, stitching, and sewing." Then her face goes blank. She holds the phone up so Dad can see. He glances, nods, and returns to his beer. "You'll have to send me that one," Mom says, handing the phone back to Liver.

Everyone is quiet for a while. My uncles dig back into their food and Dad lights another cigarette. A cold wind blows in from the lake, throwing the last pile of leaves into a whirlwind.

"The first year is the hardest. The first birthday without them, each holiday without them, especially when it's their favorite holiday." Uncle Liver reaches into the cooler for another beer. He cracks it open, takes a drink, and says to my dad, "When Mom died, that first Christmas was so hard. Sad. On all of us. Didn't even feel like Christmas without her. Remember how much that old lady loved Christmas? Holy shit. She'd have a tree up soon as we finished Thanksgiving dinner. Had Pops outside, hanging lights up along the roof and all along the windows. They always made sure to make it special."

"Things will slowly, slowly, get a little easier," Uncle Ricky promises.

Mom and Dad nod, like they're on autopilot. Mom squeezes the armrest of her chair. Dad guzzles his beer until it's empty. My phone vibrates and I don't know if I've ever been happier to get a text in my entire life. It's from Khiana. I swipe across the screen to open my phone.

Hey nerd

LOL what's up?

Nada, I need to go pick up stuff for my Halloween costume. Wanna come with? I'll come pick you up

Yeah

Don't sound so enthused

I am. Trust me. When do you want to go?

Twenty minutes cool?

Perfect

"Hey. Umm. Do you guys mind if I run to Bemidji?"

"For what?"

"My . . . friend Khiana needs to go pick up stuff for her Halloween costume."

"Friend? Or girlfriend?" Uncle Ricky wants to know. "Wait, is this the one you snuck off to the beach with that time?"

"Did you get your studying done?" Mom asks in what I call her Batman tone.

"Yeah," I say, as confidently as I can.

Mom gives me a *yeah, right* look. "Tre?"

"Okay. I did most of it. I only need to read for like another hour. I promise to finish it up when I get back."

"She cute? How long you been dating her? You didn't even tell your unc?" Uncle Ricky rattles off a bunch of questions. Thankfully, Dad tosses an empty beer can at him. "What? Can't bond with my neph?"

"She's just a friend," I say.

"Aye. That's how it starts." Ricky reaches for his wallet in his back pocket. "You need protection? I might have some in my wallet."

"Christ!" Dad exclaims. "He's not a hornball like you were in high school."

"I'm just messing around." Uncle Ricky hands me a five-dollar bill. "Here, get some snacks on your uncle."

"Thanks, unc."

"Anytime, neph."

"All right, I'm going to run inside and get ready," I say, pushing myself away from the table and wiggling my chair backward so I can stand up.

Mom puts a hand on mine before I can make my getaway. "Can we meet your friend? Maybe after you get back from shopping. I'd like to meet her. We know everyone else you hang out with like they're family. But we don't know her at all."

I swallow. I almost say, *You wouldn't do this with Jaxon.* I almost say something about being sixteen now and deserving space. I almost say a lot of things. But both of my uncles, Dad, and Mom are waiting for an answer. "Yeah, for sure," I say, like a robot that can't break from its programming.

"Thanks, honey," Mom says, and I almost cringe at her calling me *honey* in front of my uncles. But I escape without an argument.

My first stop is the bathroom. I can't remember if I put on deodorant this morning. One quick sniff of my armpit tells me I definitely didn't. I swipe some on, splash water on my face, and for once brush my teeth for the full two minutes the dentist told me to. I mean, I seriously scrub each tooth; I even run the toothbrush across my tongue. I saw an article online a while back that said that helps with bad breath. I lean down so I can see myself in the mirror, then run some hair gel in my hands and pat down some loose strands. My phone dings. It's a text from Khiana.

Your chariot awaits

OMW

"What up?" Khiana asks.

"Nothing much."

"Do you know what you're going to be for Halloween?" I ask as I buckle my seat belt, then check again to make sure it's secure.

"I'm a little torn. I have a couple of ideas, though."

"Oh yeah? Like what?"

"Was thinking of going as a gender-reversed Baraka from Mortal Kombat, as a fun challenge to myself to see if I could pull off that level of makeup and costume design. But also, super not cute. Or I was thinking of maybe doing something more classic. Like one of the Universal monsters. Maybe the Bride of Frankenstein? I know it's a little played out, but it could be awesome if I pull off what I'm imagining for the hair."

"Dang. You've put thought in."

"Of course. It's Halloween. Best holiday of the year. By far. Christmas is so commercialized. And the music? Yuck. What about you? Dressing up?"

"I don't know. Not sure." I stare out at the blur of birch bark and pine trees along the highway and take a breath. Saying it aloud hurts in the worst way. I take a breath. "Me and my brother, we used to always coordinate our costumes. Since we were little kids. Feels weird this year." My stomach sinks. "You know? Because it's my first time ever not having him to dress up with."

Khiana puts a hand on my shoulder. "That has to be super tough. I can't even imagine."

For a while, we just chill and listen to the music playing.

Khiana slaps my leg. "Tre. I have an idea. Like, genius-level idea. Cuz you know me. That's just how I roll."

"What's the idea?"

"We could coordinate outfits if you want. I've never done that before. But when my mom took me to a comic con a few years ago I was low-key jealous of all the friends there that made their cosplay costumes even cooler by matching up with people."

"Yeah?" I fight back getting overly stupid excited in front of a girl I like.

"For sure. If you have the guts, you could do like a gender-reversed Mortal Kombat character, too, like Kitana. Or if you felt more in your comfort zone you could pick any other character, like Sub-Zero or Raiden. But, hmmm . . ." Khiana sounds like she's already piecing together our possible outfits in her mind. "That's kind of coordinated; the characters are from the same game and all, but they don't necessarily go together."

Go together. I get goose bumps at Khiana saying those two words to me. Without missing a beat, Khiana continues planning out our coordinated outfits, thankfully ignoring the fact that my eyes have changed to cartoonish flashing hearts.

"I'm thinking of two that are inseparable from the other. Like Mickey and Minnie, Han Solo and Chewie, Batman and Robin."

"Me and my brother went as Batman and Robin back in the day. He was the perfect size bigger than me at the time, and my mom worked her butt off to make our costumes herself. They weren't cheap prepackaged ones. They were legit. My family was just looking at a pic from that Halloween right before you texted me."

Khiana smiles. "That's incredible. I didn't know your mom had those kinds of skills. Her and I will have to chat."

"She'd love that. You'll have to meet her sometime."

"For sure. But only if I get to see this picture of you in a little homemade Robin costume. I bet you were the cutest." Khiana's voice squeaks. "Ooh, I got it. I got it. What if I do the Bride of Frankenstein and you could be the monster. I would love to try to do that makeup, the bolts, the stitches. Eeh!"

"For real? That would be sick. I've never gone that far with a costume. Not with, like, makeup and all that. I'm down."

"Sweet. It's a deal," Khiana says. "I'll help you find an old suit at a thrift store. Yay! This is going to be fun. What are we doing for Halloween? If we are matching, we have to go to the same place, obviously."

I remembered her social anxiety and skipping the homecoming dance. "Only thing I know of that's going on is the Halloween dance at school, but I thought you hated those things."

"Yeah. Normally, that's how it is. But the costume makes me feel free, like I'm outside of the normal world."

"That's actually the way that I feel when we hang out."

"Yeah?"

"Yeah. Like this whole past year, everywhere I go, everyone I talk to, it's always the same. People telling me they're sorry about my loss. Telling me stories about my brother. I can't ever escape from it. Even with Wes and Nate, they're the most chill and the best friends ever. But they've seen me through this whole thing, so there's still kind of that vibe. But with you, it's different. I can breathe. And just be me. Not the sad me. Not the kid who lost his brother. But who I am. Right now. Who I might be tomorrow."

"I don't know what to say."

"That's a first."

"Shut up."

CHAPTER 12

OCTOBER 30

IT'S FRIDAY NIGHT, one night before Halloween. Since the holiday is on a Saturday this year, the school dance is tonight. Khiana has been working on my makeup for close to an hour. "Almost got it." She sweeps a makeup brush across my cheek. "There."

I get up from my bed and go to the bathroom. I barely recognize my reflection in the mirror. I trace a fingertip against the metal clips across my hairline, then touch the bolts on my neck.

"Careful. You look amazing. We are for sure going to win best couple's costume." She nudges me aside to touch up her face. Her white makeup, thick dark lipstick, and hair that rises up far behind her head with the curling white streaks—it's an unbelievable re-creation of the Bride of Frankenstein.

I say, "Thank you. You really got skills. You'll be working on film sets someday."

She winks at the reflection of me standing behind her in the mirror. "I know."

After a moment, she adds, "Oh, hey, we have to get a couple of selfies before we go. Ready?" She snaps several, and we pose slightly differently for each one. "Cute. Posting these."

"Can you send them to me? Oh, and my mom is going to ask to take a few pics of us before we go. Just so you know."

"All good. Your parents are way more chill than you made them sound."

"If you say so," I say.

"Plus, they got Halloween decorations all over the house, so bonus points right there." I'd first introduced her after we'd made our plans for that night, and they'd all hit it off.

"Hello," Mom says in an almost singsongy voice with a tap on the open door.

"Urgh!" I throw my arms out in front of me and waddle left to right, doing my best cheesy impersonation of the monster.

"You guys look straight out of the silver screen. Khiana, I'm impressed. You two are breathtaking."

"Aww . . ." Khiana's hands clench over her heart. "Thanks, Mrs. Brun! That means a lot to me."

"We need to get a picture when you're ready," Mom says.

"Told you," I say to Khiana, and we follow my mom to the living room.

When we walk into the living room, Dad is standing halfway

out the back door, smoking a cigarette. "This must be your favorite holiday."

She doesn't miss a beat. "Damn right, Mr. Brun. Best holiday of the year."

Mom puts her hand on Khiana's shoulder. "Go stand over there by the picture window."

"If you couldn't tell, Lori loves Halloween—maybe too much."

"Oh, hush, or I'll sew you a Grinch outfit and force you to wear it on Halloween *and* on Christmas. Okay, picture time." Mom snaps a few pics from her phone. We both hand Mom our phones and ask her to take pictures for us, too. Khiana and I break into a series of poses. One where she looks terrified and I'm moving toward her. One where we stare straight ahead at the camera.

Then Mom says, "Okay, now do a cute one."

"A cute one?" I ask. "How are we supposed to do a cute one? That doesn't make any sense with these—"

Khiana grabs my head and stands on her tiptoes and places a posed kiss on my cheek, which she holds for a couple of seconds to make sure the picture turns out. And even though it's pretend, it still gives me goose bumps.

"You two have fun tonight," Mom says. "Don't drink and don't stay out too late."

"Okay, okay," I reply.

"Take care of him for us. Don't let him drag you to a rez party after the dance," Dad adds, flicking his cigarette and closing the door behind him.

• • •

Hip-hop music blares from the speakers as we walk into the high school gymnasium. Strobe lights flicker, and the bass rattles through my bones.

"What's the deal with this?" Khiana asks over the music, gesturing to everyone sitting at tables or huddled in small circles of friends.

I shrug. "This is how our dances are. Nobody really dances, we all just kind of chill."

"Sad," Khiana replies.

Over in the corner of the gym is a snack and refreshment table that's decorated with a pumpkin-and-bat-themed tablecloth. There is a gigantic bowl of punch and a couple of clear plastic bowls filled with candy. Our athletic director, Mr. Thomas, and our civics teacher, Mrs. Hendricks, are watching the table carefully: last year someone spiked the punch and we never heard the end of it.

"You wanna grab some punch?" I ask, pointing to the table.

"Sure." The white, wavy streak in her hair seems to glow as the strobe lights burst across the room.

Mrs. Hendricks pours us each some punch. "You guys look . . . spooky? Did you do that yourself?"

I take a sip. "Khiana did both of our costumes and makeup. She's got some skills, huh?"

"I'd say. I've been teaching here for over twenty years, and I've never seen costumes this impressive. Nice work. Good luck in the costume contests." Mrs. Hendricks toasts us with her cup of punch.

Khiana smiles, and her dimples show. I bet she's blushing under all that white makeup.

"Stay out of trouble tonight . . . but have fun," Mr. Thomas says, holding out a bowl of candy. Khiana shakes her head no, but I grab a fun-sized packet of Skittles.

Mr. Thomas comes around the table and stands right next to me. Like shoulder-to-shoulder next to me. He folds his arms and looks out at the dance floor. Mr. Thomas looks like he could be a sports telecaster, with his slightly balding, feathered comb-over hairdo, the dark brown sports coat, dress pants, and shiny black leather shoes. All he is missing is a microphone and an athlete to interview.

"Season is right around the corner, Tre. I think you have a good shot at playing some quality minutes on varsity this year," Mr. Thomas says.

"I hope so," I say, with a mouthful of colorful sugar.

"You know, I'm so old that I was the athletic director when your dad was a student here."

"Yeah, that's what he said. About you being the AD when he was here, not about you being old."

"Your dad, he was a hell of a ball player. Boy, he could shoot the lights out. He had one of the smoothest jump shots I've seen at any level."

"He said that, too," I say, deadpan. Because it's the truth.

Mr. Thomas's eyeglasses reflect the strobe light from the DJ table as he turns toward me. He puts a hand on my shoulder and laughs.

Khiana elbows me, then lip-points toward where the other students are hanging out, gesturing to escape from the chaperones.

"I bet he did. Your dad never lacked confidence. That's for sure. Well, young man, you enjoy the rest of the dance." Mr. Thomas shoos me away like he wasn't the one talking *my* ear off.

Before we get more than two steps from the snack and drink table, Khiana balls up her hands and shakes them in excitement at the sight of Robert and his girlfriend MacKenzie's Han Solo and Princess Leia costumes. "Oh my God, your costumes are amazing," Khiana says to them.

MacKenzie and Khiana take turns pointing at and touching each other's hair and costumes. Robert grabs punch, then comes and stands next to me while Khiana and MacKenzie compliment each other.

"What's up, Tre?" Robert asks with a nod.

"What's up, Robert? Love the costume," I reply.

Robert looks like Han Solo on steroids. With his broad shoulders and big biceps, he wouldn't need a blaster for a fight. You'd never guess he was a hooper. He's half a foot shorter than me, but damn, when he is on fire, he can shoot the lights out from the three.

"Thanks; MacKenzie's idea," Robert says. "I wasn't even going to dress up. Yours is pretty cool. Looks like movie type stuff."

"Was all Khiana. She's really into costumes and makeup."

"Excited for tryouts next week?"

"Yeah."

Music pounds through the speakers. Robert is one of the

quietest people I've ever met. He was the sixth man on varsity the last few seasons. He'd back up Dallas or Mike if they ever needed a break or were in foul trouble. He finally became a starter for the first time when my brother passed. And now, this year, I might be the player who gets in his way of being a starter again.

"Catch you two later," MacKenzie says, taking Robert's arm in hers and waving as they go to sit down at a table. Robert gives me the guy head nod.

"Do you want to dance? It's okay if you don't want to. Normally, I don't dance, but I have kind of always gotten a kick out of doing the opposite of everyone else. Since no one else is dancing . . . what do you say?" Khiana reaches toward me.

"Yeah. I have to tell you something first, though."

"Yeah?"

"I have no clue how to dance. I've never actually slow danced before."

"That's okay. I'll lead. It's super easy. If you can play basketball, you can dance."

"Okay." I take Khiana's hand and she leads us out onto the empty gymnasium floor.

We make our way to the DJ table, and Khiana asks for a slow song. As the banging beats fade out, a slow Halsey song comes on.

Khiana steps closer to me and places her other hand around the back of my shoulders, and I rest mine on her lower back. "There you go," she says. We start to turn in slow circles, and I'm trying not to land one of my size-thirteen shoes on her feet.

"I thought you said you didn't know how to dance?" Khiana asks.

111

"I don't. I'm just copying what I've seen in movies."

Kevin joins us with his date, this blond girl he invited from some other school. Dallas, Mason, and Mike all come out with their girlfriends, and suddenly the dance floor is busy.

"We did it," Khiana says, nodding at the quickly filling dance floor.

"That was all you."

After a couple of songs, I excuse myself to go to the bathroom.

As I'm pissing, Dallas walks in and up to a urinal, thankfully a couple down from me. Even though it's the Halloween dance, he's dressed normally. Baggy black Adidas hoodie, loose-fitting jeans, and basketball shoes.

"Holy shit! Frankenstein. Killer outfit." His head flops back. His eyes glaze over.

I don't bother to correct him that I'm the monster, not Dr. Frankenstein, because that would be super nerdy.

"Having a good time?" Dallas asks.

"Yeah, man, you?" I ask, shaking it and flushing.

Dallas flushes and comes over to the sink where I'm washing my hands. He pats me hard on the shoulder. "Shot then, bro?" He pulls a flask out from his inner pocket.

Should I say *yeah* and risk getting in trouble, ruining Khiana's night, and possibly getting suspended before the season starts?

"Scared?" he asks with a chuckle. "It's cool if you don't want none."

"I'll take one." I throw a paper towel into the trash can. Dallas hands the flask over, and I take a swig, my eyes shut tight as it burns going down. "Phew."

Mason and Mike walk in just in time to catch my reaction, the bottle still in my hand. They're not in costume either. Now I feel like a dork, at least in here with them, being the only one dressed up.

Mason damn near yanks the flask from my hand. "Howah, didn't expect to see Frankenstein drinking in here."

Mike gives me a fist pound. "What up, Tre? Your costume is next level."

"Thanks."

The flask gets passed over to Mike next. His Adam's apple bobs, and the gulping sound is almost cartoonish. Dallas reaches for his flask. We watch him polish it off and stash it in the waistband of his jeans. As we leave the restroom, Dallas hands me a piece of gum. "Don't want the chaperones to smell liquor on your breath, especially Mr. Thomas."

Across the gym, I spot Khiana laughing at the snack table with Jason Voorhees and Michael Myers. Or Wes and Nate—that's their costumes every year.

"Hey," I say over the music.

"Your costume is . . . wow," Wes says, lifting his hockey mask and studying me from head to toe. He leans in close to examine my fake stitches and the bolts on my neck.

"Thanks! Jason again, huh?" I ask.

Wes pulls his mask back down. "Hey, it's a classic. And we don't all have Khiana's costume and makeup skills."

"Aww . . . thanks, Wes." Khiana takes a bow.

The music comes to an abrupt halt followed by a *boof boof boof* of our principal tapping the mic. "Good evening, ghosts and ghouls . . . and regularly dressed students. I hope you're all having a fun Halloween dance. I would like to take a moment to recognize our student council for raising the funds for this dance. Can we get a round of applause?" We all half-heartedly clap and look at the orange and black balloons, the clump of fake spiderwebs and plastic spiders in the corner, and the couple of pumpkin and bat decorations scattered along the walls. "And now . . . it is time to announce the winners of our costume contests."

Khiana does a couple of little jumps.

"Best couple's costumes go to . . ." We glance around the room at the other couple's contestants. Kevin and his date are dressed up as old-school gangsters. I'm guessing they're Bonnie and Clyde—their costumes look pretty stylish. MacKenzie has her arms wrapped as far around Robert as they'll go, leaning one Leia bun carefully on his massive shoulder.

Khiana squeezes my hand. Her eyes close.

"Frankenstein and his bride," our principal booms.

Khiana squeaks and throws her arms around me. My face flushes as she pulls me toward her and gives me a kiss on my cheek. But the buzz from the alcohol pried me from my body. For once, I don't care about what anyone thinks. And it feels fucking amazing.

CHAPTER 13

NOVEMBER 2

IT'S THE FIRST evening of basketball tryouts. I'm standing outside the gym, nerves running up and down my body. I feel a pat on my back. "Don't worry about it, Tre. You got to go in there and do your thing." Nate pulls the pick from his Afro and puts it into his gym bag. "I'm the one who should be worried. I don't want to spend another season on the B-team."

"Let's do this," I say. Inside the gym, I am shocked to see it packed with students trying out for the team.

"What the fuck?" Nate exclaims.

"Holy shit," I reply. "I didn't realize this many guys even went to our school."

"Only four real hoopers anyway," Kevin says as he walks past and heads into the locker room. Me and Nate try not to laugh as we follow him.

As we leave the locker room dressed in our basketball gear, Coach says, "Everyone line up against the bleachers."

Coach Whitefeather stands in the middle of the court. He's all limbs, like a scarecrow. His black-and-gray hair is pulled into a short ponytail. He's wearing a black T-shirt and blue jeans and dad-style New Balance tennis shoes. "This isn't basketball tryouts. This. Is. Boot camp." He surveys the group of us sitting against the flat, folded-in bleachers. "Some of you are not going to make it or won't be able to hang. Most will quit. Some will go home and cry to your moms. But those who survive . . . you get to come with us." Everyone looks stoic as fuck. Maybe they think he's bluffing. "We're going to start with circuit training. Each section of the gym will be a different exercise. Sit-ups. Push-ups. Jumping jacks. Wall climbers. Leg raises. Wall sits. Sprints. And when we finish with that, we'll run dribbling and shooting drills to gauge where you are, skills wise."

We are about twenty minutes along. One guy runs for the exit, gets to the door just in time, and pukes his guts out. I don't know if it was the realization that he was too out of shape, or if he was too embarrassed, but he grabbed his bag and left. Nobody laughs. Nobody mocks him. Everyone keeps doing whatever drill they're in.

Coach blows his whistle when we hit the half hour mark. Sweat drips down my brow and I'm breathing heavy, but I'm good. This is what I've been working for. I was doing all of those drills by myself, all summer. Almost everyone walks to the one water fountain and waits in line, hunched over. I sit down next to my gym bag and grab my water bottle out of it, and take a couple of sips, careful not to drink too much. Guzzling a bunch of water when you're working out this hard will mess you up. That's what Jaxon told me once, and I've stuck by it.

"You must have worked hard this summer," Kevin says, sitting next to me with a blue Gatorade.

I smirk and nod. "Yeah, I put in the work."

"Fuck. You got even faster than you were last year. Making us look slow during those wind sprints." Kevin twists the top of his Gatorade bottle off and slams half of it.

"My bad," I say.

"Nah, you're good, bro. Wish everyone took this as serious as you did. Guys mess around all summer, run a few pickup games here and there, and expect to be ready for the season. That's not how it works. Keep hustling hard, Tre. We need to be pushed this year. We could use fresh blood on the team."

Coach blows his whistle. "Break time is over. Everyone line up at half-court. Time to finally play a little basketball. There are twenty-five of you in here," Coach says, still counting as we all scramble to get to half-court. "Starters from last year are going to be captains and will be picking their teams. Not looking for anything fancy. Don't bother trying to be flashy or show off. That won't get you anywhere. I'm looking for high IQ players who play team ball and hustle hard. Kevin, Mike, Robert, Mason, Dallas, pick your teams."

The starters huddle up under one of the baskets. We can't hear what they're saying, but when they come out of their circle, Dallas points at me. "I got Tre." He waves me over.

Each starter picks players until everyone's team is decided. The team I'm on is up first against the team that Kevin fielded.

"First team to fifteen wins. Call your own fouls. Winner stays on the court," Coach says, handing a basketball to Dallas.

We start hooping and everyone except Dallas and Kevin looks like they're moving in slow motion. Everyone else is still breathing heavy from the exercises we started off with. That little water break we had was all I needed. I don't feel tired anymore.

I was able to show how fast I was during the sprints, but it's hard to display your basketball skills doing push-ups and sit-ups. Now's my chance to prove I belong on varsity.

This feels almost too easy. I'm getting whatever shot I want, stealing lazy passes, grabbing rebounds, and blocking shots. After I score a few buckets, the opposing team starts doubling me, which lets me set up Dallas for easy layups and wide-open jumpers. We smoke Kevin's team. We stay on the court for the next hour, undefeated.

After tryouts, I sit in my car, waiting for the window to defrost. My mind is replaying the first-day tryouts. Hoping that my hard work from this last year pays off. Hoping that I look worthy. When my car finally warms up, I buckle up and drive home.

"Hey, Tre," Mom says, glancing up from her laptop.

"How'd tryouts go?" Dad asks as he cracks open a beer.

"Pretty good, I think." I open the fridge.

"I made dinner before jumping on here to do my online classes. Your dad even helped cook for once. Fresh deer meat from the hunt he and your uncles went on last week and Red Lake wild rice I bought yesterday. It's in plastic containers in the fridge. Dish yourself up."

I fill my plate and grab a glass of water, but I'm unable to take a bite. My stomach is too tense. I can't stop wondering if I impressed Coach Whitefeather.

"I wouldn't worry so much, son. As long as you're working hard and making smart plays, you'll make varsity," Dad says as he takes a sip.

"How can you be so sure?"

"There's no way you don't make it this year. You're my son. You were born with my skills. Just like Jaxon was. Top two scorers in school history, and the first two to lead the Warriors to district championships."

I try not to roll my eyes. It's like he thinks he's Odin, Jaxon was Thor, and we live on Asgard. Guess that would make me Loki. I force down wild rice.

My mom stops typing and puts her hand on my shoulder.

119

"Tre . . . I know you love it more than anything, but at the end of the day, it's only a game. It's—"

"It's not a game, Mom. *Call of Duty* is a game. This is my ticket to college, and my ticket out of here. On top of that, everyone thinks of me as Dad's son and Jaxon's brother. I can't fail. I can't come up short."

Mom lifts my chin up. "You're way more than that. You can be and do anything you want. And anyway, you definitely got my looks and smarts. You're welcome for that."

Dad sits next to her. "Hey now. He got my last name, and my basketball skills. I helped."

We share a much-needed laugh.

Mom adds, "All I'm saying is, you shouldn't obsess so much about it. There are so many good things in your life other than basketball. You're an honor roll student, one of the smartest people I've ever met. You were reading books to me when most kids are learning to talk. And you're driven, self-motivated. No one was waking you up early every day this summer and forcing you to go and work out so hard. You did that. And that determination will carry over to anything else you want. You can do anything you want with your life. You hear me? Anything. So please, don't take what I said as me not believing in your basketball dreams. I hope they come true for you. Just keep in mind that you'll have a lot of options. A lot of kids don't."

"That's true," Dad puts in. "I know we talk nonstop about basketball around here. But your mom is right—"

"Per usual." Mom folds her arms and fights back a smile.

My phone vibrates. It's a text from Khiana.

Want to go see a movie?

Yeah

Can you pick me up? We should still be able to make a 7:00 o'clock

Yes, let me make sure my parents will let me go

Okay. LMK

I set my phone down. "Can I go see a movie with Khiana?"

"If you're so worried about making varsity, maybe you should focus on getting as much rest as possible," Dad says, moving to the back door. He cracks it open partway, leans halfway out, and lights up a cigarette.

"We're going to watch a movie. That's basically resting. You used to let Jaxon do whatever he wanted, with whoever he wanted. Now that I'm sixteen, I can't even go see a movie."

Dad takes a drag of his cigarette. "Maybe I should have been more concerned about him. Maybe I was trying too hard to be his best friend. Maybe I should have tried harder to be his father. Maybe . . . he'd still be here." With that, Dad walks out the back door.

"We worry about you, Tre. That's all," Mom says. "We've been around a lot longer than you have. We know what happens to a lot of promising young kids around here. Especially in my line of work. Do you know how many familiar faces I see? Kids who used to be sports stars, kids who used to have all the potential in the world—and now they're addicted to drugs, alcoholics, had babies super young. Some of the most talented, brilliant people around here slipped once and never really got back up."

"Well, I'm not them. That's not going to be me. I need you guys to believe in me. Trust me. I don't want to mess up my life. So can I go?"

"Yeah. Buckle up. Be safe. And try to be home as close to ten as possible. Deal?"

"Deal. Thanks, Mom." I shoot Khiana a quick text letting her know I can go to the movies. I take the quickest shower of all time, dry off, and get dressed.

When I come back to the kitchen, Mom is washing the dishes.

"Hey, I'm sorry. I didn't mean to hurt Dad's feelings. Again. Or yours."

"He'll be fine. Go, have some fun. Tell Khiana I said hello."

"I will." I kiss Mom on the cheek, zip up my coat, and start to trot down the stairs.

"Do you even have any money?" Mom's voice carries from the kitchen.

I pat down my pockets, realize she's right, and jog back up.

"Here, honey. This should be enough cash for your movie ticket, and snacks and drinks for you and Khiana."

"Thanks, Mom." I smile and jet out the door.

• • •

Khiana's grandma lives down the main highway on the way to Bemidji.

"What's up?" Khiana says, hopping in my car. "The parents set you free, huh?"

"Yeah."

"I remember those days. Nothing like being a sophomore. My mom used to be super strict. Before I could leave, she'd check my homework to make sure it was done, interrogate me about anyone I ever wanted to hang out with, make sure I was home by nine. It made dating damn near impossible."

"I can relate. My parents—especially my dad—grill me if I get home even a minute past my curfew. When you and I first started hanging out, he had a million questions. I wish they trusted me. They used to let my brother do whatever he wanted."

"I know it sucks. But I bet they'll chill soon. My mom got more relaxed with her rules with each school year, as long as I stayed out of trouble and got good grades. You okay?"

"For sure."

"You seem off."

"Maybe I am. I'm sorry. I'm tired. A full school day and then basketball tryouts wiped me out."

"We don't have to go to the movies tonight. It's not too late to turn around."

"No, I'm good. I promise."

"You're going to be busy all the time now, aren't you?"

"If I make varsity, yeah. I've never done it before. But it used to feel like Jaxon was either gone, chowing down food, or sleeping all basketball season."

"I hope we can still squeeze in time to chill once in a while. You're one of my favorite people, and the only person I hang out with besides my mom and grandma."

"We will. You're one of my favorite people, too."

Me and Khiana agree to split everything. She buys the movie tickets and I buy us a tub of popcorn, two sodas, and Sour Patch Kids before sitting in the middle of the back row of the theater. Khiana grabs a handful of popcorn. "Sweet. We got here at my favorite time to arrive—right after the half hour of stupid commercials and previews, but before the movie starts. Ooh, here we go." The movie starts with a white screen and a voice-over.

"Thanks for spilling my Red Bull that day," Khiana whispers as she rests her head on my shoulder for one second before sitting up and grabbing another handful of popcorn.

CHAPTER 14

NOVEMBER 6

IT'S THE LAST day of tryouts. My last chance to show I belong. I'm sore as all hell from the past week of torture, but we have one final scrimmage before it's over.

My team is down, 18–20. The first team to twenty-one wins the game.

Mason dribbles the ball up past half-court. The guy guarding him can't play defense for shit, but it's too late to switch.

"Ball game right here," Mason says.

No one comes up to set a pick. No one cuts to the basket. Mason dribbles the ball real low, crossing it back and forth between his legs. He takes a hard dribble to his right, and his defender goes for the steal. In a blink, Mason flicks the ball behind his back and drives to the basket. I flash like I'm coming to stop him, and he throws the ball to who I was guarding, which was exactly what I was hoping for. I tip the ball right into the hands of one of my teammates.

I demand the ball as I sprint up the court. Mason chases after me. It's me and him, side by side. We cross half-court, then the three-point line. Right as we hit the paint, I spin toward the basket. With Mason's hand in my face, I bring the ball up to lay it in and he swings to block the shot. I bring the ball back down and fly under the basket and put the perfect spin on the ball to bank in a reverse layup. With that basket, the score is tied, 20–20.

Next basket wins.

This time I pick up Mason for the length of the court, trying to steer him away from his sweet spot, that middle-of-the-floor area. I'm all over him, my arms are outstretched, and I'm low to the ground. Mason slaps my arm away, hard, leaving a lasting sting. "Get off me, rookie. You don't want none of this." His cocky grin has faded, replaced with a scowl.

I swipe at the ball, and it bounces off his knee and flies out of bounds. I fight back a burst of excitement. Everyone else is finished scrimmaging and is sitting on the sidelines, watching.

Mason mean mugs the hell out of me. Like I shouldn't have done that or something.

Nate picks it up and gets ready to take it out. Under my breath, I say, "Aye, man, me and you, right side of the court. Pick-and-roll. Mason is pissed. He's going to be all over me, overplaying me. When you set that pick, I'm going hard to the basket, but roll and be ready."

Nate nods. Everyone in the gym starts to hoot and holler.

Coach asks, "What's the score?"

"20–20," I yell.

Nate goes to inbound the ball, but Mason is all over me, hands flailing in every direction.

"Don't choke, rookie," Mason barks at me. "Don't choke."

I catch the inbound pass with my left hand and then secure it with both, cradling the ball tightly for one second. I collect myself, look ahead, and start dribbling up the court.

"Show him what's up, Mason," someone calls.

"Take it away!" someone else yells.

Fuck no. This is my game to win. Nothing is going to stop me. I angle my body so I'm dribbling with my right and leaning into Mason with my left shoulder as I make my way across half-court. He has fast hands. For the last few seasons, I've watched him take the ball away from people seemingly at will. In my peripherals, I can see Coach Whitefeather staring at us, arms folded. As I dribble, I worry if I've made varsity. I worry if I'm on the cusp. I worry whether this final play will make or break it. I drive hard to the right side of the court.

Bad idea. There is a cluster of people moving around over there. I wave my left hand, signaling for them to get out of the way. They clear out, leaving Nate and Kevin, and me and Mason. At a glance, Nate knows the exact moment to come up and set a pick on Mason.

There's a sliver of room, and I take it to the basket. But Mason slips around the screen. Kevin overreacts and is draped all over me as I drive. I go for the layup with my right hand. Kevin is high up in the air on my left side, going for the block. Mason is stitched to my right side, reaching in to steal the ball. I'm blanketed by two of the best players in the state, both doing everything they can to stop me. And they do that.

They stop me. But not how they're hoping to. I flick a no-look bounce pass directly behind me. I hope Nate has cut to the basket. If he has, I will look like a magician. If he hasn't, I will look like an amateur. I turn and see Nate lay a smooth finger roll against the backboard. It swishes through the net for the game-winning basket.

After practice, I scarf down dinner at home, shower, get dressed, and drive over to Wes's to hang out. We're all bored, but at least we're bored together. Which is better somehow.

"Sucks that we have to wait all weekend to find out who made varsity and who is on JV," Nate says, leaning back into the couch and scrolling on his phone.

"Yeah . . . time is going to go super slow," I agree.

"What would you think of shooting another interview for the documentary?"

"I don't know, man. I'm kind of out of it, zombie mode right now."

"Okay. I understand. It's just that—"

I shoot Wes a look. It's one part eye roll, one part death stare. We go back to staring at the TV screen, a live stream of a gamer playing *Death Brigade*.

Nate looks up from his phone. "What do you guys want to do tonight? Getting sick of watching this dude play. How about we have another *Death Brigade* marathon? What's Khiana up to? We could use her help again, if we do game."

"Games or movies," Wes says. "My dad doesn't want me going anywhere this weekend on account of the snowstorm that's supposed to hit tonight. If it gets real bad out, you guys are welcome to stay. It'll be like old times."

"Bro, I live right down the road. No matter how bad it gets, it's like a three-minute walk home to my place," Nate replies. "And so much for inviting Khiana over. Don't want her to risk driving if it's going to storm soon. Guess I'm stuck with you two."

Me and him go back to staring at our phones.

Wes scribbles in a notebook. "Whenever I watch documentaries, the best ones include tough interviews, from tough moments. That's what makes them compelling. Special. Those clips."

"He's not going to let this thing go. You should just get it over with," Nate says.

Wes shakes his head. "No. It's okay. I'm just saying."

I think about this documentary that Wes showed me last summer. It was about this guy who was a former mega-famous pro wrestler. The filmmaker showed how he was bankrupt, living in a run-down mobile home, scraping to get by, and that the world had forgotten him. But the wrestler had decided to get back in shape and try to get into the sport again. As he fought to stay sober and work out and make his comeback, he got injured. They shot an interview in that moment—when his comeback looked like it was hopeless. And his breaking point messed me up. I had to leave to go to the bathroom to hide my tears. Wes is probably right.

I say, "Yeah, man. We can shoot."

"Really?" Wes says, clearly fighting back excitement.

"Yeah. What else are we going to do? Plus, you're probably right. About the moments like these. We need to make this documentary—"

"Award-winning," Wes says.

"Nay. Award-winning, he says. Say that, eh?" Nate kids, and we all laugh.

Wes hops up and gets his lights turned on and his phone in the tripod.

"And, we are shooting," Wes says, focused on his phone screen. He moves one of the lights an inch. "You completed varsity tryouts this week. Question number one, how do you think you did?"

Nate is pretending to be playing on his phone, but I catch him sneaking a glimpse.

"I, umm . . . I think I did pretty good. I held my own against the five remaining starters. Made smart plays to win games in scrimmages. Showcased my dribbling, passing, and shooting skills in the drills we did. And I feel like I had the best conditioning."

"If you had to put money on it, would you say you made the cut?"

My head nods like a fishing bobber, but it's not in an agreeing way, just a lost, confused sort of way.

"He definitely made it," Nate says. "Without a doubt. One hundred percent. He was killing them out there. He showed up Mason so many times. Wish you could have seen how mad dude—" We both shoot him a look. "What? Sorry. You can edit that shit out. Tre, you know you made varsity. Stop fronting. Stop being so scared to say it. Own that shit. The best players, the Jordans, the Kobes, the LeBrons, they know they're the best on the court when they step on it. You gotta have that mentality, bro."

"Definitely edit all that out," I say.

"Man, shut up. I'm speaking the truth over here. I was there all week. Not only will you be on varsity, you'll be a starter."

"Your friend seems to believe in you. *So* back to my question: Do you think you made varsity?"

Nate's eyes are Cookie Monster wide and he's nodding at a ridiculous pace. I fight back laughter, and it feels nice. Then I realize I'm fighting back tears. Nate believes in me so much. And Wes is shooting a documentary about my basketball journey because he believes in me that much, too. "I love you guys. Thanks for being there for me. And for having my back. And believing in me, even when I don't believe in myself. I'm lucky as fuck to have you two as my best friends." Wes looks up from his camera screen.

Nate sets his phone down for the first time all night. "Love you, too, bro. You're more than my friend, man. You're like a brother to me. I know you're going to crush it this season. You put in that work, all damn summer. Wish I would have worked as hard as you did. It was clear in tryouts you were in insane shape. You looked like you barely even got tired when we were all dying. Proud of you. Next summer I'm going to be there with you, side by side during those workouts."

"Yeah, right." Wes tosses a rolled-up dirty sock at Nate.

Nate hurls it back. "For real. You'll see. This guy inspired me. Next summer, I'm committing to the Tre Brun workout regimen. Aye."

"Yeah. I'd say yeah." I collect myself. Wipe my eyes with the cuff of my hoodie and take a big breath. "To answer your question, I believe I made varsity."

CHAPTER 15

NOVEMBER 9

THE SECOND THE end-of-day school bell rings on Monday, me and Nate grab our backpacks and run to the gym. This afternoon is the announcement of who made varsity, followed by the first real basketball practice for both junior varsity and varsity. We round the corner of the hallway leading to the gym and see the list of names posted right outside the gym doors. There's a line of a dozen or so guys waiting to check it.

"You know you got this." Nate puts his hand on my shoulder as we wait in line. "If anyone should be worried, it's me."

A couple of guys exchange fist bumps as they walk into the gym. A couple more shake their heads and walk away. Basketballs thump. Inside, Coach is rebounding for Kevin as he works on his midrange jumper. Dallas is already in his basketball gear and stretching his legs. It's finally our turn, me and Nate.

We walk up and read through the names. The obvious ones are listed first, almost like they're in a bold, bigger font. Mason, Kevin, Robert, Dallas, Mike. The rest blur. A slow, painful realization sinks in. Something about your name calls out to you, whether it's someone gossiping or it's on a list. You somehow always hear or see it right away.

My name? It's not there.

"Hey, man," Nate says, rubbing my back. "Don't sweat it. Look, there are both of our names on the top of the JV team list. We'll dominate on junior varsity together. Shit will be more fun, us hooping together. I bet we go undefeated."

I tune him out. Everyone who made JV walks down the hall to the old, dark, cold gym they use for practice. Everyone who made varsity walks into the nice gym where varsity practices and plays their games. The players who didn't make either team head toward the exit.

"Tre? Where the fuck you going?" Nate asks.

I can't bring myself to answer him.

Moments later, I crank the heat in my car. Should I quit basketball? Or should I go back inside and give it my best on JV and show Coach how wrong he was? I picture having to tell my dad that I didn't make varsity. It's too much to handle.

Fuck. Fuck. Fuck.

When I get home, I walk in as quietly as I can, hoping to avoid my parents.

"Aren't you supposed to be at practice?" Dad asks as I'm turning down the hallway to my bedroom.

I keep walking. "No."

"Why not?"

"I didn't make it." I slam my bedroom door. Fucking parents always asking the most obvious-ass questions. Why the fuck else would I be home this early? I hurl my gym bag against my bedroom wall. I put my headphones on and turn some music on.

Khiana texts me.

Are you okay?

Ofc

Why wouldn't I be?

I heard you didn't make varsity

The blinking little dots mean she's still texting. I swipe out of our text thread and mindlessly scroll through my social media, making sure to flick quickly past any posts about who made the team. My mom walks in and sits on the edge of my bed. I take my headphones out but keep staring at my screen.

135

"Hey, honey," she says, in the voice she's used every time I've ever been sick or scraped a knee. "Are you okay? Do you want to talk about it?"

"No." Texts from Khiana and Wes pop up.

"Well, whenever you're done being all crabby, come on out to the kitchen. I made Indian tacos." Leaving my room, Mom shuts the door behind her.

I open Khiana's text first.

> Is it cool if I come by? It's okay if you don't want me to. But I'd like to be there for you

Then I look at Wes's text.

> Hey bro . . . I'm really sorry that you didn't make varsity

I text Khiana back first.

> It's all good. I'll be fine. Come on over if you want. Would be cool to see you.

Then I reply to Wes.

> Thanks bro

> It is what it is

> Maybe this basketball thing isn't meant for me

> I get why you'd feel like that. But I believe in you man. You got the skills. You know I wouldn't bullshit you

> I know this sounds crazy, but I think an interview about getting cut will add some grit to our documentary. Not today. But maybe when you feel ready. Remember the last one you didn't want to shoot? That's our best one yet. I've been editing it.

> This interview will make the film extra special, especially after you win state next year

Reading Wes's text pisses me off and makes me feel better at the same time. Like, this dude is still thinking about *his* documentary when I'm hurting, but at the same time it's nice hearing he has faith that I can ball. I walk into the kitchen. "Hey, Ma . . ."

"Hey, crab ass," she says, focused on a bubbling pan of grease.

"Is it cool if Khiana and Wes come through?"

She turns frybread with metal tongs. "If I say *yeah*, will you stop being crabby?"

"Deal," I say as I text my friends.

Khiana gives me a hug. Wes sets down his tripod and his camera equipment and daps me up. "Hungry?" I ask. They both nod.

I tap Wes on the arm. "Aye, bro, I don't want to shoot any interview for the documentary this eve. But I get your point from your text. I'll let you know when I feel up to it," I say.

Wes puts a hand on my shoulder. "For sure, bro. Don't sweat it."

"Thanks."

"Oh my God, it smells good." Khiana barges past us toward the kitchen.

We all sit down at the wooden table in the kitchen. Khiana, in between me and Wes, arranges her plate and Pepsi just right, holds her phone up, and takes a couple of pics.

"Maybe I'll be a food blogger someday. And I can say it all started with an Indian taco." Khiana laughs, and her thumbs blur as she crops, edits, and posts her pic to her social media.

Wes picks up his phone and likes her pic the second she posts it.

My phone vibrates. It's a text from Nate.

> Where the fuck was my invite? You know I love Indian tacos

> Sorry bro. Next time. I promise

> I'm just messin. My ma brought home Little Caesars so you know I'm Gucci BUT FR I hope you aren't too bummed about not making varsity. I promise we'll have more fun as teammates on JV anyway. We going to be killing it out there

And I'll be all right. Been through way worse.
Appreciate you tho

"Nothing wrong with playing on JV again," Dad says as he cracks open a beer. "You had fun last season. Most players don't play varsity until they're juniors anyway. Totally normal. Plus, there won't be the pressure of fitting in with the varsity team. This group of guys have been playing basketball together since they were in third grade, so they have a certain chemistry together. You'd be the new guy, playing different than they're used to. Might be tough to figure out how to play together so fast. The new guy gets blamed for everything in that sort of situation. This is their last season together. But next year the team will be yours."

"I guess," I say with a dismissive shrug. Embarrassed to be talking about my failure, especially in front of Khiana and Wes. And especially since my dad and Jaxon became starters on varsity in eighth grade. The only two guys in the history of our basketball team to ever get called up to play on the varsity team before they were even in high school. Not me, though, I guess. I can't even make the team as a sophomore.

My mom sits down next to me with an Indian taco and a Pepsi for herself. "Oh, Christ, Ed. Can we have one dinner without talking about basketball?"

"Either way, I didn't make the cut." I pick up my taco with

both hands. The golden crust, the aroma of ground beef, melted shredded cheddar cheese, tomatoes, lettuce, and a dab of sour cream smells so good.

"Mmmm . . . Mrs. Brun, this is seriously good frybread," Khiana says. "My grandma Doris always used to brag that her frybread was the best in all of Indian Country . . . but I think you've got her beat."

"Thank you, Khiana. I wouldn't tell your grandma that, though." Mom winks at Khiana. "We'll keep that review between us."

I nod at Khiana; she nods back with a knowing look. Who makes the best frybread is a never-ending point of pride on our rez, but also as safe as talking about the weather.

Wes is murdering his taco like he hasn't eaten in a week. I elbow him. "Damn, fam, don't forget to breathe."

"Shutupdude," he says through a full mouth.

My dad still hasn't taken a bite, but chugs the rest of his beer. "Well . . . you didn't start playing basketball until recently. Don't be so hard on yourself. Jaxon was so good because he was playing since he was in diapers. You were always wrapped up in your video games and comic books. Kept trying to tell you that you should get outside more. Asked you a hundred times to come play ball with me and your brother. Would have developed more of your skills by now."

He's always comparing me to Jaxon. He never gives me any respect. My friends are here, watching all of it. Ignoring Dad, I say to them, "Speaking of video games, do you two want to come check out my collection of retro games? My uncle Ricky gave me his old Nintendo and a shoebox full of games."

"Hell, yeah. I love old-school games," Khiana says.

"I wanna see," Wes adds, dabbing grease off his face with his napkin.

Mom notices Wes is done eating already. "Do you want another one?"

He pats his belly. "That's okay, I'm stuffed. Thank you, though, that was amazing."

Dad finishes his beer and cracks a new one. "Tre, don't get all sad about getting cut from varsity. Just go out there and have fun playing JV, study hard, enjoy basketball the way you used to enjoy video games. And maybe start thinking about a path other than basketball for yourself after high school."

I don't want to get into an awkward argument in front of my friends, even though Dad saying that hurts as bad as when I realized I didn't make varsity. "Good idea," I say.

Wes asks, "Did you know Michael Jordan got cut from varsity in tenth grade, too? I was reading about that while doing research for my documentary." I give him a finger slice of the neck, a *please stop talking* look, and he makes the all-teeth *eek* emoji face.

With that, I dig back into my taco, my comfort food.

Sometimes all you need is a good piece of frybread to heal your soul.

CHAPTER 16

NOVEMBER 13

ONE WEEK HAS passed since I didn't make varsity. But damn, it still stings. Even a week of torching my JV teammates at practice every day hasn't made me feel even a little better about my basketball skills. Wes is hyped, though. I hit him up earlier and told him we could finally shoot the next interview for the documentary.

Nate helps Wes set up and adjust his light stands in my parents' downstairs den. "There we go. It will look identical on video."

"Okay," I say, sitting down on a stool in front of the plain white backdrop Wes brought.

"You sure you're up to doing this? We don't have to if you really don't feel like it."

"Nah, I'm good. Do you think the audio will pick them up?"

I point at the ceiling. My parents are talking above us, and even though we can't hear what they're saying, you can still make out the muffled sound of voices.

"Hmmm . . . let me do a quick test video. Recording now. Say anything."

"If you can hear them in this video, I can go ask them to be quieter for the next ten minutes."

Wes records me sitting, doing nothing but probably looking awkward. He plays the video back, listening for background noise before assuring me we're good to go.

"And we're rolling. Tre, you didn't make the final cut on varsity. Why do you think that was?" Wes asks.

"I, uh, I really couldn't tell you. I felt like I played hard, made the right moves, and outperformed pretty much everyone."

Wes looks up at me. "What are your next steps?"

"I'm going to focus on improving my game. This past week of working on my game with my JV teammates has shown me I can really hone my skills at this level. I'll keep getting better."

"I dig it. I like the premeditated, good guy, say-the-right-thing response. We have it in the can, as they say. But now, for the sake of options, tell me how you really feel."

"You sure you want him to go off?" Nate asks.

Wes raises a finger to his lips. "Shhhhh . . ."

Nate shakes his head. "Okay."

"All I can think about is how excited everyone on the rez is for this season. Everyone thinks this could finally be our year to go to state. And I'll be watching instead of playing. It hurts, knowing I won't be helping them. That I'll be a fan, not the second coming of my brother that my dad hoped I would be. I—"

From upstairs, Mom calls, "Coach Whitefeather is on the phone! He wants to talk to you."

"What's he want?"

"Well, how in the hell am I supposed to know?"

I grab the downstairs landline. "Hello?"

"Tre?"

"Yeah."

"Did you hear about Mason and Mike?"

My worst fears pop into my head. I can't stand Mason, but damn, our world would be rocked if something bad happened to him. I have flashbacks to when my parents told me about Jaxon. "No. . . . What happened?"

"Those idiots were out drinking and got caught. Now they're suspended for the next two games."

"Oh man. That was . . . dumb."

My mom and dad come downstairs. Like I wasn't already freaking out. Now I've got to talk in front of my best friends *and* my parents.

"Yeah. Real dumb. Now we're short a couple of guys. Figured I'd invite you to suit up a few games on varsity. Monday at practice, we can show you some plays, and then Tuesday we play Clearbrook. They've got a good team this year. Do you want to help us out?"

My thoughts and feelings blur like a tornado. Roots rip and cows fly. I want to jump up and down and shout, "Yes, of course I'll play on Tuesday!" My voice is calm. "Sounds good."

"Good. Oh, and Tre?"

"Yeah?"

"I know you might have been mad about not making varsity. I had my reasons. But it was never about talent. I knew you got some skills. You got me?"

"Yeah." My thoughts go wild, wondering what in the hell those reasons could have been. But also, it doesn't matter. I'm on varsity.

"I'll see you Monday, then."

"Okay. . . . Thank you for the—" *Click.* I keep talking since everyone is staring. "—opportunity. I appreciate it. Yeah, yeah, no problem. No, yeah, of course." I hang up the phone.

"Well?" Dad asks.

"He asked me to play with varsity for the next couple of games. Mason and Mike are suspended for the next two games because they got caught drinking."

"And?" everyone asks at once.

"I said *yeah.*"

"That's what's up," Nate says. "You should have been on varsity in the first place."

Wes is recording the moment, never missing a beat.

I grab my phone and text Khiana.

> Guess what?

> What?

> I'M ON VARSITY NOW

OMG FR?

YES

I'm excited for you. Now you don't have to be acting all emo about not making it lol jk

Shush 😊

"Here." Dad hands me three twenty-dollar bills. "Go out for pizza. See a movie. Have fun." He almost always has the expression of that one grainy picture of Geronimo. But right now, right this second, his face is as proud as it used to be when Jaxon would make a big play.

"Cool." Still in shock, I grab the cash.

Mom hugs me. "There you go, Tre. I'm proud of you."

"Mom. You're—"

"Embarrassing you. I know. I don't care. That's what moms do." She finally lets me go, and Dad puts his hand in the air, calling for a high five. "Nice. You'll show them you should have been out there this whole time."

"Thanks, Dad." I slap his hand and ask my friends, "You guys want pizza?"

"I call shotgun," Nate says, running up the stairs.

CHAPTER 17

NOVEMBER 16

IT'S BEEN THREE days since I found out I would be playing a few games on varsity, and my mind has been racing the entire time. As I get into my basketball gear for practice, I look around the locker room and worry about what the guys on the varsity team think about me suddenly taking a spot, maybe taking some clock from one of them. Of course, that is something to worry about later; I still need to play well enough to prove I belong. No one says anything to me. Everyone is quiet as they throw on their practice gear. I lace up my basketball shoes. Here goes nothing.

I'm the first player into the gym. Only one row of lights is on, which makes the space really dim except for down by one of the baskets. I jog over to the rack of basketballs that are under the lights. I take one dribble, then spin the ball in my hand.

Coach walks in and clears his throat. "Hey, Tre. Welcome. Go ahead and set that back down for now?"

"Yeah. My bad."

"Don't sweat it. Go wait for the rest of the team against the wall over there."

I sit down, and now the single row of lights seems like one of those scenes in a movie when the detectives are interrogating a possible bad guy. This can't be good.

Coach Whitefeather paces in front of us like an army general, pointing to the wall any time anyone comes out of the locker room. Coach does a head count once everyone is seated.

"We aren't going to put up with bullshit. If any of you want to smoke cigarettes, drink booze, skip school, there's the door. When you wear that Warriors jersey, you represent me, you represent your school, you represent your family, but most importantly, you represent your people. If you can't handle that, then go on home." No one gets up, no one moves, no one says a thing. "Those knuckleheads are out the next two games. But they mess up again, and they're kicked off the team. Now let's get to work."

"You rolling with us?" Kevin asks.

"Yeah." I check out the court, waiting for him to say some dumb shit.

"Good," he replies.

As we gather around the basket, Coach says, "We're going to take practice slowly. All of you are returning players, and you know our playbook, but we need to teach it to Tre. We won't be running any drills, just walking Tre through as many plays as we can squeeze in. When he gets in the game, he is going to run point guard for us."

Point guard. I'm going to be the point guard for the Red Lake Warriors. Epic. I feel like Spider-Man in *Infinity War* when Iron Man tells him that he is now one of the Avengers.

We work our way through all the movements of the play. My head is spinning as I try to keep track of where each of my teammates moves to. Even running it through in slow motion, I feel lost. "You got it?" Coach Whitefeather asks.

"Yeah," I say, too afraid to say no.

"Run 44–2," Coach says. Seems simple enough. I got this.

Or so I think. Forty-four is a formation that has ten plays on one side of the court. And then another ten identical plays, but on the other side of the court.

"All right, guys, that's enough of running the plays tonight. Let's put it into action and run some scrimmages. See how much Tre remembered."

After practice, I stop and stare at the empty seats, feeling chills across my shoulders and down my arms. This place is going to be packed tomorrow.

"Don't overthink it, bro," Dallas says. "Same exact game you've been playing. Now there will be a bunch of people watching. Don't let it psych you out. What are you doing later?"

"Nothing."

"I can stop by if you want. All of last year's games are posted online. I could walk you through plays and break them down for you. Might help."

A mean gust of wind and snow rushes at us when we open up the gym doors.

I zip up my jacket and pull my hood on. "Thanks, man, that would be dope."

When I get home, I shovel down my mom's chicken-and-wild-rice soup and guzzle a liter of water, take a quick shower, and get dressed. As I'm pulling a hoodie over my head, I hear a text notification on my phone. It's a text from Dallas.

Just pulled up at your parents

Cool cool, I'll be out front to let you in

When I open the front door, Dallas asks, "What's up, niij?"

"What's up, bro?"

"Brought us snacks."

"Nice."

"Dallas Charnoski," Dad says like LeBron James walked in the door.

"Boozhoo," Dallas says.

"State this year?" Dad asks.

"You know it." Dallas hands me the bag of snacks and hustles into the living room, his eyes on the picture of Jaxon throwing down a reverse slam. "Holy shit, I remember that dunk."

"Yup. Jaxon could fly," my dad says.

"Hell, yeah, that was against Bemidji his sophomore season. He picked the pocket of their point guard, then raced down the court and flushed it. He had like thirty points that game."

Dad slightly adjusts the frame. "Thirty-three."

"My dad said you used to be as good as Jaxon was. He showed me a YouTube video of one of your games. It was kind of grainy, but it was still dope. Saw you cross someone over so bad that they fell and then you splashed a step-back three."

Dad is beaming with pride. "Yeah, that was against Blackduck, my junior season. Dropped forty-eight that night."

"You want to go watch those games?" I ask, trying to steal Dallas away before Dad launches into the entire back catalog of both his and Jaxon's playing careers.

We go downstairs to the den and pull up last season's games online on the small TV that we have down here. Dallas asks, "You want Takis or Chili Cheese Fritos, bro?"

I turn on the TV. "Takis."

"Pop?" he asks, holding up a grape Sunkist.

I grab it and fall back into the couch, trying not to be starstruck. I've been watching this guy ball on people for years now. It feels like I'm sitting with a celebrity. Damn, Tre. Chill.

"Hey, we didn't even cover this at practice," Dallas says, jumping up. Standing next to the TV, he goes into a detailed explanation of their, I mean *our*, tip-off play. Then the rest of the night, he shows me the plays we ran in practice, rewinding, pausing, crunching on his Fritos the entire time. "You nervous about tomorrow?"

"A little."

"Don't sweat it. If you want to get some serious clock, leave everything on the court. I'm not the best, but I play harder than everyone else. I get the loose balls, the garbage points, and I bust my ass on defense. Bring that energy tomorrow night and you'll be good."

CHAPTER 18

NOVEMBER 17

THE FINAL BELL of the school day rings. I carefully place a small God's Eye that I made in my Ojibwe Arts and Crafts class into the top of my locker. The yellow, white, and baby-blue-colored yarn is wrapped and tied around sticks, forming a diamond shape. I'm getting better. The first one I made was a mess—looked like a cat had torn it to shreds. Now that I'm on my third one, I think I've got the hang of it. It's my favorite class. Only one that takes my mind off basketball.

"How many points you going to score tonight, bro?" Nate asks, yanking me back to reality.

I shrug. "I just hope I don't do anything too silly out there."

"You deserve to be out there. Remember that. But for real. Don't shoot any airballs."

"Shut up," I say, and we both laugh. "Crush it out there with the JV tonight."

"You know it. I'll catch ya later, bro," Nate says, and we fist-pound.

"Congrats on getting called up to varsity. Good luck out there tonight, Brun," Mr. Thomas says as he and a couple of teachers walk by. I wave and say thanks.

Wes and Khiana come around the corner.

"You ready to shoot our interview?" Wes asks, holding a notebook and his phone.

"Ahh, shit, man. I forgot we were doing that."

"Hope you don't mind if I'm there while you guys do the interview. You're not going to get all bashful if I'm watching, will you?" Khiana asks.

"Nah. It's cool. Let's go, though. I need to still get home and eat dinner. I'm starving. Where are we going to shoot?"

Wes says, "I got the keys to that room that used to be for theater and band."

Khiana tells him, "If you ever need an assistant for editing, let me know. I helped an ex edit a music video and it was fun watching how something like that comes together."

"Yeah, I'd love that. Takes forever to edit a short clip. Would be nice to have a second set of hands and eyes."

I get this weird feeling in my stomach realizing how well they click. "Is the door unlocked?"

"No, but the principal trusted me with the key. After a lot of requests, emails, calls from my dad, and an essay on why I could benefit from this unused space." Wes pulls out his keys, unlocks the door, and turns on the lights. "It's a shame we don't have theater or band anymore. My dad still talks about how much he loved both."

Me and Khiana help Wes with setting up his lights, backdrop, and tripod. Once we're ready, Wes asks questions about my first game, the pressure and the expectations. Khiana offers a couple of suggestions for questions, which Wes passes on.

The lobby to the gym is filled with fans buying tickets to the game, getting snacks from the concession stand, and buying this year's team apparel. I twist and turn my way through the crowd. Glass cases filled with trophies and team pictures are positioned outside the gym. One of them is filled with pictures from my dad's era. It's wild seeing him look my age. In one image, he's holding up a trophy for setting our school's all-time record for points. In other photos, he's holding up season MVP trophies and All-Conference trophies.

I move to the next case—the one they call *Jaxon's*. His Warriors jersey hangs behind the glass, almost like his ghost is keeping it afloat. I take in his three MVP trophies, his top scorer trophy, and his All-Conference trophies. I press my hand to the glass and whisper, "I hope I make you proud tonight, big bro. Wish you were here."

I peek into the gym in time to watch Nate use a spin move for a layup. The crowd roars for the basket and it feels as loud as the last play-off game. Half the seats are already filled. I look up to Dad's spot. That's what Jaxon used to call it. Half-court line, all the way up to the top row, against the brick wall, on the same side of the gym as the team benches. Dad's chomping on popcorn, chatting with my uncles. Mom is usually next to him, but she has online classes tonight.

Along the wall against the baseline sit the Elders, a lot of them in wheelchairs. They never miss a home game.

"Tre," Dallas calls, waving me over. He's surrounded by the rest of the varsity team. Relief washes over me. Thank the Creator for Dallas. Time races by as I sit and cheer on Nate and the rest of our JV team as they give Clearbrook a first-half beatdown. After halftime ends, Dallas says, "Come on, bro. Time to go suit up."

When I walk into the locker room, Robert is stretching his legs. He looks up and nods at me. Kevin is wrapping athletic tape around a swollen middle finger. The rest of the guys are goofing off, making jokes as they slowly get suited up.

Dallas sets his gym bag down in front of a red locker. He turns and twists the combination lock until it pops open. Inside is a scattered mess of empty Gatorade bottles, granola bar wrappers, and a pile of socks and boxer shorts. Dallas looks over at me. "Sorry about the smell. I really need to take this shit home and wash it. Do you have a locker assigned yet?"

"I don't have one yet. JV didn't get lockers. Our gym bags are our lockers."

"That one is free. We've had the same lockers since ninth grade. That one was . . . that one was your brother's." Dallas looks down at the floor for a second. Pausing. He takes a breath and tightens his shoestrings. "But make sure and buy yourself a lock before you start leaving stuff in there."

"Cool. Thanks," I say, and open the door to set my bag inside. There is a Post-it note dangling on the back of the locker.

Never stop trying to get
Better than before
Smarter than yesterday
Stronger than you ever thought you could be
J.B.

This really was Jaxon's locker. I reach in and press my fingers against the note, hoping it will make me feel a little close to him for one moment.

"Nervous?" Startled, I jump and turn to see Coach White-feather.

"Nah," I say.

"Okay, Tre. I hope you shoot better than you lie. Come on back to my office. We got to get a jersey for you."

His office has a desk with a computer, an old-fashioned phone, and a box that is overflowing with bottles of hand chalk, markers, erasers, and whistles. On his wall is an American Indian Movement flag, his college degree from Bemidji State University, and grainy, framed pictures of Red Lake Warriors basketball teams. Then I spot one of him and Jaxon. My brother is holding up his 2,000-points trophy and they're both grinning. Coach opens his closet and pulls out a large cardboard box. "One jersey left, number ten." He tosses it to me. It's red with black and white on the letters and numbers.

I feel like Rey holding a lightsaber for the first time, like maybe I'm a Jedi now.

Coach grabs a pair of trunks and hands them over, then digs out another uniform. This one is mostly white with red-and-black trim. "Your away uniform."

"Thank you," I say, still mystified by the idea of holding *my* varsity Warriors uniform. I run my fingers across the jersey over the word *Ogichidaa*. It means *Warriors* in Ojibwe.

"Pretty ace, huh? Those jerseys are new this season. Thought it would be cool for us to have our team name in Ojibwe. Feels like the word is clearer, stronger, means more."

I stand there looking at the jersey, my jersey, still in awe. When I come back to reality, I wonder if I should excuse myself, or if he has more to say.

Coach glances up and notices me still standing there. "I suppose, before we get this season underway, I should take a minute to tell you what happened with you not making the varsity team originally. Have a seat." He points at one of two chairs facing his desk. "Like I said on the phone, it wasn't about talent. You got the skills. I was taking a gamble on a couple of things. I didn't want to mess with the chemistry of this team; the core of the team has been playing together since they were in diapers. There's a certain type of magic that comes with that amount of time together. I was worried bringing you on board might mess that up."

Coach digs out a cigarette from a drawer and fiddles with it but never lights it. He stares at it, then continues, "More importantly, I didn't think it was fair to throw you into the fire like that. I figured it was best for you to have one more season of fun and develop your game without a spotlight on you the whole time. I know the pressure that is on you to follow in the footsteps of your father, and especially your—"

Coach stops talking and lets out a sigh. My dad does the same thing sometimes when he's having a hard time talking about Jaxon. I know my dad cries, but he never wants anyone to see it. Looks like Coach is the same way.

"I get it, Coach. It's okay. That makes sense to me. I'm just happy to be here, and I hope I don't let you down."

Coach Whitefeather's eyes get watery. "You won't. I know you won't. I just wanted you to know that I never doubted your skills. I know how serious hoopers like you take that sort of thing."

Coach watches the look on my face with concern in his eyes. He sits down at his desk and leans forward, his hands clasped. "Couple of rules we have on this team. Pay attention when I'm talking; try to learn something new every practice, every game. Play as hard as you can. And this next set is my most important: stay out of trouble, no drinking, no smoking, take school serious, keep your grades up. You have to be passing all classes to be able to play. You got me?"

"Yes, Coach. I do. My brother used to tell me sometimes he thought the only reason some of his teammates stayed in school was because of your rules. My dad said the same thing about back in the day, that being on the team made him keep his grades up and not get into any sort of trouble."

"Good. Glad to hear a few people agree with me around here. One last thing," Coach says, shooting me a serious look.

"Yeah, what's that?" I ask.

"I'd like for you to start the game tonight. After watching practice yesterday, it's clear that without Mason, you're the best ball handler we currently have. And after watching you play alongside our starters, I could see something magic going on out there. Think you feel comfortable enough with the plays?"

"Yeah. I have a couple of them down, a couple I'm still figuring out," I say.

Coach looks at my rapidly tapping foot, then up at me. "You're playing with a team of vets. They will help you. I'll help you. Run the plays you have memorized. In between time-outs and half-time, I'll refresh your memory on some of the other ones."

I'm nodding, way faster than anyone should ever safely move their head. My left foot is still tapping away like a bunny rabbit's.

"It will be fine, Tre." Coach looks at his watch. "You better hurry and get suited up. I'll be out there in a minute to walk you guys through tonight's game plan."

"Yes, sir." I shake my head as I walk out. Sir? Ugh. Why'd I say that? I never say *sir*. So corny. In front of my locker, I slide out of my clothes and into my uniform. When I look down again at the red-and-black jersey—the word *Ogichidaa* across the chest—goose bumps flash across my body. All of a sudden, I'm that short, nerdy middle school kid again, the one louder than everyone in the gym every time Jaxon posterized someone.

And now, it's my turn.

"All right, everyone. Sit down and listen up." Coach White-feather paces. "Clearbrook is a scrappy team and they're disciplined. That coach over there has been there forever. He knows his stuff. And that town is a bunch of racists who hate Indians. Hate us. They don't want to beat you because of basketball. They want to beat you because they hate you. Their parents hate you. And their grandparents hate you even more. That gives them an edge on you guys, if you don't come out and play hard right from the jump."

Coach grabs a marker and draws the outline of a basketball court on the dry-erase board. "Keep your thoughts within these lines. Nothing that happens outside of these lines matters. You got me? *Keep your thoughts within the lines.* You can use that advice for a lot of things in your life." The buzzer blares, echoing into the locker room. The cheering of the crowd grows as the JV team walks in. "We're only running the set of plays we showed Tre at practice for the first half, so he will know what in the hell is going on. When we reconvene at the half, we'll give him a refresher of JD. Bring it in."

Everyone stands up and forms a circle, with our hands intertwined together at the top. "That crowd out there, they're still holding on to that last play-off game. But tonight is the start of a whole new season. Forget about last year. Start fresh. Now let's go out there, play hard-nosed defense, and play team basketball. All right?"

Everyone hoots and hollers.

Holy shit. This is it.

• • •

The announcer bellows, "Welcome to tonight's game between the Clearbrook-Gonvick Bears and *your* Red Lake *Warriors*! And now, the starting lineups."

Breathe, Tre. Breathe.

The announcer lists the visiting team's starters and coaches to the sound of golf claps. Our coach points to each player as they run out onto the court and assigns one of us to guard them. "And now, the starting lineup for the home team. Standing at six foot four, a sophomore making his debut, wearing number ten, Tre Brun!"

I leap up from the bench and run through the tunnel of my teammates, giving high fives to their extended hands as I pass by. I run over and shake the opposing coach's hand, then jog to half-court and wait for the rest of my teammates to be introduced.

The crowd keeps cheering as the referees get ready for the tip-off. I've never been on the court with a packed gym, I've always been in the stands. People all around talk, laugh, clap, cheer, and whistle, the sounds mashing into a single inhuman voice. Like static. In the top row, Dad is looking right at me. We nod at each other, and it brings me a small comfort.

Dallas yells something, but I can't hear. I shrug and point to my ears. He laughs and points at my shoes. One of my laces is untied. Shit. I kneel and tie it as fast as I can. The referee takes note and holds his hand up, letting the other two referees know to hold tight. My hands are clammy, making it harder to get ahold of my shoelaces as I struggle to tie them tighter this time. Phew. Okay. I nod at the ref as I stand back up.

The referee tosses the ball up in the air. Here we go!

Kevin jumps and tips the ball to me. Rounded leather snaps into my fingertips. Two defenders streak toward me. The sound of the crowd is cut by sharp squeaks of basketball sneakers stomping, turning, and stopping on the wood court. The thumping of the basketball matches my heart rate as I dribble away from my opponents, keeping my body between them and the ball as I spin. Dallas races down the court. I throw a bounce pass ahead of him, hoping I've timed out his speed. He catches the ball and lays it up. Relief washes over me. The first play went okay. I can do this. I'm fine.

Back on defense, I try to block a shot from their point guard, swiping at the ball, but I slap his forearm. The referee blows his whistle. Less than one minute into my first varsity game, and I've already picked up a foul. Great.

Clearbrook's point guard makes both free throws to tie it up. I bring the ball up the court and call out a play, but I go the wrong direction. My teammates yell at me, but the more they yell the more confused I get. Robert runs over, asking for the ball. I break the play and pass it to him. He crosses over his guy like we are on the playground and goes to the basket for an easy two. My screwups start to feel like dominoes falling as I botch the next couple of plays, too.

After I pick up my second foul, Coach Whitefeather screams for a time-out. "You're running around out there like a goddamn crackhead on the first of the month. Tre, I'm sitting you down."

I grab a spot on the bench. The scoreboard reads 7–5. The guy I was guarding makes both of his free throws. 7–7. I notice the time on the clock. I made it two whole minutes before getting into serious foul trouble. You only get five personal fouls in high school ball before you are out the rest of the game, and I have two already. SMH. Way to go, Tre.

Without me in the game, our team runs the plays smoothly. They score effortlessly, like they are playing against little kids. Robert calls a play for Kevin to post up down low. Kevin takes a couple of hard dribbles to the right, fakes left, spins right, and fades away for an easy two.

"Deer hunter," Coach Whitefeather calls.

Our team gets into a full-court press. Clearbrook panics and throws a high pass that Dallas picks off. He hits Robert for a layup. It's almost like watching an instant replay as our full-court press continues to haunt Clearbrook over and over, leading to turnovers for them and layups for us. Like a defenseless, starry-eyed boxer up against the ropes and getting his lights knocked out, their coach hollers for a time-out.

Our cheerleaders start a routine that I've heard my entire life, and our fans start chanting along. I glance at the scoreboard. We are up 17–7. A part of me feels glad that we have taken control of the game. Another part of me worries that my teammates did it without me.

As the first half ends, Coach Whitefeather walks by. "I couldn't put you back in with two fouls, worried you'll pick up your third one just as fast. Saving you for the second half." Then he barks orders to the players on the court.

We enter the locker room at halftime, up 45–24.

Coach Whitefeather grabs a marker from the whiteboard, twirling it slowly. "If we want to go to state this year, we can't rely on our press to do it for us. A good team will break it. We need to play better team defense. Christ, you guys aren't helping each other out there. Good teams rotate. Good teams help each other out." A couple of the players nod. A few study their shoes or stare into space while sipping from water bottles. With a stomp, Coach says, "Tre!"

He's got my full attention. "Yeah?"

"These are the first five plays of forty-four. We're going to review them real quick."

I only had one day of practice, and I feel like a pimple on your forehead on school picture day. I pay super-close attention as Coach scribbles on the whiteboard, drawing lines, Xs, Os. "You good, Tre?" Coach asks.

"Yeah."

"Okay, good. We're going to go with the same five that we started with. Bring it in."

We stand in a circle and put our hands together in the middle. Kevin shouts, "One, two, three," and everyone simultaneously says, "Warriors!"

Clearbrook gets ready to inbound the ball, and I'm even more nervous than when the game started. Their point guard says, "Kansas," and swings the ball over to the wing. They set a screen on me. Kevin and I switch, and I end up guarding their center, who's way the hell taller than me—at least six ten. They see the mismatch and toss it over to him.

He posts me up, takes a couple of dribbles, then spins to the basket. I swipe at the ball, knocking it down the court. Dallas grabs the ball and passes it across the court to Robert, who drives to the basket. Defenders collapse on him.

He goes up on one side of the basket, tucks the ball away as he floats under the rim, and twirls the ball up on the other side. It hits the backboard, but a little too high. I leap in the air; the ball rims out into my hand. For a second everything slows down. The gym is on mute.

I've never been this high in the air before. I slam the ball through the rim. Hard.

The normal speed of the world and the sound of the gym returns. I beat my fist against my chest and run back up the court. Our fans are jumping up and down, screaming and cheering.

Clearbrook's point guard races down the court and flings up a three-pointer from a few feet beyond the arc. The shot misses, and I grab the rebound and dribble downcourt. Dallas is on my right side and Kevin on my left. As we cross our three-point line, I fake passing to Dallas, then throw a no-look alley-oop into the air for Kevin, who hammers down a nasty two-handed dunk that leaves the backboard shaking.

The Clearbrook players look like they just saw a monster—five monsters.

Everything is going great until I pick up my third foul contesting a jump shot.

"That's three on you, Tre!" Coach shouts, holding up three fingers. "You only get five!"

The Clearbrook player makes their free throws and, as we're going back up the court, he nudges me and winks. I give him a shove, not a hard one, a small one to let him know what's up. As soon as I extend my elbow a little, he flails like he got hit by a car.

The referee blows his whistle. "Personal foul on number ten."

Coach Whitefeather hollers, "Jesus Christ!"

I spend the rest of the game on the bench, worrying that I blew my chance to keep my starting spot on varsity. When the game ends, kids rush down from the stands and race toward Robert, Kevin, and Dallas like they used to for Jaxon. I remember waiting an hour after games to give my big brother a hug. The kids are holding mini basketballs, game programs, and T-shirts, and some even offer their forearms to be autographed. Nobody asks me to sign anything.

When I walk in, my mom stops typing. "How did the game go?"

I dig through the fridge. "We won."

"Nice. Congratulations, Tre. There's leftovers."

"I'm not hungry." I grab a Gatorade, crack it open, and chug half of it.

"Sorry I couldn't make it. My online class did a review of the study guide for tomorrow's test in my Advanced Policy Analysis, Advocacy, and Contemporary Issues class."

"The name of that class makes it sound like the test is going to be hard as hell. I'd be stuck at home studying, too. And it's all good. You didn't miss much." I'm tempted to bring up how she never missed one of Jaxon's games. But I don't.

"Still. I want to be there for you. I'll look through the schedule and figure out how I can make as many of your games as possible. Your dad was there. He sent me a couple of pics of you. They were all blurry, though."

"Nice. Where is Dad, anyway?"

"He said he was going to have a couple with your uncles. You know how they like to talk about the games until one of them passes out." Mom rolls her eyes. "At least they're at Liver's and not over here. God, they used to keep me up until three in the morning laughing and talking really loud. So annoying."

"Oh yeah, that's right. They should make a podcast." We both laugh.

"Love you, Tre."

"Love you, too, Mom."

I dip for my room. I fall into my bed and can't believe how tired and sore I am and how my bed has never felt more amazing. I throw on my headphones and scroll through social media on my phone and smile when I spot my lob pass to Kevin on a bunch of people's stories.

CHAPTER 19

NOVEMBER 20

"**R**EADY FOR TONIGHT?" Kevin asks, in between bites of a protein bar.

"Yeah. I think," I say.

"You think? We're playing Bemidji tonight. We've never beaten them before. Maybe tonight we'll break the losing streak. You getting the plays memorized?"

"I spent the last two nights watching games from last season."

"Thatta boy." He grabs a gallon jug of water out of his locker. "See you on the bus."

Nate nods at me when I get on the bus and slaps the open spot next to him.

As I'm sitting down, Kevin calls, "Christ, you want a B-team jersey, too? If you're varsity, you sit back here in the last few rows."

Nate rolls his eyes, then nudges me out of the seat and waves me off like he's shooing away a fly.

Seconds later, Kevin pats the open seat next to him. "Gotta get to know each other a bit if we're going to be teammates all year. Assuming you stay on varsity. Which I'll fight for if I need to. You got skills, Tre. No one's ever thrown me an alley-oop like the one you did. Easily the best dunk of my career." Kevin is wearing a North Face jacket, a matching beanie, and winter gloves. I've never even owned a pair of gloves. My mom used to make me and Jaxon wear socks on our hands when we'd go out to play in the snow. I set my gym bag down and squeeze in alongside him.

When the bus takes off, I unzip my bag and pull out the issue of *Slam* magazine with Steph Curry on the cover that has the article I've been meaning to read. I flip through until I find the book-marked page. There's that model-looking, seven-foot-tall white boy from Crestview Christian Academy. Oh yeah, and that ridiculous headline. *God's Son: A Basketball Prodigy.*

Skimming through, I notice that he is a senior, and that he has committed to Duke University next fall, but most NBA scouts expect him to stay only one season before becoming a top draft pick—more than likely the number one pick. His name is Jacob Griffin, and whoever wrote this article has declared him the best basketball player to ever come out of Minnesota.

Kevin leans over to look at the article. "I saw some highlights of that guy online. Insane bro. He can do it all. Handle the rock like a point guard, shoot from deep, leap out of the building, pass, defend, everything. Wish I was that tall, with those skills. If we somehow get to state, I hope we don't have to play against him. Probably poster all of us."

"We have to beat Bemidji first," I say.

"Did you know that Bemidji has never come up to play us in Red Lake?" Kevin asks. "Heard they're scared to come up here."

"Yeah. That's what my dad told me, too."

"Your dad's team almost beat them back in the day, huh?"

"Yeah. He talks about it all the time. Lost by one point. Bemidji hit a half-court shot at the buzzer."

"Damn."

"He always brings up the two free throws he missed early in the game. Haunts him."

"Shit. That would haunt me, too. I mean, can you imagine how good it would feel to finally beat Bemidji? To be the first rez team to ever give the pretty white boys an L. Be historic."

"You guys almost had them last year. I cheered so hard that I lost my voice."

"Would have beat them if we'd had Jaxon with us. I'm sure of it." Kevin glances away.

I want to try to lighten the mood and say something stupid, like, *Well, now you're stuck with me.* But who knows? Maybe I'd make things worse. I open my *Slam* magazine back up.

"What are your goals?" Kevin asks.

"What do you mean?"

"For basketball. What do you want to accomplish?"

A couple of our teammates turn around in their seats to hear my answer.

The first thing that comes to my mind is the truth. That I want to be even better than Jaxon was. That I want to beat Bemidji. That I want to win the state championship. Go D-1. Make it to the NBA. If I say so, I'm afraid I'll be laughed right off the bus.

"Well?" Kevin asks.

"I don't know. Guess we will see. This probably sounds dumb, but if I get really lucky, I'd like to get a scholarship for college or something like that. But whatever."

"Those are my goals, too. Been recruited by a bunch of schools since that regional championship game. Division Two schools, but shit, they've all been offering full scholarships." With a smirk Kevin adds, "Shit, that or rez league MVP straight outta high school."

Rez league is what we all affectionately have coined the men's basketball league on our reservation. It's equally known for flashy layups and fast-break threes as it is for the heated arguments and fistfights. It's a mixture of wannabe hoopers, scrubs who love the game, and of course, the ghosts of former high school stars. It's our NBA.

Not one basketball star from our rez has ever gone on to play college basketball or pro basketball. Rez league is all we've got once high school ball is over.

Our bus pulls into the Bemidji High School parking lot. Cars are parked all along the edges of the winding road. Every single spot of their football-field-sized parking lot is filled. An endless line of people waiting to get into the game curves around the side of the school.

"Holy shit," Dallas says. "I've never seen this many people at a regular season game."

When we step down off the bus we are greeted with whistles, war whoops, and cheers. People pat us on the back as we walk past them and into the gym.

This. Is. So. Cool. I'm geeking out on the inside while calmly nodding and high-fiving fans as we walk in like I've been doing this for years.

"Let's go, Warriors!" someone shouts.

The referee tosses the ball up to start the game.

Kevin tips it to me. I throw a bounce pass ahead to Dallas. Two Bemidji defenders catch up to Dallas and jump to block his shot. One of them bumps into him as he's laying up the ball, but there's no whistle from the ref. I jump and get my hand on the missed shot, tipping it up and banking it in.

Bemidji races up the court, moving the ball quickly from player to player as they set screens away from the ball until one of their players ends up wide open for an easy layup.

"Forty-four, one," I say as I dribble the ball up the court.

This time I know exactly what we're doing. Dallas fakes one direction and then cuts through the lane, sets a pick for Kevin. I throw the ball to Kevin, who turns and faces his defender, who is almost seven feet tall. Kevin shoots the ball extra high to avoid getting his shot blocked. Kevin's shot hits the back of the rim and bounces high. Dallas tips it back to me and the ball lands perfectly in my hands, just the way I like the grooves to feel across my fingertips.

But I hesitate. I worry about missing the open shot. I pass to Robert, who is wide open; he shoots a three-pointer that swishes in.

With the clock winding down in the first half, Bemidji has the ball and is holding it for the final shot. Their point guard passes it off to the wing. I chase him through the lane and over to the corner. Their center sets a pick for a guard who cuts to the basket. I leave my guy to help out like Coach told us to. He catches the pass and then bulldozes right into me.

I crash onto the hardwood floor with a thud. The ref's whistle blows.

Dallas races over and kneels next to me. "You all right?"

I'm fighting for air but nod. We crisscross our arms, clasp our hands together, and he yanks me to my feet.

"Blocking foul on number ten," the ref says to the scorers' table.

I hunch over, push my hands into my knees, and gasp for air as Bemidji sinks both free throws. Their mascot, Paul Bunyan, runs to the edge of the court beside me, points at me, puts his hands on his belly, and laughs. When the buzzer sounds at the half, the score is knotted up at 53–53.

I collapse into my seat in the locker room, staring at the cold, cheap linoleum floor. Breathing hurts. I wonder if I've cracked a rib or something.

"Tired?" Coach asks.

"No, I'm good," I say, though I want to crawl into a casket.

"You already got three fouls. You're playing out of control, looking like a rabid rez dog fighting over a fucking bologna sandwich."

· · ·

Minutes into the third quarter I go for a rebound, but I'm out of position and commit my fourth foul. A second stringer rips off his warm-ups and runs over to check in.

Coach calls my name and points to the bench.

Bemidji catches fire, hitting back-to-back three-pointers and getting fast-break points.

Coach screams for a time-out. "You know why they went on that run? Straight-up outhustling you guys. I don't give a shit. I'll sit all of you. We can lose this game, if that's what you want."

We are down, 62–55.

Kevin catches a pass with his back to the basket. With a taller defender on him, he power dribbles, picks the ball up, does a couple of fake turns, and then commits to spinning and fading away to his right. Their center jumps up and blocks the shot. Their point guard grabs the ball, runs up the court, and stops on a dime for a midrange jumper. It misses, but their power forward leaps into the air and slams the ball through the rim so hard the entire backboard sways. The Bemidji side of the gym erupts like a volcano.

"Goddamn it!" Coach Whitefeather throws his clipboard to the floor. "Tre. Go in there. And don't foul out."

I run to the scorers' table to check back in.

Dallas pulls up for a high arching jumper that bricks. A cloud of players fight for position underneath. Kevin gets his fingertips on the ball and slaps it out to Robert. He's open, but defenders are running at him. He hits me with a no-look pass. I'm deep from the rim, but this is in my range. If I make it, I'll look like Steph Curry. If I miss it, I'm going to look like an asshole for shooting from this far out. Fuck it. I let it fly.

Swish. Nothing but the bottom of the net. I fist-pump in celebration. Damn, that felt good.

Back on defense, I sneak down to the baseline to help out Kevin. Bemidji's center never sees me coming. I swipe the ball away from him and throw a one-arm football-style pass to Robert for a wide-open layup to end the third. For the first time in almost two games, I finally feel like I matter. For the first time, I sort of, kind of feel like I belong.

With two minutes left, the game is tied up 77–77. I study the floor, dribbling near half-court. I feel like a chess champion plotting his next move. I check the clock, then yell out, "JD!" My teammates run to their spots.

I pass it to Robert, set a back pick for Kevin, who curls around and catches the ball on the wing. When two defenders rush at him, he dumps it to me. It catches me off guard. I was sure he was shooting and wasn't ready for a pass. I fumble the ball, regain control of it, but suddenly, Bemidji players surround me.

I go up strong for a layup as their center slams into me. As I crash toward the hardwood, I throw up a prayer. The ref blows his whistle as my shot soars into the air. The ball hits the back of the rim, bounces high into the air, lands on the front of the rim and sits there for a second, like someone pressed pause. Then it rolls in. And one.

I hear my dad's voice cut through the boom of cheers from our fans. "That's how it's done, Tre!"

I get up and walk to the free-throw line, then glance up at the scoreboard. We are up, 79–77, with a minute and a half left. We need this free throw.

Everyone lines up along the paint and the ref passes me the ball. My hands are sweaty. Holding the ball against my hip with my elbow, I try to wipe them off on my jersey. Holy shit. We could beat Bemidji. We are right here in this game. We could be the first Red Lake squad to ever beat them. Not even my dad or Jaxon could beat them. But tonight, I could. Come on, Tre. Focus.

I take a couple of dribbles like I always do. I take a deep breath, stare at the rim, imagine my shot going in, and shoot. It swishes in. 80–77.

They set up their offense. I fight through screens while keeping an eye on the ball on the other side of the court. Robert and Kevin both go after the ball handler while their center rolls to the basket. I see the play unfold before it happens and leave my guy to go and help.

I sprint from the opposite side of the court as their center catches the pass. He takes a hard dribble outside of the paint and rises for a one-handed slam. I jump off both feet and go up after him. My hand knocks the ball out of his hand, but I feel our hips bump. Before we even land, I'm already praying that the ref let that one go.

The whistle blows and a referee says to the scorers' table, "Shooting foul on number ten."

I throw my head back in the air and stare up into the bright lights.

I walk to the bench to watch the rest of the game—helpless.

Applause. *Really* loud applause. Our fans are on their feet, cheering for me even though I fouled out. My teammates jump up from the bench and give me high fives. I fight back tears. It's weird to feel sad, angry, and happy, all at the same time. I throw a towel over my head and sip on a water bottle as their center sinks both of his free throws. 80–79.

Someone in the Bemidji crowd yells, "Hey, Brun."

I turn and see them holding up a sign that reads, *Lumberjacks vs. Warriors, 53–0.* Someone next to them is holding up a sign that says, *Undefeated. Forever.* My first instinct is to flip them off. But I hold it in. I look back out at the court. One minute to go in the game. Come on, guys. Please pull this off.

Kevin takes two dribbles to the left and spins right. One of Bemidji's players swipes the ball away and passes the ball ahead to a teammate for a layup. We are down 81–80.

Robert drives to the basket for a layup. He's hit as he goes up but there is no call from the ref. His shot rattles in and out. Bemidji's center grabs the rebound, throws it into the air. His teammates circle around, jumping up and down. The buzzer sounds.

We could have won if I hadn't fouled out.

I'm sitting in the locker room, hunched over in my chair, staring at my shoes as my teammates leave to get on the bus. There's a towel draped over my head. Black Nikes pass by. Someone pats my shoulder. Red-and-black Adidas shoes stop. I'm broken inside. Defeated. Stupid. Lifeless. But my teammates pat and tap, comfort me without words. They're saying *good game. It's okay.*

There's a heavy thud in the chair right next to mine, followed by the chomping sound of what must be an apple. "Aye, you did your best, Tre. Hold your head up," Kevin says, chewing loud as hell. He puts his arm around my chair.

"Thanks," I say, but so quiet I'm not sure he heard.

"It's only the second game of the regular season." *Chomp.* "Ain't like we lost in the play-offs." *Crunch.* "We still got twenty"— *chomp*—"more games to go. Can't take losses like these so hard." *Gulp.*

"I know. I just . . . I really, really wanted to beat those guys."

"We will. We will. When it matters most. To go to state." Dude is a total Captain America type. A glossy red apple appears in front of my face. "Gotta replenish. See you on the bus." I take the apple and feel Kevin's gigantic hand pat my back. "Hurry up and get dressed. You don't want to be the guy everyone on the bus is waiting on. Learned that lesson a long time ago." Kevin's size-fifteen Nikes disappear, and the chomping sounds slowly fade away.

It's quiet. I must be the last one left. I sit up and pull the towel off my head and look around at the empty locker. Only hours ago, we were all fired up. Thinking tonight would be the night we would finally beat Bemidji. Ugh. I grind my teeth.

Only an hour ago we were in here during halftime, thinking we still had a chance.

I set the apple on a chair and take my jersey off, holding it in my hand and looking at it. Do I even deserve to wear it? Maybe they would have won if Mason and Mike were playing instead of me tonight. Maybe I'm not as good at hooping as I thought I was.

I toss my jersey into my gym bag, pull off my trunks, and slip into some jeans and a hoodie. The door opens up and a gust of cold air sweeps in. "Dang, bro, what you doing in here still? Taking the longest shit of all time?" Dallas asks in a joking voice. "I'm just fucking with you. But for real. The guys are all waiting. They want to get to McDonald's."

"I know. My bad. I'm ready."

"Kevin give you this?" Dallas asks, grabbing the apple off the chair and inspecting it like a detective at a crime scene.

"Yeah, he—"

Chomp. "He's never shared an apple. Or any of his snacks. With any of us before. That big bastard must really like you," Dallas says, chewing and talking with his mouth open.

"Yeah, you can have it," I say, slapping him on the arm.

Dallas looks at the core, then realizes he just ate my apple. "Oh shit, I'm sorry. I'm starving. After games I can't wait to eat. Come on, let's go." We walk out of the locker and down the long, dark hallway. "Good game out there tonight, no bullshit. I know you're a little bummed. I remember when I lost my first couple varsity games. Shit stung. But the longer you play, the more you'll realize only the play-offs really matter."

"Yeah, man. I know. I just thought we had them."

"We did," Dallas says, like he's both proud and sad at the same time.

We walk out of the hallway and into the dimly lit, empty gymnasium.

"Was fun as hell, though, right? Having those rich white boys all shook like that?" Dallas says with a laugh.

"If I wouldn't have fouled out, we'd be walking out of here as the very first Red Lake team to beat them."

"And if I would have hit my free throws. And if Kevin would have made his layups. And if Robert would have been hot tonight instead of ice cold. We're a team. We win together. We lose together. Don't beat yourself up." Dallas puts an arm around my shoulder. "Now let's go get some fucking McDonald's. I'm dying for a twenty-piece and some fries."

CHAPTER 20

NOVEMBER 20

I'M LYING IN my bed, trying not to think how damn close we were to beating Bemidji. I'm trying not to think about my stupid fouls. Or each play that could have gone our way. I'm hoping that scrolling endlessly through social media will be enough of a distraction. But it isn't. I remember the nasty film of sweat on my skin. I sniff my armpit and jerk my head from the stench. I should probably take a quick shower. I should also text Khiana.

WYD?

Playing PlayStation. How'd your game go?

We lost

Oh well. I'm sure you did your best

I tried

You want some company?

What would my mom and dad think about her coming over so late? The pit of my stomach feels funny, but I want to forget about basketball for a while.

Fuck it.

Yeah . . . that would be nice

When Khiana's headlights hit my bedroom wall, I slowly tiptoe to the front door and open it as quietly as I can.

She turns her lights off and gets out of the car. Khiana's wearing baby-blue Care Bears pajama pants with a white cotton tank top and a Misfits hoodie. Something about her being in her pajamas turns me on. Will this be the night we finally hold hands, cuddle, make out, or more? "Hey," she whispers.

"Hey," I whisper back.

On the front step, she wraps her arms around me, and I hug her back. And we keep holding each other. Everything I was stressing about disappears. Moments later, we get cozy in my bed, prop up against pillows, and take turns scooping ice cream out of the same container as we watch stand-up comedy on Netflix. "Khiana?"

"Yeah?"

"I, umm." I want to ask her if she likes me like I like her. Or if she's ever even thought about that. Or if we will only be friends.

She loads up a scoop of ice cream, then hands the container to me. "What is it, Tre?"

Come on. Just ask. "Thanks for coming over. It's nice."

"I'm nice."

"You are."

"That was it?"

"Yeah."

Khiana scans my expression, our eyes lock, then she lights up. "Tre. No. We can't."

"What? What are you talking about?"

"I know that look."

I shift against the pillows behind me. "What look?"

"The doe-eyes, falling-in-love look."

"No. That's not . . . what? You're silly."

"Tre, it's okay. I think you're great. That's why I'm here. I love our friendship. But I'm done with high school in a few months, and then I'll probably leave for California." She folds her arms. I don't know what to say. She adds, "Dude. Seriously. It's cool. If you're cool with this"—she points back and forth between us—"then it's all good. We're all good, okay?"

"Okay."

"Now hand me the ice cream. You've had it for way too long."

CHAPTER 21

NOVEMBER 23

I SPENT THE WEEKEND streaming Marvel superhero movies but not really watching them. They were just on in the background. A comforting distraction. My mind won't stop replaying the heckling Bemidji fans, my mistakes during the game, the dumb fouls I committed, how quiet the locker room was after. How bad it felt, in my heart, in my gut, to lose that game. And now it's Monday and school just ended but there is only half an hour before basketball practice. Not enough time to go home or do anything really. The school hallway is madness as students who don't play basketball or aren't in an after-school activity are speed walking out the door. I open my locker and grab a book for civics that I left over the weekend. I thumb through it for a second, checking how many pages I need to read to be caught up with the class. At least seventy. I really need to read it tonight. I stuff it into my backpack, then pull out my winter coat and put it on because it's easier than carrying it around.

Kevin and Dallas come around the corner, and passing classmates high-five them, fist-pound them, or move far out of their way.

Dallas and Kevin nod at me. I nod back. The loud, distinct thump sound of a basketball being dribbled on linoleum booms from down the narrow hallway, out of sight. But the thud is getting louder as it bounces and echoes against the white brick walls. Mason comes around the corner, doing a slow crossover dribble. Mike is alongside him, pretending to play defense, slapping at the ball.

For a second, I consider taking off in the other direction. The library is that way. I have to catch up on my reading. I shut and secure the door of my locker.

"We're about to go get in some shots before practice. Want to come with?" Kevin asks, adjusting his gym bag.

"What up, Tre?" Mason asks before I can answer Kevin.

"Nothing. Just—"

"Nice work out there the last couple of games," Mason says, and it sounds like he means it. Dallas and Kevin look confused.

"Oh, umm, thanks," I say, hoping my face doesn't show how puzzled I feel.

"You did pretty good. Not too bad for being tossed right into the fire like that." Mason lightly backhands my chest like a friend after a funny joke.

"Dallas and Kevin and Coach all helped me a lot," I reply.

Mason says, "Be cool if you can learn the plays and get some clock under your belt. Maybe we can get you some experience this year during some of our blowout victories."

My chest gets heavy, but I shrug. "I'm just happy to be on the team."

Mason smiles and gives me a fist pound. "Right on, I can't wait to get out there and take my starting spot back tomorrow night against Nevis. Was bullshit that we got in trouble. Ain't like you guys never drink."

Kevin looks confused. "I don't drink. Hate the stuff."

"Hopefully no one else gets in trouble the rest of the season," I say. "I mean, we almost beat Bemidji without you and Mike." Mason's eyebrows drop. I add, "I'm just saying that if we almost won without two of our best players, then we should for sure beat them to go to state this year."

Mason laughs. "*Our* best players? This guy went from JV to starting to the coach already."

Kevin circles the group to stand behind me. "He's right, though. We did almost beat Bemidji without you guys. So, by the end of this season, if we all come together, we should end up on top."

"This guy." Mason points at Kevin and shakes his head with a what-the-fuck-ever smile. "Fucking world could be ending, and he'd find a reason to be happy."

Mike puts a hand on Mason's shoulder and slowly guides him down the hall toward the gym. "Let's go get some shots up before practice, then. We might be rusty from the week off."

"I don't get rusty," Mason replies in a huff as they walk away.

Kevin turns and watches Mason and Mike until they walk

into the gym. "He's scared of you, that's all. He's got his pride. Would bother him a lot if he lost his starting spot to a first-year player." Then he messes up my hair like a sitcom dad after a heart-to-heart.

Dallas adds, "Don't let him bother you. Play your game. Let it work itself out. It's not up to Mason, or any of us. It's Coach's decision. I'm sure he'll let us know tonight at practice. Come on, let's go."

"A couple of you may have a problem with this, but I don't give a shit," Coach begins. "It is what it is. We're staying with Tre as our starting point guard tomorrow night against Nevis." With that, Coach grabs a marker and starts to draw on the whiteboard. "We're playing Nevis, in their house. They're one of only two teams that beat us in the regular season last year."

Mason shakes his head and starts to rock back and forth in his chair. "How in the hell are you going to start Tre over me? He hasn't done shit in the last couple of games. He had his chance. *I* should be starting."

I stare at my shoes, and Coach replies, "You've got to earn your way back into the starting spot. You messed up. Big-time. Let this whole team down, hell, the whole rez. You can earn it back by staying out of trouble, keeping your grades up, and outworking Tre."

Mason stands and moves to the middle of the locker room. "Shit. This is *my* team." He pounds his chest. "I've earned it. I know the plays better than he does. Me and these guys been playing together since we were kids." Mason gestures to Kevin, Dallas, Robert, and Mike. Then he flings his hand in my direction like he's flicking a mosquito. "Tre's played *two* games with them."

"Two games, thanks to you," Coach replies. "Now drop your little prima donna hissy fit. I've got some coaching to do."

Mason flips his chair and storms out.

CHAPTER 22

DECEMBER 5

"**WE MUST BE** almost done shopping, right?" Wes asks, kneeling on the linoleum floor to riffle through his shopping bags, mouthing names under his breath.

Nate, Khiana, Wes, and I agreed to do our holiday shopping together, hoping to make it less painful and more like hanging out. We stopped in front of the massive Christmas tree in the middle of the mall. The artificial tree is double the height of a basketball rim and decorated with tinsel, strings of blinking white lights, candy canes, and red, silver, and green bulbs. Santa's Workshop is located in front of the tree, with Santa himself poised on a gigantic red-and-gold throne overseeing the elf helpers directing an enormous line of kids who are shouting, screaming, pointing. We are in a cyclone of screaming toddlers, colliding shoppers, and Mariah Carey's "All I Want for Christmas" on repeat.

"And I'm done." Wes sighs with relief. "Thank the Creator."

I grab a couple of Wes's bags off the floor so he can stand easier. "I'm almost done." I return the bags to him. "I only need two more gifts."

Hands on her hips, Khiana says, "You guys are silly. What is this, the nineties? I got my shopping done weeks ago online. I only came with to get out of my grandma's house for a bit."

Nate digs into his jeans pocket and pulls out a wad of cash. "My grandma won playing keno at the casino last night. When I said I was going Christmas shopping, she gave me a couple hundred bucks and told me to get gifts for everyone in my family."

As a teenage girl and her mom pass by, brutally criticizing each other's fashion sense, I peer into his shopping bag. "And so far, you've only got gifts for your grandparents and mom and dad, right?"

"Yeah. Thinking about how I can spend the smallest amount on my annoying-ass brothers and sisters, and then I can pocket the rest."

In an evil voice, Khiana says, "Santa is watching you."

Except for Nate, we all laugh. "Yeah, right," he says, rolling his eyes as he thumbs through a handful of crisp twenties.

"No, for real, look." I point at the mall Santa. He's got a black-gloved hand in the air, running his thumb against his fingers like he's asking for Nate's money.

Nate stuffs the cash into his pockets. "Hell nah. This my money, Santa. You got your own ways."

"Where should we go next? The shoe store?" I nudge Nate as we dodge shoppers zooming past us in every direction. "Maybe you could get them winter beanies."

"Or socks," Nate mutters.

I add, "How about going to the bookstore? That's by the shoe store."

"Okay," Khiana says with a dismissive laugh. "Wes, since you're all done, want to hit the arcade? After this Christmas hell-hole, I could use some Skee-Ball to unwind."

Wes nods. "Yeah, that sounds cool."

I say, "I just need to grab one book . . . for my mom. Then I'm done. We can meet you two at the arcade."

Everyone agrees. Wes and Khiana go one way. Me and Nate the other. I take a glance back and almost expect to see Wes and Khiana holding hands. They aren't.

Nate pulls me out of the way of frantic shoppers. "You good?"

"Yeah, I was just scoping out the mall."

Nate purses his lips like he's fighting the urge to call me out on my little lie. But he doesn't. For once. A Christmas miracle. We pass holiday pop-up kiosks. We make sure to avoid eye contact with the guy in a Santa hat ringing a bell for donations. We weave through shoppers until we reach the bookstore. We survived.

"Jingle Bells" is blaring so loud that I might lose my hearing or my mind. The display tables up front are decorated with Christmas lights and wreaths, featuring Christmas books front and center. People whiz in and out. They manhandle the books. I beeline it to the graphic novel section like I'm driving to the basket with hundreds of defenders eager to hack me. Instincts kick in as I dodge the other shoppers. Unfortunately, Sam isn't at the counter today. I hope she still works here. It would be a bummer to never see her again.

Thankfully the manga, anime, and comic-book section, tucked in the far corner, is less hectic. I thumb through graphic novels, wondering what Khiana may already own. "Aye, do you think it would be weird if I got Khiana a Christmas present? Like even something small?"

Nate gives me a side-eye, clearly knowing that I didn't come to this store for my mom. "I mean, no. Not if it's small. But I hope you got me something first and spend what's left on her. I could use some new Jordans. And not them knockoffs where his arms are flailing in the wrong directions." Nate goes into a pretend jump shot.

I hold up a manga graphic novel. "I was thinking of getting her one of these."

Nate crosses his arms, apparently amused. "You still feeling some sort of way about her? Or nah?"

"Nah. She's a friend. We talked it over. Besides, it seems like . . ." I dig through the comics again to avoid eye contact.

"Like what?" Nate asks, arms still crossed.

A mother and two kids squeeze between us; the kids are pulling on their mom's jacket, telling her over and over what they want for Christmas.

I grab a graphic novel that screams Khiana vibes. On the cover, sexy lady vampires are sucking the blood from dudes in business suits. Khiana is all about badass, powerful women. Hopefully she doesn't have this one already. "Got it." I hold it up like a trophy and lead Nate to the store counter. "I'm ready to get out of here. Where else do you want to stop?"

"I'm getting all my siblings the same thing—winter beanies from Walmart."

"What happened to buying them here in the mall?"

"Too expensive." Nate waves his hands dismissively. "Those little fuckers don't deserve Nike beanies. They're always stealing my shit and messing around in my room."

"Damn, bro. You're ruthless."

"Hey, you're lucky you don't have a—" Nate chokes on the next word.

He looks one part sad as fuck, one part ashamed. I hate that he feels bad, so I change the subject. I point at the candle store directly in front of us. "Moms like candles, right? I can't think of what else to get my mom. It's whack, but I give up. I'm going to grab her one."

Nate's smile is knowing and sad. "Yeah, moms love candles. All girls like candles."

Nate helps me navigate through the jam-packed store filled with women picking up candles, sniffing them, and commenting on each scent before moving on to the next. Together, we pick out a lavender-scented candle and a pine-green one with a Christmas bow on it.

Then we make our way out of the store, twisting and turning

in the walkway to push through the chaos of the mall. Nate says, "Want a quick game of arcade basketball? I bet I still have the high score."

"Maybe some other time. I'm starving."

"Chicken. Let's go find Wes and Khiana and get out of here."

We split up. The arcade is loud. Shrieking kids and the bings, dings, and boops of arcade games is a welcome relief from nonstop Christmas music. A group of little kids almost run into us with fistfuls of tickets to exchange for candy or cheap plastic toys. It's like *Lord of the Flies* in here. Not a parent in sight. And no Wes or Khiana either. Which is weird, because she's usually easy to spot. She is like a spotlight, the way she shines. But as I duck around arcade machines and kids, no luck.

Coming around the Skee-Ball and air hockey, Nate shrugs. "Maybe they bounced. I wouldn't blame them. There's only like two games in here worth playing."

A screech cuts through the noise. Khiana and Wes tumble out of the comically small photo booth, laughing their asses off. They don't even notice us standing right in front of them.

"Oh my God, I can't wait to see if those turned out," Khiana says.

Wes almost jumps when he finally notices me and Nate. Brushing his knees off, he says, "Oh, hey. I didn't see you guys."

"Hey, you two ready to go?" Nate asks, tapping his stomach. "I'm starving."

"Yeah, just one minute," Khiana replies. "We need to grab our pictures."

Nate asks, "What are you guys hungry for? I'd be down for McDonald's."

Wes shakes his head. "Man. We always eat at McDonald's. What about Taco Bell?"

Khiana's nose wrinkles. "Gross. I'm not riding all the way back to the rez with a bunch of teenage boys after a round of Taco Bell."

Meanwhile, I'm standing there, speechless.

The photo booth grumbles and shoots out their photos. Khiana picks them up carefully, keeping a thumb and her pointer finger delicately on each side of the strip.

Wes takes a step closer to her to examine the pics.

Did they take cute, couple-type pics? Faces pressed against each other, a head on a shoulder, a kiss on the cheek or on the lips? It's like my bags suddenly weigh one hundred thousand pounds each.

Nate jumps in. "McDonald's, it is."

Khiana busts out laughing and slaps Wes's chest. "You're the biggest dork." She shows him the photo strip, and Wes laughs just as hard as Khiana. In between gasps he holds them up for me and Nate. Khiana made cute, glamour-shot poses—like in her cosplay pics—while Wes picked his nose, stuck his tongue out, stuffed his fist in his mouth, and pressed his thumb against his nose, lifting it like a pig snout.

Suddenly, a twenty-piece McNuggets with fries sounds good.

We walk out of the arcade. Khiana tugs the sleeve of my hoodie. "You going to hang out with us when we get back? After I teach those two how to properly wrap a present, we're going to play video games."

"I didn't know you were hanging out after," I say.

"We were talking about it the whole way here, remember?" she replies. "There's a *Death Brigade* tournament tonight. You must have been zoned out."

"My bad. I've been doing that a lot. I've been super tired lately."

I hold the mall door open for Khiana and the guys. It's snowing and a cold wind makes us all shudder.

Khiana pulls her hoodie on. "Come on, I'll help you wrap your presents, too. We could really use one more for the tournament."

"I don't know if I could stay awake. I've been struggling to stay up past ten on the nights that we don't have a road game. Even then, I pass out on the cold-ass, bumpy school bus rides home. I don't think I'd be any fun, or any help."

Nate slaps my arm. "Come on, bro, when did you become such an old man? I'll buy us a stack of energy drinks. Suck it up, it's Saturday night."

"I wish I could. For real. I've legit never felt this exhausted, and I'm sore as hell. We didn't get back from Warroad until midnight, and I was so revved up I didn't fall asleep until two. Plus, I have to get up early tomorrow."

"On a Sunday? For what?" Nate asks.

"My dad got the keys to the gym, so he's going to open it up on Sunday mornings and help me work on shooting and dribbling drills. You guys are welcome to join us."

"Hell no," Nate replies. "I'm not waking up until Monday morning. Baby Jesus made Sundays for us to rest."

CHAPTER 23

DECEMBER 25

"**MERRY CHRISTMAS, TRE,**" Mom says, waking me up. I struggle to open my eyes and lift my head from the pillow. Peeking out from under my blanket, I ask, "What time is it?"

"Time to open presents. Come on."

I rub sleep crust from my eyes and yawn. "Okay, be right out."

Moments later, I'm faced with Dad, standing in front of the decorated tree. "Merry Christmas, Tre."

Bing Crosby's "White Christmas" is playing, and the smells of pine and cinnamon rolls fill the air. Dad and Mom love the holiday. They don't mess around. The day after Thanksgiving, they decorate the tree, hang the lights up outside, and start playing carols.

I take a seat on the couch. "Merry Christmas, Dad." Mom joins me.

With a big smile, Dad hands me a gift. "Here you go."

As soon as I touch it, I'm pretty sure I know what's inside. I study the silver-and-white wrapping paper with snowflakes and snowmen.

"Well?" Dad says. "Open it up."

I pull the paper off the package and then pause to brace myself before tearing through the rest. It's a Nike shoebox. I crack it open—basketball shoes. My jaw clenches and my eyes well up.

"Honey, what's wrong?" Mom asks, rubbing my back.

"Every Christmas, Jaxon always got a new pair of shoes as his main gift. I always got like comic-book stuff. But his gift was new Jordans or new LeBrons. That was *his* thing."

Dad sits down and puts his arm around me. "It's weird," I say. "Having Christmas without him. If he was here, this would have been his gift."

Mom rests her head on my shoulder and wraps her arm around me, too. "I know, sweetheart. I know. We all miss Jaxon."

"First set of holidays are the hardest," Dad says. "When I lost my mother, the whole first year was real tough. This year, every holiday, every season, even going to the basketball games. It hurts. It's all really hard."

Tears fall onto my arm, and Mom trembles, breathing in short, sharp bursts.

"Remember how mad Jaxon used to get whenever I borrowed his shit . . . I mean, stuff?"

"Goddamn, he used to hate that," Dad says. "I don't know how many times I had to run down the hallway and save your skinny ass from him." We all laugh.

Catching her breath and wiping her eyes, Mom asks, "Remember how mad you both were that Christmas when there was only one gift under the tree, and it had both of your names on it?"

I shake my head. "I don't know how you expected the two of us to share one Xbox. Jaxon basically took it over after that. He'd challenge me to a game of one-on-one. The deal was if I beat him, I could keep it for a week. But I never did beat him."

Suddenly, Dad stands up and walks out of the living room.

"He okay?" I ask.

"Yeah. He's one of the strongest people I've ever met. He's probably going to grab a smoke. Do you want to open another present?"

"Of course."

Mom grabs a couple of other gifts and sits back down. I tear right into the wrapping paper to reveal a couple of graphic novels that I had been hinting for, and a Batman Funko Pop!

"Tre." Dad comes back holding the LeBron shoes that my brother got for Christmas last year. "Jaxon only wore these in last year's Christmas tourney. He had his highest-scoring game of his entire career. You guys wear the same size now. Thirteen," Dad says.

"I remember. He was killing it those . . . last games." Trying to ignore the lump in my throat, I thumb through my *Deadpool Vs. Thanos* graphic novel.

All of a sudden, Jaxon's shoes are between me and the book. "I think he'd be okay with you borrowing these. You can wear the ones we got you at school—that way they won't get all beat up—and you can wear his during games, like a good-luck charm." Dad's eyes are sad, but he has a small smile. "Wear them next game. See what happens. Bring a little part of him with you."

CHAPTER 24

DECEMBER 28

TYING MY SHOELACES tight, I stare at Jaxon's shoes. *Come on, bro. I need you tonight.*

Coach announces, "We're playing Minneapolis. They've won the state championship three out of the last four years."

I study Jaxon's shoes, trying to summon his strength.

"This is going to be a test out there tonight, boys. Not too often you have to go against a state champion, especially a state champ like Minneapolis. Small-town teams like us never beat big-city teams like them. Shit, I wouldn't be surprised if we caught an ass whooping. But sometimes you gotta play a team like this to know where you really stand. Don't know if that makes sense to you young bucks, but it does to me." Coach Whitefeather grabs a dry-erase marker and draws some Xs and Os.

When we line up for tip-off, I cannot believe the size of their center. He looks like Shaquille O'Neal. He has bowling ball shoulders, and his muscles are massive and defined. Even Kevin looks small next to him.

Minneapolis's center easily wins the tip. Their shooting guard blows right past Dallas like his feet are stuck in cement. Kevin catches up and cuts him off, but he throws the ball high. Their center throws down a vicious highlight-reel dunk. Guarantee you that one ends up going mini viral online.

Their crowd erupts.

The rest of the quarter, Minneapolis plays harder than us. They move like lightning, and we look like we're playing underwater. They hit us with a bunch of flashy crossovers, no-look passes, stepback threes, and dunks. We fall behind by ten points.

When the second quarter starts, they seem unhappy that they're only up by ten, so they completely change their style of play and slow the game way down. Setting picks off the ball, moving the ball until they get it to their center.

Each time they dump it down to him, he busts out a variety of twists, turns, pivots, and pump fakes. They are scoring almost every single time down, and the game has ground to a halt.

We are getting zero fast-break points, which is a huge part of our offense.

Stuck playing in a slowed-down, half-court set, we struggle to match their scoring. Any time my teammates drive to the basket, their center steps up to block or alter the shot. Their guards are playing stifling defense, waving their arms all over, deflecting passes, knocking the ball out of bounds. They're making it nearly impossible for us to even get into our offensive sets.

Coach Whitefeather yells for a time-out after they go on a 7–0 run. I glance at the scoreboard as we walk to the bench. Three minutes to go in the second, and we are down 47–32.

"They're playing harder than you, that's all. You can beat them, but you've got to match their intensity. You gotta go at them, play your game, and quit worrying about getting dunked on. You think our people drove five hours from the rez to the cities in a snowstorm to watch you play scared?" We shake our heads, shrug, and walk back onto the court.

Their center curls off of a screen and catches the ball at the free-throw line. In a split second, he takes one hard dribble and rises high into the air. Kevin stands in between him and the basket, waiting to take a hard charge. Their center soars into the air, his nut sack right in Kevin's face. Kevin crashes to the ground as their center throws down a monster dunk that threatens to rip the rim off the glass. The ref blows his whistle and calls a blocking foul on Kevin.

At the free-throw line, their center takes a couple of dribbles, picks the ball up, looks over at Kevin, and winks at him. Then, with a smirk, he sinks the shot.

"Let me know if you want me to sign that poster after the game," he says to Kevin.

We scrap, scratch, fight, and claw with everything we've got, but we are unable to put a dent in their lead. Walking into the locker room at the half, I look up at the score: 38–57.

• • •

We are gasping for air and slamming water as we watch Coach Whitefeather pace like an angry parent who's stepped on a Lego. He stops in front of me and puts his hand on my shoulder. "Tre, stop being afraid of your own teammates or of the crowd, or of messing up, or whatever the fuck you're afraid of." He's right. I am afraid. Of everything he mentioned. "Tre, you're like a clone of your brother. You have the same moves he had. You shoot the ball the exact same. But he was cold-blooded. Ice in his veins. Fearless. He wasn't afraid of missing a shot or messing up. You can be like that, too. Let go, just hoop. Take over this game like Jaxon would have. That or come have a seat next to me and we'll give the reins back to Mason."

Mason stares at me, like he's trying to burn me alive with Superman's heat vision.

"I will," I say. "I'll do it."

Mason starts laughing. "Let's see what you got, rookie. I'm ready to take my spot back."

"Mason, go sit down. The rest of you guys, get out of his way. If they double him, you know he's going to kick it out to you for open shots. Trust him."

As we walk back out to the court, Dallas pats my arm. "You got this, bro. Forget about the crowd. Forget about everything. Hoop like you would back on the rez. Let that ball fly."

Minutes later, Dallas inbounds the ball to me. I dribble to half-court and yell, "Iso!" which means isolation. Everyone clears out of the way. This is it.

The Minneapolis point guard taunts, "Oh, you want some of this? You think you can score on me?"

I stare him down, dribbling between my legs. I drive hard to my right, but my defender is stitched to me. I cross the ball back to my left. I take a quick step back and shoot a three. As the ball leaves my hands, I know it's good. *Swish.*

Dallas jumps into the air with a fist pump. "There we go!"

They inbound the ball to their point guard, and I'm right in his face, pestering the hell out of him. Every direction he tries to go, I'm already in his way. He picks up his dribble to pass, but I'm all over it, arms waving, making it impossible for him to find a teammate. He throws a high pass across the court that Dallas picks off.

We have a two-on-one break.

Dallas drives until their point guard goes to stop him. Alone now, I step behind the three-point line and wait. Dallas kicks it out to me and for once, with zero hesitation, I let the damn thing fly. *Swish.* Fuck yes!

The Minneapolis coach calls a time-out. Dallas and Kevin raise their arms as they walk to the bench, gesturing to our crowd to stand, which they do, cheering wildly.

The scoreboard reads 44–57.

The next several plays, I give everything I've got. Playing hard-nosed defense, getting stops, and driving to the basket for buckets or kicking it to my teammates for open shots.

When the third quarter ends, we are down 53–60.

Coach Whitefeather says, "Tre, do that one more quarter and we can win this damn thing." My teammates pat me on the shoulders and give me high fives. Well, everyone except for Mason, who is still on the bench.

With two minutes to go in the game, we're up by one point. I set up the offense. Robert screens my defender. I take two hard dribbles toward the basket, then rise up for a dunk. Their center leaves Kevin to contest my shot. He soars into the air at me, and right when we are about to collide, I switch the ball to my left hand. He crashes into me, but I take the contact, hang in the air an extra second, and loft a teardrop of a shot into the air.

The ref blows his whistle as I hit the floor. The ball rolls around the rim. It circles around once, it circles again, starts to roll out, then sinks in. Our crowd roars.

I knock down my free throw, putting us up by four.

Their point guard pulls up for a three-pointer from several feet back. I get my hand all up in his grill, but his jumper swishes in. Kevin pulls up for a contested midrange jumper that rattles out. Their center grabs the rebound and throws an outlet pass to a guard for a layup.

We are down by one point, 80–81. Twenty seconds left.

Coach Whitefeather says, "Four corners. Go for one shot."

Everyone runs over to different corners, clearing the floor for me and my defender, like a game of one-on-one. My mind shifts to one thing: scoring on this guy. I forget about everything else. It feels like the rest of the gym is dark, and a spotlight shines on the two of us.

I'm dribbling the ball in the middle of the floor. Their point guard stabs at the ball, nearly knocking it away. The crowd starts to count down.

Back on the rez, I've played this exact scenario through my mind a million times.

"Five."

"Four."

Kevin runs toward me to set a pick, but I wave him off. I dribble between my legs, twitching and jerking my shoulders like I might drive either direction in a flash.

"Three."

"Two."

I drive hard to the left, stopping on a dime to cross the ball over to my right.

My defender bites on the fake and stumbles like a baby deer on ice.

"One."

I release a deep three-point shot. The gym is silent. Waiting. Wondering who won and who lost. Except for me. I'm not wondering.

That. Shit. Is. Money.

Cash.

Money.

I throw both of my hands up in the air, fists clenched in celebration.

SPLASH.

My teammates run at me, tackling me to the ground, all piled up.

"Good fucking shit!" Kevin screams with an ear-to-ear smile on his sweaty face.

I'm yanked to my feet, and all I see are familiar faces from my rez flooding the court, all wearing red-and-black Warriors shirts. They're shaking my hand, high-fiving me, hugging me. Their eyes sparkle. All I can think about is how proud Jaxon would have been. And how I wish he could have seen me do my thing. Like I used to watch him.

Wes, Nate, and Khiana fight their way through the crowd.

Wes has his cell phone in hand, recording, as always.

"Khiana?" I say. "I didn't know you were here."

"I wanted it to be a surprise."

"How many times did we daydream that moment?" Wes asks, phone in hand, recording.

"Told you that you belonged, bro," Nate adds. "Holy shit, when I saw that shot go up, I was praying for it to go in, fam, no bullshit. I can't believe you took out Minneapolis. The dynasty."

Older fans shake my hand. Younger fans dap me up and ask for selfies.

The cheerleaders from the other team nudge their way through. One of them with long, curly black hair walks up to me. "Hey, that was wild. I can't believe you took that shot."

"Thanks," I reply.

"Well, anyway, I wanted to say great game. I followed you on all of your social media accounts—you should follow me back."

"Thanks," I say again.

"Talk to you later, Tre," she calls, hanging on to the sound of my name as she walks away with the rest of her squad.

Even though we're friends, I wonder what Khiana is thinking. I know how I'd feel if some hot guy hit on her in front of me.

Khiana rolls her eyes. "Well, Tre. It's official. You are a bona fide high school sports star. Like in every teen sports movie ever."

"Gross, right?" I say.

"Tre?" calls a gentle voice from behind me. I turn to face a little girl with long black hair.

She holds up a game program and a pen. "Will you sign this for me?"

"Of course." I get down on a knee so that we are eye-to-eye. Whoa. I'm signing my very first autograph. This exact moment played through my mind a thousand times. It's surreal.

"I like your Indigenous Baby Yoda shirt," I say to her. She giggles, covering her mouth. I can't help but laugh with her. "There you go." I hand her the game program and pen.

By the time I stand, kids have surrounded me, holding game programs and pens, or cell phones, raising them up. I sign autographs and take selfies.

"We're probably going to take off," Wes says, his eyes never leaving his phone as he records the swarm of fans. "We're all hungry as hell."

"How did you get here?" I ask Khiana.

"I came with Wes."

Are they together? I wonder. Like *together* together? Did I not text or hang out with her enough? Do they have way more in common? Wes is still recording me, which snaps me out of it. "Cool, thanks again for coming. Have a safe ride home, you guys."

I get right back to taking selfies and signing my name. In the distance, Wes is getting a wide-angle shot of the crowd around me. Khiana smiles and waves at me.

CHAPTER 25

JANUARY 9

EVERY WEEKEND AFTERNOON should be like this. The living room is filled with the smell of fresh-baked garlic bread, ground beef, marinara sauce, and my mom's famous blueberry pie that has blueberries that she and my dad picked from the forest on the rez. The kitchen table is lined with snacks, summer-sausage-style deer meat, crackers, cheese, and veggies that have gone largely ignored. My uncles, Ricky and Liver, are at the kitchen table, telling their old sports and party stories, occasionally laughing at something so hard they almost fall out of their chairs. Dad steps in and out of the kitchen area to be a cooking helper, but he's more of a taste tester, so Mom keeps kicking him out. Me, Nate, and Wes all squish together on the couch, shoulders pressed against each other, chomping on snacks, watching the Timberwolves take on the Memphis Grizzlies.

Today feels like a holiday. Except better. Nate and Wes hit me up last second and asked if I wanted to chill. Mom and Dad put together the snack plate for us. Then my uncles popped in, and when my mom realized she had a full house, she began whipping together spaghetti.

Now our home is filled with family, friends, and laughter. It hasn't been like this since before Jaxon died.

The game we are watching ends with a final full-court heave by the Timberwolves that hits the back of the rim and flies off into the stands. "Oh man," Nate says. "I would have lost my shit if that went in."

"I thought it was good for a minute there," Wes adds.

A Subway commercial comes on. We shuffle around on the couch until we are comfortably uncomfortable. Only a couple of years ago, we used to all fit on this same couch perfectly. I grab my phone off the padded elbow of the couch. The rips—Jaxon used to call them battle scars—are still there from when we used to pretend we were pro wrestlers jumping off the top rope. Damn, that used to piss my mom off.

I smile and start scrolling through social. A couple of likes pop up in my notifications. Nate has liked my most recent video. Wes made me a compilation of clips of my best plays of the season and paired it with an upbeat hip-hop track.

Nate gives Wes a fist pound. "Nice work, Wes. This comp

video of Tre is legit. You're gutsy, bro. Going down onto the base-line, or wedging your way into the front row. I get closetraphobic just thinking about it."

Wes's thumbs blur as he texts someone. "Thanks, fam. And I think you mean *claustrophobic*."

"That's what I said," Nate mutters.

"Holy. This guy is getting popular on social media. Tre, ain't you have like one hundred followers before the school year started? Now you got almost seven hundred. That's like the whole rez. But also, I see a lot of white chicks following you, too."

"Yeah, it's been wild. Mainly since last month. Since Wes here started helping me with the highlight clips. He knows how to get the most views."

Wes finishes his text and sets his phone on his lap. "Thanks, guys. It's good to have my genius appreciated. But if you think those little clips are impressive, wait until you see the—"

Nate rolls his eyes and says with a grin, "We know, we know. The *documentary*."

Wes elbows him and takes the last cracker and cheese off his plate.

"For real," Wes says.

"Damn, Tre, I was thinking you had bots following you. But you got a grip of hotties following you on here. Check out this dime from Bemidji." Nate shoves his phone at me and Wes. We both nod. He adds, "That's it? Look at this bikini pic, I've never seen a—"

"Shhhh." I put a finger to my lips and head tilt toward my parents.

Nate mouths, "Sorry." Then he goes back to scrolling on his phone.

Mom is pretty chill, but she doesn't put up with talking about girls like that.

Nate holds up his phone screen for us. "Khiana's trip looks dope." He swipes from one image to the next. "The gigantic arcade and amusement park inside Mall of America, and this pizza slice she's holding up is as big as her face."

Wes leans over me for a better look. "That amusement park is fun. I went with my mom and dad, back when I was like ten or eleven . . . seems like forever ago now."

Nate says, "Maybe we can go there in March. If Tre takes us to the state tournament."

Uncle Ricky chimes in from the kitchen table. "What's this *if* stuff? This is the year we're going to state. No doubt in my mind. Ain't never seen anyone hoop like Tre. Can't anyone stop him." He chugs what's left of his beer and belches. "Excuse me."

I give Nate a *thanks a lot* look. "No pressure," I mutter, then squeeze my way out from the couch to get myself Kool-Aid from the pitcher on the table.

Uncle Ricky fist-bumps me. "Been fun as hell watching you this season, neph. Holy shit, you're everywhere now. Every time I open up the local paper, there's a picture of you, skying for a dunk, next to an article about how you dominated another game. Every time I'm online, someone has shared a highlight of you. I always make sure to comment on those and point out that you're my nephew."

Uncle Liver grips his phone like he's trying to crush it. "Came across a post on one guy's page, had a shit ton of comments. Had everyone all fired up. He was saying that you had the potential to be the best Warrior of all time, and the first to lead us to state. Bunch of people started chiming in, some saying your old man here is the GOAT, a few younger ones saying it was your bro. Others brought up a few other Red Lake hoop legends. Next thing I knew, I was arguing with strangers." Uncle Liver chuckles to himself and pats my arm. "And your handles and range, looks like watching an NBA player. No bullshit, neph. You've got natural talent and have been putting in the work. Been nice watching you out there."

"Thanks, Uncle Liver." The compliments make me nervous. "I appreciate it, unc. I'll be right back." I jet down the hallway to the bathroom and lock the door. I lean down in front of the mirror, take a couple of deep breaths, and splash water on my face. Staring at my reflection, I wonder if I have what it takes. Maybe I've just played a few lucky games. What if I choke in the play-offs? What if I never get us to state? What if I let them all down? Jaxon always seemed so cool, like his fame and pressure were normal. Fucking Superman. *I wish you were still here.*

Back in the living room, my uncles and dad are *still* talking about basketball.

Uncle Ricky adjusts his navy bandanna. "Your dad wasn't throwing down dunks like that."

"Hey, I could get up. If I was as tall as Tre, I would have had dunks, too."

"Nay," my uncles say at the same time super loud, and we all bust out laughing.

Mom comes over and rubs my shoulders, which is kind of embarrassing in front of the guys. "That height came from my side of the family. My dad was six foot four, and my mom was five foot ten. So, you're welcome."

I shift away. "Thanks, Mom."

"Next game on Tuesday against Nevis, eh?" Uncle Liver says. "We keep getting to games earlier and earlier, but the gym is packed quicker and quicker. Hard finding a spot to park if you don't get there right when the JV team is starting. We're talking a line of cars down both directions of the highway as far as you can see."

I turn to Nate and Wes for confirmation. Just sounds too surreal.

Wes comes over with his empty paper plate and grabs crackers, cheese, and the deer meat summer sausage. "It's wild. I lost track of time gaming the other day after school, finally noticed it was almost seven, and so I raced up to the gym. I had to park at The Trading Post and walk the half a mile to the game up that icy old hill."

Mom's voice cuts in from the kitchen. "Dinner is ready. Hope you boys are hungry."

We line up for spaghetti, garlic bread, and salad. Everyone lingers at the blueberry pie, but Mom has a rule about eating dinner before dessert. Her cooking tastes extra, extra good today.

CHAPTER 26

JANUARY 12

BETWEEN THE CHEERS, war whoops, and whistles, it's the loudest game ever. I grab a towel and water bottle.

Dallas pats my head. "Stand back up, bro. You got to wave to the fans, take a bow or something." I stand and face the fans behind our bench. Dallas grabs my hand and lifts it high, like I'm a boxer who just won a fight. Everyone cheers louder. We turn toward the other side of the gym, and they get just as riled.

I say, "This is wild. What's the big deal?"

"What's the big deal? That last run we had out there . . . Think about it, Tre. We were up seven. Then you went off and hit four threes and threw down those two dunks. That put you at forty-nine points. Only four behind breaking the all-time school record of fifty-three—*Jaxon's record*."

Kevin daps me up. "That was sick, Tre. Fucking sick. Who do you think you are, Steph Curry?"

Coach pats us on the backs. "Good game, boys. Nice job putting them away. Now take a seat so we can get out of here."

We sit and watch our bench players have fun. The score is 94–77, with three minutes to go. It's a basketball tradition to rest the starters when a game is basically over—when no matter what happens at that point, the other team can't possibly come back. We watch as Nevis hits a three-pointer. The folks who traveled to see them play cheer like that was the buzzer-beating, game-winning shot. Dallas and Kevin chuckle. So do some of our fans. Dallas says, "Really happy over one three, eh?"

They get into a full-court press. One of our guys dribbles into the corner and is trapped by two Nevis players. He panics, dribbling it off his own foot.

Some of our fans cuss. Some throw their hands up in exasperation. Nevis runs a play for their shooting guard, a double screen on the baseline for a corner three; they call the play gopher. Same play we snuffed out almost every time. But our bench players seem rattled. Nevis hits another three. Their fans get even louder than they were on the last shot.

Coach paces in front of us. He glances at the scoreboard, shaking his head. "Fuckers left their starters in there. Can't hate on them too much for not giving up, I suppose."

Two minutes to go.

Coach shouts to our on-court teammates, "Four corners." It's a play meant to use up as much clock as possible or to allow a player to clear out the floor and cook a defender without defenders or teammates in the way. Four of our players run to their spots, one in each corner on our side of the court, with our backup shooting guard dribbling in the middle. As they pass the ball to whoever's open, Nevis scatters to try to steal. A referee blows his whistle and calls traveling on one of our players.

Kevin shrugs. "He did shuffle his feet before dribbling."

Nevis pushes the ball down the court, passing and cutting, until they get an easy layup.

94–85. Coach presses a hand into his face.

Nevis fouls one of our guys. He goes to the free-throw line but bricks both shots. As soon as they get the rebound, Nevis calls a quick time-out.

On his clipboard, Coach shows our bench players what he thinks Nevis will run as their next play. He tells them how to better defend it this time.

Nevis runs gopher again. This time our defense is moving around the screens, but one of our players slips to the floor. Nevis hits another three. Suddenly we're only up six points, with a minute to go. As he jogs back up court, the player who hit the shot winks and points at me.

Coach taps my shoulder. "Tre, sub in."

I stand to pull off my warm-up jacket and jog over to the scorers' table. Our crowd cheers as loud as they did during that standing ovation. I turn, expecting to see the other starters alongside. "Just me?"

The buzzer sounds and the referee signals me in. I wave out our backup point guard and direct a teammate to inbound the ball to make sure I gain possession.

"What do you want me to run?" I call to Coach.

"You got this." With that, he sits, shrugs, and grabs popcorn from a fan behind him.

I catch the pass. Two Nevis defenders immediately surround me. I've got an open teammate in the corner, but what if they make another mistake? I dribble backward, retreating toward the half-court line. Once I've had a little room to breathe, I rush the defenders. I throw a stutter step, then spin away, leaving them in the dust. The lane is wide open. Nevis's defenders hurry to stop me, but it's too late. I take flight. Cocking the ball behind my head, I rise. Nevis players jump, too, but they're nowhere near as high.

Bam! I throw down the meanest dunk of my life.

I almost jump back in the air in celebration. I almost start clapping with the crowd. Then I remember the assignment. Nevis inbounds the ball, seemingly unfazed. I chase after them.

Their shooting guard dribbles while waving off screens, like he can get by me without help. I used to watch this guy battle Jaxon. That's how I was shutting him down all game. I know his favorite moves. He drives to his right, crosses over to his left, and—damn it. He didn't pull up for a jumper like usual. He used a stutter step. Left me standing there like a statue. He goes for a layup.

I recover in time. My hand pins the ball against the backboard. I pull it down and glance up court. I cross half-court and survey the floor.

The Nevis crowd turns vicious. "Overrated!" "You're not your brother!"

The Nevis defender calls, "Yeah, what they said."

Fuck this. Fuck them. I fake driving right, once, twice, then throw a crossover at my defender. He crumples to the court.

After a throwaway glance at him, I shoot a three. The buzzer sounds. The shot swishes in. My teammates flood the court. Dallas and Kevin squeeze the air out of me.

"Fifty- four! You broke the school record."

CHAPTER 27

JANUARY 22

THE BUZZER BLARES. I toss the ball to the ref as Dallas runs up and gives me a fist pound. Fans flood onto the court asking for autographs and selfies. Even white kids.

The scoreboard reads 98–74.

Another snowy, cold night on the road in northern Minnesota, another win in the books. Life is blurry. Basketball games seemingly every other night, practice after school on nights we don't have games, long bus rides, getting home at one in the morning, only to wake a few hours later to get ready for school.

On the bright side, we rattled off seven wins in a row. I've dropped over twenty points in a few games, over thirty in a couple.

My coach is happy, the entire rez is happy, and I'm . . . a zombie. I smile for one last selfie with my arms around a couple of fans wearing shirts for the opposing team.

In the locker room, I wince as I pull my jersey off. Dark bruises are scattered across my rib cage. When I pull down my trunks, there's a grapefruit-sized bruise on my outer right thigh.

With a hint of respect, Kevin says, "Few more like that and you'll look like a cheetah."

"McDonald's or McDonald's?" Coach Whitefeather asks with a snort-laugh. By the time our games are over, we're lucky if there's a small-town McDonald's open.

After wolfing down Mickey D's, we refill our pops for the ride home and waddle carefully like giant, sportily clad penguins across the ice through the parking lot. Passing a car full of girls, one shouts, "Tre, you're a snack!" I smile and wave.

Kevin slaps my side, right on my bruised ribs. "Howah, Tre, pulling all the chicks."

"Fuck yeah, eh?" Mike nods. "I should start shooting from half-court, too."

Laughter rises from the team. Mason says, "You could hit full-court shots all night, and it still wouldn't help you pull any chicks, bro."

"Ho—fuck you then," Mike says, dragging out his vowels, exaggerating our rez accents.

"Grab her digits real quick, if you're so cool," Mason says like he's calling out a bluff.

I shrug. "Not interested."

As we climb on the bus, Mason says, "Supposed to be a superstar and he's too scared to talk to white chicks. How you going to be a starter on the Red Lake Warriors and still be acting like a nerd?" Mason shakes his head in disgust.

I want to tell him to shut up, but I've seen him knock out a few people at school for far less. I lean my head against the cold leather bus seat and close my eyes. They burn, maybe from being so damn tired, maybe from all the sweat that dripped into them.

A vintage Taylor Swift song fights to be heard through the blown bus speakers and crackling static of the FM radio. Mason says to Mike, "Probably your favorite song, huh?"

"It's *your* favorite song. I heard you jamming to this when you pulled up to school the other day. Turned it down all quick when you saw me."

"Psshh," Mason says, crinkling his eyebrows. "Taylor Swift is pretty hot, though I prefer my girls browner and curvier."

Mike smacks my arm. "Aye. But for real, when Tre goes to the league, he'll probably forget all about us and be dating a famous singer or celebrity, eh?" I swear to God, we can't even ask each other a remotely serious question without hitting each other first.

Mason replies, "Tre ain't going to the fucking league, you dumbass. No one from our rez ever goes anywhere or does anything. There's always a new superstar who scores a few baskets and everyone acts like they're going to be the next LeBron. Look around our rez at the former *superstars*. When we're done playing, we go to work at the casino, or slang weed, or end up alcoholics, hooked on drugs, or dead. But none of us go the fucking league. Ain't that right, Tre?"

I want to disagree. But maybe he's right. Maybe I am in fantasy land. Colleges are afraid to sign rez kids. They believe these outdated stereotypes—that we can't live away from home or we can't handle the schoolwork or that we're all a bunch of drunks. "Rez league MVP," I say, and thankfully, everyone laughs.

I pull out my phone, put in my headphones, and turn on oldschool Lil Uzi Vert. Hopefully, I have enough service to zone out on social media. Khiana has posted a story featuring her and Wes, filming each other and laughing their asses off. That has to be her bedroom—it's definitely not his. I click to his account and find the companion video, shot from his angle. Are they dating now? Have they messed around? I stuff my phone into my backpack.

"Hey . . . Tre," Mike whispers. "You should come party with us tonight. There's a party at Shane Brown's. Going to be fun. You in?"

"Yeah, you should roll with." Dallas leans over the seat behind me. "I'll pick you up on my way."

I worry about the party getting busted. I worry about getting in trouble and suspended from the team. I worry about losing Mason and Mike, too. Coach swore that next time he'd kick them off the team. I'm always worrying. About everything. I don't want to be alone. I need a distraction. Fuck it. I'll go, but I won't stay long.

"Yeah, sounds dope." Mason is right. I'm not going D-1 or playing in the NBA anyway.

. . .

Dallas's headlights go dark right before he pulls into my driveway. He's a champ at this whole not-waking-the-parents-up thing. I zip up my hoodie and tiptoe downstairs. The last step creaks. I freeze. One. Two. Three. Nothing. In slow motion, I turn the doorknob.

"Tre?" Mom's raspy, half-asleep voice.

"Yeah?"

"Where are you going? It's late."

"I'm going to go hang out with Wes for a little bit."

"Well, don't be up too late," Mom replies. "You need your sleep."

Outside, the full moon bounces off the snow, reflects off the beer can in Dallas's hand.

"Tre," Dallas says, like a game show announcer. "What's up?" He digs a beer out of a cooler in the back seat. "Here you go, fam." I crack it open, take a drink. We clink our cans together, and Dallas says, "Cheers. You ready to party?"

"Always." I take another drink, trying to be cool.

"Aye." Dallas knows I'm full of shit, but it's all good. He backs out and cranks up Juice Wrld. As we ride, he belts out the first couple of lines and holds a pretend microphone to me.

I shake my head. He hits me in the arm. "Come on, man!"

So, I start singing, and we fight back laughter. I'm hanging out with a hero of mine. The fresh snow and full moon look like a movie setting, and for once, the rez is peaceful. There are no other cars out, not even a cop car. We turn down a dirt road and drive

227

until we spot cars and trucks lined on both sides of the road. The bigger the party, the more likely it is to get busted.

"Aye." Dallas grabs my attention. "It's all good, bro. The guy whose house this is, Shane, he's tight with most of the cops around here; used to be one until he ripped up his knee in an accident. Plus, he loves us. Comes to every game. You got nothing to worry about."

"I wasn't worried."

Dallas walks in first and is greeted by cheers, hoots, and howls. Following right behind him, I get fist bumps and approving nods.

Mason and Mike are sitting at a small plastic and metal table, playing cards with a couple of older guys and girls who look familiar. Each one of them has a McDonald's cup filled to the brim with a brown drink.

In the kitchen, a loose circle of people from school are passing around a blunt and laughing. Guys from the football team are in the living room, getting rowdy over a game of *Fortnite*. Most of the girls' basketball team stands together in a loose circle, staring at their phones, nodding to the music, passing around their own blunt. Beyond that, the crowd streams up and down the hallway, in and out of the bathroom and bedrooms.

I have no clue what to do or where to go.

"Tre." Mason waves me over. I worry that he's drunk and going to be even more ballsy than normal. I worry that he'll say shit that will take away any cool points I might have earned by hooping the way I've been. Instead, he stands up from his card game to give me the close handshake, pat-on-the-back gesture. He hands me a cup filled with ice and brown liquid. "Southern and Coke. Go ahead. You can hang on to that one. I'll get another."

I watch the card game and listen to the music until the alcohol eases my nerves.

"Tre. Did you see this?" Mason asks, showing me his phone screen. "Looks like your best pal and your crush are in love."

On social media, Khiana and Wes are using one of those so-cute-you-want-to-vomit picture filters. She's on his lap, and they both have cartoonish freckles, fake horn-rimmed glasses, and bear ears. No way that's platonic. For a second, I forget how to breathe.

"That's your chick, right?" Mason asks like he's waiting for my heart to break.

"Nah, man. We're just friends."

"You sure?" he presses, like he wants to see me crumble.

"Yeah, she's cool, man. Her and Wes have a ton in common. I was wondering when they were going to figure that out." I say it like I knew that all along, and maybe I did. But I can't process this, not here and now, and definitely not in front of Mason.

Dallas barges in and sets a bunch of tequila shots in front of us. I grab one. Then we knock back a couple more. I lose track of how many drinks I've had. But my lips feel numb, and I'm no longer steady on my feet. Everyone around me is laughing, rapping along to music, and I'm just sitting here, gripping my phone. I know better than to message Khiana right now, but I can't help myself.

I text her.

> So you and my best friend huh?

> I thought you didn't want to date since you're moving when you graduate. Or was that just what you told me since you didn't want to date me?

Bubbles pop up on the screen. Then disappear.

"Shots for four of the best Red Lake Warriors. After me, that is. . . . Aye." This older guy with a beer belly, wearing a Warriors shirt, laughs to himself. He sets a bottle of Jose Cuervo and glasses on the table and pours.

"Cheers," Dallas says as we all clink our glasses.

Almost everyone at the party has their phones out, capturing videos and pictures of us.

I want to ask them to not post anything, but I don't want to sound like a huge nerd either. So, I throw back my shot and almost puke it up.

Dallas pats my shoulder. "You all right, bro?"

I'm holding a balled fist up to my mouth, praying to the Creator I don't hurl all over the table. My eyes burn and get all watery.

Breathe. Breathe.

Don't throw up in front of Mason, Dallas, and Mike—the three most infamous party animals at our school. Through blurred vision, I watch another shot poured in front of me.

"To winning state," someone says, and everyone repeats it in a group chant. We clink our glasses again and drink another.

• • •

The next morning, I struggle to walk, still feeling dizzy and a little drunk. I wave Dallas goodbye. He laughs, nods, then puts his truck in reverse and drives away. I take a deep breath, hoping to sober up even just a little. The sunlight bounces off the fresh blanket of snow. It's so fucking bright, it makes the pain in my head throb even more. Damn. I wish I could have made it home before my parents woke up. But I was having too much fun. Ugh. I shake my head at myself and walk inside, afraid as all hell of how my parents are going to act.

"Well, look what the cat dragged in. Where in the hell were you?" My mom sets a spatula down on the side of a frying pan and puts her hands on her hips. The smell of scrambled eggs and blueberry pancakes fills the air. But instead of smelling good, it makes me feel sick.

At the table, Dad is burning a hole through me with the look on his face. "Why didn't you come home last night? You didn't even call or text. We were worried sick about you," he barks.

"I'm sorry. I didn't mean to. I fell asleep at Wes's. Dozed off watching a movie."

Mom's shoulders drop from looking tense to relaxed, but she gives me the same concerned look she used to when I was a little kid and scraped a knee. "Oh my God, honey. You look awful."

"Something you're not telling us?" Dad asks, but he says it like he already knows what that is. Every time I glance at him, he is staring at me, impatiently waiting for an answer.

"I'm just really tired. And really sorry. It won't happen again."

I take off to my room before they can continue their interrogation.

"Aren't you hungry?" Mom yells. "Breakfast is almost ready!"

I shut my bedroom door, plug in my phone, turn on some soft music, and collapse onto my bed. Hopefully they'll leave me alone and let me sleep for an hour or two. When I close my eyes, the room spins. My tongue feels sandy. I'm dying for water or Gatorade, but if I drink anything, it's coming right back up.

Who knows what people from the party last night posted on social media. I'm terrified to look. And even if it stayed offline, I'm pretty sure everyone will be telling everyone else all about it. On my rez, the walls have ears, the trees and their leaves have ears, the pebbles on the road have ears, every speck of sand along the beach has ears, every deer, bird, dumpster-diving bear, and every rez dog has ears . . . for gossip. There's no such thing as a secret on the rez.

CHAPTER 28

JANUARY 25

MONDAY MORNING AT school and I still don't feel one hundred percent. Partying over the weekend really kicked my ass. First few hours of class were a battle just to stay awake. Thankfully it's finally lunch break. Halfway done with the day. I still have no appetite. I should eat something. We have a game tonight, and I'll need energy. But I can't stop thinking about Khiana and Wes.

With my hood up and my head down, I speed walk out of the school.

Dark clouds blanket the sky. Cotton-ball-sized snowflakes fall, swirling as I hurry to my car. I start the engine and rub my hands together as I wait for the air to warm up.

Wind spins up clouds of snow, giving me privacy. Fellow students rush to their cars.

They're holding tight to their hoods and scarves.

I lean my head back and close my eyes. I want to ditch school and lie in my bedroom, curtains drawn, lights off, music blaring in my headphones. But I can't do any of that. If I don't attend school this afternoon, I won't be able to play tonight.

Tap, tap, tap. Wes knocks against the passenger-side door. I gesture for him to get in. He does, warming his hands on the vent. We sit in silence, watching the snow swirl. Finally, I can't take it anymore. The question explodes. "What's up with you and Khiana? Fuck, man, I can't believe you would do this." I look over at him. "Really? *Really?*"

He meets my gaze. "I didn't mean to fall for her. I knew you had feelings for her."

"So then you went ahead and started dating her anyway?"

"It just kind of . . . happened."

"Oh. It just happened."

"Yeah, man. It just happened. I don't know what you want me to say. I'm sorry. You were gone all the time, her and I started talking more, and before we knew it—"

It's not that simple. "Seems she's into whoever pays her the most attention. When it was me, she liked me. Once it was you giving her attention . . . oh, guess what, then she liked you."

"She never liked you, not like that."

"What? Did she say that?"

"She didn't need to."

"You're a real friend, you know that?"

"I didn't mean to hurt you. Neither did Khiana."

"Whatever, man. It's all . . . it's whatever."

"Tre, I know things are crazy for you right now, but try to focus on getting through this next month. You've come too damn far to let anything mess with that. You should keep your mind on basketball and school. And maybe stop partying with those guys, you know?"

Anger takes over. I slam my hands into the steering wheel. "My life isn't some stupid fucking movie you get to direct, okay? Maybe you should chill on trying to give me advice."

Wes gets out and says, "It's only stupid because you're the one writing it. You're the one fucking up your own story. Not me."

"Fuck you!" I yell. Wes slams the car door.

Later that night, during pregame warm-ups, my mind is a hot mess thinking about everything that just went down. I have to focus. Maybe stretching and some deep breathing will help. I leave the layup lines, walk over to half-court, and sit, stretching my legs into a V shape. I reach with both hands toward my left foot, hold it, breathe out, then switch, reaching to my right foot. Hold it. Pause. Breathe. It's working. My thoughts slow down. Now that I've had a chance to calm down—and my hangover headache is finally fading—I feel like an asshole for how I acted toward Wes. I can't help but worry that I ruined things between me and Khiana.

I hate myself right now. I switch my stretch over to the other leg.

"Tre," Coach Whitefeather says gently. "Don't look now, but to the left of your parents is the coach from the University of Minnesota. He called last night to tell me he was coming to watch you play. I'm going to make sure we get you extra shots, to showcase you. But don't overthink it, kid. Play your game."

What? Whoa. I rub my eyes and look again. Seeing the Gophers coach is a trip. I've never seen someone from TV in real life before.

The referee tosses the ball up, Kevin tips the ball into my hands, and I race up the court and hit Robert on the wing. He pulls up for a three with a defender flying at him.

The shot rattles in, then rolls back up, swirls around the rim, and falls out. I time the miss perfectly and jump. As my fingertips start to guide it back in, an elbow hits my back and I crash to the floor. There's no call from the ref, and for a second, I almost throw my hands up in frustration; then I remember the U of M coach and keep my cool.

From the hardwood floor, I watch Clearbrook get a layup.

Dallas passes me the ball. Kevin cuts hard to the basket, and I find him with a bounce pass. He rises for a dunk but one of their players slams into him, knocking him to the ground. There's no whistle from the refs. Kevin grunts, holding his left knee. His dad puts an arm around his mother, who has her hands together in prayer.

The Clearbrook crowd cheers, applauding the dirty play.

Without thinking, I shove the guy who fouled Kevin. He falls on his ass, and the Red Lake crowd jumps to their feet, cheering on my retaliation. Like magnets, players from both teams crash into each other, with me in the middle.

Refs jump in, trying to break us apart. Coaches rush onto the floor to help pull us away from each other. As we separate, a ref blows his whistle and points at me. "Technical foul on number ten." The gym splits between booing and applause.

"Why didn't you call anything when my teammate got slammed to the floor?" I yell. "Or when I got shoved the play before?"

Dallas runs up between us. "Don't blow this shot in front of the Gophers, bro."

"Those were common basketball plays," the ref says. "You blatantly shoved someone during a dead ball. Unacceptable. And furthermore, watch your mouth. Next time you'll be gone."

Kevin, limping, is being helped off the court. Coach calls a time-out. "Tre. What the hell are you doing? That's no way to act. Especially in front of the U of M coach sitting here watching you play. You want to blow your chance? Word gets around about players who are hotheaded."

"But Coach, these refs are—"

"Drop it, Tre. Don't let it happen again. If you ever feel like that, take a breath, walk away, come sit down, anything but that. Now listen, this time-out is almost over. I need you to play center. You're the only other player on our team with the height to handle that position. Mason, sub in. You're taking the reins at the point-guard spot."

"I don't know the plays from the center position," I say, almost to myself.

"Yeah, you do. You're always finding Kevin. Imagine where he would be moving to when Mason calls out a play," Coach says in a huff before sitting down.

Later, their crowd is every bit as hyped as ours, maybe more. I'm posting up, asking for the ball, but Mason keeps bringing it to the other side of the court, opting for midrange jumpers for himself or getting the ball to Robert. Without Kevin to clog up the middle, Clearbrook gets easy layups and putbacks off of offensive rebounds.

The quarter ends with the score tied at 24–24. Coach barks orders, but I'm thinking about how I've probably already blown my chance at impressing the Gophers coach. I don't see Wes here recording. I wonder if Kevin is okay.

Slap slap slap. Coach claps his hands together hard, right in my face. "Snap out of it, eh? You look like a fucking zombie out there. Wake up or come sit down next to me."

The rest of the half is a shit show, with us taking bad shots, getting beat on defense, and getting outhustled. We walk into the locker with our heads hanging, down 38–51. Mason kicks a chair so hard it flies across the room. Kevin is icing his left knee, grimacing.

Coach Whitefeather storms in, coming to a harsh stop right in the middle of the room. "Pressure too much for you?" I assume he's talking to all of us. "Too much now that the big bright lights of the play-offs are right around the corner? Or is it that Gophers coach that's got you all shook?"

Dallas taps me on the leg. Mason says, "Fuckin' refs are on bullshit out there."

"Well, you guys got yourselves into this mess of a game," Coach says. "Might as well let you get yourselves out of it. You sure as hell ain't listening to a word I say."

"Christ," Mason mutters.

There's a long, awkward silence until Coach adds, "Mason, you're going to start the second half at point guard. Tre, I need you to forget that you aren't at your precious point guard spot and play ball. Like you used to. Hustle like you're still trying to prove you belong here."

"I never stopped playing hard," I say under my breath.

Coach tosses the eraser and marches out of the locker room.

CHAPTER 29

JANUARY 26

WALKING INTO SCHOOL the next morning, I spot Khiana and Wes across the parking lot. He says something to her, fighting a smile, like he's trying to play it cool. He always does that when he tells a joke. She throws her head back like whatever he said is the funniest thing she's ever heard.

"Your pal snagged your chick already, eh?" Kevin asks, holding himself up on crutches.

I shrug a tired, IDGAF shrug. "What did the doctor say?"

"Knee sprain. Thankfully. Could have been worse. I'll be fine."

"Shit, man, I'm glad that's all it was."

"Me too. Hey, I was just messing with you about Wes and Khiana. You okay?"

"Yeah, I'm good. All that matters is the rest of this season."

"Good," Kevin says before hobbling away. I walk down the hall, avoiding eye contact with all of my classmates. It's one thing to walk through school after a big win. Feels embarrassing walking through here after taking an L. I open my locker, hang my coat, and put my winter beanie on the top shelf.

"Can't believe you guys lost last night." Nate slams his locker door. "Shit was ugg-ah-lee."

"Yeah." My phone vibrates. It's a text from an unknown number.

This is Blair Howe, a journalist for Slam magazine. I am reaching out to notify you that we have selected you to be a story in an upcoming issue. I'm wondering if we could chat so that we can line things up.

"Duuuude . . ."

"What, man?" Nate asks. "You get some nudes?"

"What? No." I hand the phone to him. "This is from *Slam* magazine."

"Oh shit . . . Holy shit."

As Wes and Khiana approach, Nate shouts, "Tre is going to be in *Slam* magazine!"

I'm in shock, and I'm not ready to talk to Wes and Khiana. I grab my phone from Nate and bounce.

Standing in front of the door to my next class, I text back to the sportswriter.

I would be honored and humbled to be in Slam magazine. It's my all-time favorite basketball magazine. And a dream come true.

Great! Glad to hear. We checked in with your principal and basketball coach, and it appears next Monday they'll set aside the time for us to do the interview and photo shoot with you.

I have one small request that I hope won't blow my chance to be in your magazine.

What's that?

Can my team be part of it? Like part of the photo shoot and included in some of the story.

The bell rings. I stuff my phone in my pocket and enter my English class. At my desk, I feel my phone vibrate. I pull it out of my pocket, hold it under my desk—out of the teacher's eyesight—and steal a look.

Sure. We can get some shots of them and get their thoughts. That will give us options for final editing decisions.

I text back as fast as I can.

Thank you. I really appreciate it

Then I jam my phone back in my pocket and pull out my
notebook for English class. If I don't jot down notes in class, I end
up daydreaming the entire time. Jaxon had the same problem. He
shared that tip with me when I was struggling with school.

Pencil in hand, I start scribbling notes, doing my best to pay
attention. The teacher is talking about how we're going to read
Romeo and Juliet.

Halfway through, she pauses her lecture. "Yes, Sean?"

The entire class looks over to see why he's raising his hand. I
mean, he probably wants to ask for the bathroom pass so he can
escape from this boring class and roam the hallways. But hell, this
is the most exciting thing to happen so far in this class.

"How come we have to read Shakespeare?"

"Well, Sean, if you had heard anything I had said, you would
know that Shakespeare is one of the greatest storytellers in all of
history. It's important to not only read and marvel at his writings,
but to have a base-level knowledge of his work. It gives you perspective."

"Well . . . it would be cool to read something I can understand."

"That's what . . . haven't you been listening at all? Each day I
will go into detail in breaking it down to have it make more sense."

"I don't even like reading. I'd rather watch Netflix or play

Xbox. But if I *have* to read, I just wish it could be a story I'd understand without someone explaining it ten times."

"Sean . . . part of our appreciation for notable fiction from—"

"Excuse me. Sorry for interrupting class," our principal says over the speaker system. "But something of this magnitude deserves a moment. Our very own Red Lake Warriors are going to be featured in an upcoming issue of *Slam* magazine. To celebrate, we've shifted today's lunch to pizza, and we ordered ice cream and cake from The Trading Post. Now, back to learning. Goooo, Warriors!" Getting the text from the *Slam* journalist felt like a dream, but something about hearing it over the loudspeaker makes it more real. I don't know who starts it, but a slow clap gets faster and louder until the whole class has joined in. A couple of guys in the second row high-five.

Our teacher says, "How about that, Tre? What an honor! You must be thrilled."

"Yeah."

"You have to promise to sign a copy for me when it comes out."

"Sure." I bury my face in my book.

"Where were we? Ah yes, the Montagues and Capulets—"

Sean leans and whispers, "Aye, Tre, thanks for getting us cake and ice cream."

That afternoon, Coach Whitefeather paces as usual, smirks as usual. "You think you're hot shit now because you're going to be in a magazine, eh? Just a bigger bull's-eye on our back. You've been struggling to beat these local farm-boy hick schools around here.

Those other teams, if you haven't noticed, are playing beyond their capabilities because they want to beat us so bad. This magazine bullshit is going to make that ten times worse. Plus, who knows when Kevin is going to be back to full strength. We have to prepare like he isn't coming back."

Kevin is seated in his street clothes, his crutches resting against his legs.

"Play-offs are right around the corner. These guys been scouting us all year, sending their spies to tape our games. Happens every time we get on a play-off run. We bump into a team that has our playbook memorized. For the next few practices, we're going to learn a whole new offensive set. Going to call it ma'iingan. The wolf. Now let's go."

We hop up and walk out onto the court.

"You know why I named this set ma'iingan?" Coach asks a few minutes later. We have no clue. "Because . . . wolves travel in packs, hunt in packs, kill in packs. Their strength comes from each other. You guys ever see a pack of wolves chase down a larger animal? They circle them, trick them, take them down together. That's what we need to do. This new set is all about making the extra pass, lots of screens, lots of back cuts. If you don't have the ball, no more standing around with your thumb up your ass."

As we cruise out of the gym after practice, Dallas says, "We're going to have a little *Slam* magazine announcement party. It's at Shane Brown's."

"Oh, man. I don't know."

245

"Niij, it's not every day a team from a rez gets to be in the biggest basketball magazine in the world. We got to at least have a couple drinks."

My stomach clenches as we take the last couple of turns to Shane Brown's party.

"You all right?" Dallas asks as he polishes off the last of his Coors Light.

I crush my own can. "Of course."

Tupac's "To Live and Die in L.A." is blaring so loud from Shane's house that we can hear it almost as clear as if it was coming from Dallas's truck speakers. He turns the engine off and slaps me on the arm. Gesturing to two cars parked ahead, Dallas says, "See. I told you. Shane, Mike, and Mason. Maybe one or two other people. Nothing to worry about. Now, let's celebrate."

Shane greets us. "What's up, legends?"

Mason and Mike nod at us, then get back to playing *Call of Duty*.

"Mixed drinks or beers?" Shane asks. Then he belches loud as hell.

"Going to stick to the beers tonight, bro. Gotta be ready for the play-offs. Aye." Dallas slaps Shane in the beer belly and grabs a couple of Bud Lights out of the fridge. Dallas tosses one to me, and we crack them open.

Over the music, Shane says, "Hey, you guys, pause that shit for a minute."

"Hold on a sec," Mason replies. "About to snipe this fucker."

We watch Mason back up his claim by getting a head shot on Mike. "Four in a row. Can't touch me on this game." Mason stands from the couch with a drink in his hand. He asks Shane, "What you want, you chubby ol' fucker?"

"Christ. Fuck you." Shane chuckles. "Come on over here for a second."

Shane holds his mixed drink into the air, and we all follow suit. "To *Slam* magazine. Cheers."

We all say *cheers* in unison.

"Fucking big-time, guys. Big-time. Everyone on the rez is going to get one of those magazines and hang the cover on their walls. Badass. Proud of you guys. You don't know this yet because you're still young, but being a Warrior is like being part of a club, part of a family. All of us that played before, we watch you with a lot of pride. We cheer on each team, season after season, hoping that they'll do what we couldn't. When yous got to the regional championship last year, holy shit, that was ace. And now, *Slam* magazine . . ."

"Fuck *Slam* magazine." Mason gulps his Southern Comfort with a splash of Dr Pepper. "All I ever wanted since I was a little kid and watched you guys lose in regionals was to suit up in a Warrior uniform and get revenge for you all. But now, this is it for me. I'm not going to play college ball. This will be the last time we play a meaningful basketball game. We have to win state. For us, for the former Warriors, and for the entire rez."

"Fuck yeah," Shane says, staring into his brown drink like it's a Magic 8 Ball.

I take a sip of my beer. These guys are my heroes. It still blows my mind that they're my teammates. It's a punch in the heart, the thought of any game being our last together. I think about what Mason said, about this being it for them.

"All stiff already?" Mike asks me, and everyone chuckles.

"Nah, man," I say, and take another drink.

As a car pulls into his driveway, Shane says, "Christ, who's that now?" He goes to the window. "Fuckin' crack open one beer, and everyone on the rez magically appears."

Dallas nudges him aside and peeks out. "That's Kevin."

Minutes later, Kevin hobbles in, but without crutches. Mason throws a combination of fake punches at his ribs. "Never thought I'd see you at a party. Especially with that bad knee. How'd you even drive here? Or did your mom drop you off?"

"Christ. My mom would kill me if she knew I was partying over here. And it's just my left knee. Only need my right one to hit the gas and brakes." Kevin rolls his eyes.

"Why you here, then?" Mason asks.

"To make sure you guys don't get in trouble again," Kevin replies.

Shane offers Kevin a mixed drink. "Here you go, bro. You ain't playing for a while anyway."

Kevin shakes his head no. "That's okay, bro. Even if I'm not playing, I still don't want to drink. Promised my parents I'd wait until at least after high school. Almost there."

"Play some cards then or what?" Mason asks.

We're a couple of games in when more cars pull up and more people come inside to party.

Mason, Mike, and Dallas get up to greet their friends, who're seniors at our school.

"Hope too many more people don't show up." Kevin leans over to me so that no one else hears him. "I ain't trying to get tossed in jail right before the play-offs."

"Me neither. Hey, if it gets too crazy here, you mind giving me a ride home? Dallas won't leave no matter how many people show up."

"Yeah, man. I got you."

With each game of cards, we finish another drink, and another carload of our classmates shows up. Each time the door opens, everyone cheers and woos.

"*Slam* magazine," someone says.

"State champs," someone else says.

My lips are numb. The beer tastes like water.

"What's up, Tre?" I look up at Nate and Wes.

"What's up, Nate?" I say, avoiding eye contact with Wes.

They make their way into the living room to mingle. I elbow Kevin and gesture to Wes. "Can you believe this guy? My best friend, but he starts dating the only girl I've ever been into."

"That's the alcohol talking." Kevin puts a hand on my shoulder. "Deal with it another day."

I open another can of beer. This one is my sixth. Wait, seventh? I've lost count. My teeth grind, and my hands are balled into fists. Wes spares me a worried glance. I stand, but the room wobbles like a fishing boat on a windy day.

"You okay?" Dallas asks.

"Yeah." I steady myself with my hand on the table and move toward the living room.

Someone grabs my wrist. Kevin. "Where you going?"

"Nowhere," I say, pulling my arm free. I take slow, careful steps, weaving my way through circles of people until I'm standing behind Wes. I tap him on the shoulder. Hard.

When he turns, his eyes are wide. He places a hand on my arm, but I slap it away.

He begins, "Tre . . . it's not what you think."

Nate muscles in as close as possible without touching. "Tre. Drop it, man."

"Drop what? I'm just talking to one of my best *friends*."

Nate says, "I'm telling you for your sake to let it go."

"For my sake? What's this guy going to do?"

"Tre," Wes says. "I would never do anything to hurt you."

I bust out laughing. "Yeah, right."

Everyone goes quiet, circling us. Someone turns down the music. A couple of people hold up their phones, ready to take a video of whatever happens.

"You should get the fuck outta here," I warn Wes.

"You're the one who should leave, Mr. Basketball Superstar. Don't you get suspended for two weeks for drinking?"

"Are you fucking threatening me?"

"No," Wes says.

"Fuck you, man. We've been best friends since kindergarten. But I guess that doesn't matter to you."

"Of course it matters. And we *are* still friends. Look—"

"No, you look. For real. Look around this room." I hold my arms out. "Everyone in here, hell, everyone at our school, they all think you're a weird-ass-looking light-skinned boy. Only reason no one ever fucked with you is because I've always had your back. And this is how you repay me? By stealing the girl I fell for?"

"I didn't steal anyone. And maybe that's all true. And I am some weird-ass-looking light- skinned boy. But at least I'm myself. I'm not afraid to be who I am; I'm not trying to be someone else."

"What's that supposed to mean?"

"I'm just saying."

"What the fuck ever. Fuck you, Wes. Fake-ass friend. Get the fuck out of here."

"Fight. Fight. Fight." Everyone pumps their fists. More phones ready.

I finish my beer, crush it in one hand, then throw it at Wes. It smacks his forehead.

He punches me.

I grab my lower jaw; the pain is instant and sharp; the sting stays like an echo. I shove him down, jump on top of him, and throw wild punches at his face. People try to pull me off, but I keep slipping free to punch again. Suddenly, strong arms grab me from behind. Wes punches me right in the face. Someone yanks me off like I'm a toddler.

Mason.

CHAPTER 30

JANUARY 27

AS I'M GRABBING my backpack out of my locker, Dallas says, "That's a nice little shiner."

In a hushed tone, he adds, "Aye, fam, what you going to say to Coach about your eye?"

"I don't know."

"I accidentally elbowed you messing around in gym class."

"Huh?"

"That's what I'll say when he asks. He'll believe me, and then bitch at us for being stupid. Wanna bet?"

The bell rings when I walk into class, and my civics teacher, Mrs. Hendricks, pauses at the chalkboard. "Tre, what happened to your eye?"

"Caught an elbow goofing off with a friend."

"Do you want to go see the nurse? You should get an ice pack on it."

"No, I'm fine. I've been icing it."

She finally starts the class, talking about the legislative branch.

My brain is throbbing in sync with my heartbeat. My eyes burn, and my head feels heavy. I lay my arm on the desk and rest my head on it.

The sound of the bell jolts me awake. I wipe drool off my chin and shut my notebook.

"Tre . . . ," Mrs. Hendricks begins.

"Yeah," I say, suddenly gripping my books.

"You slept through almost the entire class."

"I'm tired, like I need to sleep for a week. It won't happen again."

"I've been going to Warriors basketball games since I started working here. You're my favorite player. You have a world of potential. You're going to do big things, on and off the court. You get a pass today. But don't make it a habit."

"I won't. I promise."

"Good. Because basketball isn't all there is. It's important to make sure you get what education you can get out of this place. College is harder than you'd imagine."

There's a knock and we turn to see Mr. Thomas in the doorway. "Excuse me, Mrs. Hendricks. I need to speak to Tre."

"Have a seat." Mr. Thomas gestures to one of the two wooden chairs facing his desk.

Once again, I scan the grainy old pictures of him standing alongside the basketball team—from back when he used to be the coach—along with his college diploma from Bemidji State University and pics of him with his wife and two daughters. The photo of him and Jaxon holding up the district championship trophy. "Do you know why I asked you here?" I shake my head and catch a glimmer of myself in his eyeglasses, which were probably last fashionable twenty years ago. "Well, there are a lot of rumors floating around about a party last night. Allegedly, a lot of basketball players were there."

"As far as I know, everyone was at home last night."

"Tre, it's okay."

"Huh?"

"You know, it seems like only yesterday I was a teenager myself." He leans back in his chair and puts his hands behind his head. "Believe me, I can relate."

I hate when adults say that.

"I know you were at that party last night. Hell, I didn't even have to ask anyone. Heard the entire story as I walked down the hallway on my way in today." Do I admit the guilt? Is this a trick to get me to confess?

"Drinking is an automatic two-game or two-week suspension. I mean, you know that already. That's why Mike and Mason missed the first couple of games of the season. I can't imagine how you kids didn't learn a lesson from all that."

I chew my fingernails. It probably makes me look extra guilty,

254

but I can't help it. "What are you saying? I, umm . . . I don't know what to say."

"Look. The play-offs are right around the corner. I've been working at this school longer than you've been alive. Heck, I was the athletic director even back when your dad was a student athlete here. I coached your dad, believe it or not, and in all that time, I've never seen the people of this reservation as jazzed as they are for this basketball team. This is our best chance to finally win state. So, how about we make a deal? Just the two of us."

I stop chewing my nails. "What deal?"

"Promise me that you and your teammates won't drink again until the season is over."

I lean forward, thinking it over. I want to say yes, but I can only control myself.

"I know you know the story of your dad's team." They were the first team in Red Lake play-off history to win the district tournament. Legend has it that the team and everyone on the rez spent the next few days partying nonstop. They were so hungover that they got their asses handed to them in the regional tournament. A game against Bemidji that everyone thinks they should have won. "I remember how heartbroken those players were for the rest of that school year. Hell, some of them are *still* heartbroken about it. Not living up to your potential is haunting. So . . . let's forget last night happened."

I lean way back in the chair, stare at the ceiling for a second, and exhale a sigh of relief so loud Mr. Thomas has to fight back a laugh. I thought we were so screwed. This is for real. We got one more chance to not fuck around.

"Yeah. We can do that," I say, jumping up from my seat and reaching across his desk to shake his hand. "Good looking out, Mr. Thomas."

I rush out of his office with the speed of a rez ball fast break.

On my way to my car, Khiana yells my name. She jogs to catch up. "Really?"

"Really, what?"

Her eyes are teary. "You picked a fight with Wes. Just because we fell for each other?"

"I was drunk. And angry."

"I thought you were cooler than this. When the season started, you basically disappeared on me. And that's when me and Wes clicked. We have more in common than I've ever had with anyone. Why are you being jealous and bitter? Why not be happy for us?"

"Whatever. I guess I'm just a fuckup." I blow out a breath. "It hurt finding out from your pics together. When I texted you to ask, you never replied. You owed me that much."

"I didn't owe you anything. We talked about this. I told you I wasn't looking to date. You wanted us to be something, and I didn't feel the same."

"You told me you didn't want to get into anything cuz you were about to graduate and then move. That was messed up that you'd say that to me, then turn around and date my best friend. You lied."

"I didn't lie. That was my truth at the time. I didn't know me and Wes were going to end up connecting the way we did. Plus, that gives you no fucking right to act like this." Tears stream down her face.

Seeing Khiana cry and knowing it's my fault messes me up. Suddenly, I can't breathe and can't think of how to even begin apologizing. "I'm . . . . I'm . . . ," I stutter.

"Sure you are. Leave us both alone. Okay, superstar?"

CHAPTER 31

FEBRUARY 1

THE BLACKISH-PURPLE BRUISE under my eye is fading. I pray to the Creator that my mom can do something to help. In the bathroom, I run gel through my hair, then toss it until I get the messy, rolled-out-of-bed look just right.

Mom is on her laptop at the kitchen table. "Hey, Ma? Would you be able to work a little bit of magic on this?" I ask, pointing to my eye, then looking down at the floor in embarrassment. "We have our *Slam* magazine photo shoot after school today."

"We can try to put concealer on it, but only if you tell me what really happened."

"Mom . . ."

"Tre . . ."

"Okay. I'll tell you."

I follow her downstairs and into the den bathroom, where she keeps all her makeup and jewelry and where she can take her time getting ready in the mornings without me or Dad bothering her. She has a long mirror against the wall, and a shelf full of her turquoise and beaded necklaces, rings, and bracelets. She squeezes between me and the shelf and digs around in a drawer until she finds some concealer. "So, tell me what happened."

"It's a long story."

"Give me the short version."

"I . . . messed up. Bad. I got into a fight with Wes because I was jealous of him and Khiana dating. It's stupid."

"Tre, he's been your friend since you were in kindergarten. He's always been there for you. He was your first real friend, when you didn't have any. He always loved you for who you were, not what you wanted to be. And he never left your side during Jaxon's wake. Not once." She uses a smooth little sponge to dab on the liquid concealer. "Can you find it in your heart to tell him you're sorry? And Khiana, too?" Mom stops dabbing and looks me in the eye.

"I want to. It's hard. It's like the words are buried somewhere inside of me," I say.

"They're buried behind your pride. Pride can be a good thing. Pride in our culture, in our tribe, in our heritage. That's the kind of pride that keeps who we are as a people alive. But personal pride, that ego pride can get in the way of growing, learning, and admitting when we are wrong." She tilts her head, studying her handiwork, and continues dabbing. "Sometimes it takes making some really stupid mistakes to learn how to set your pride aside for

259

a minute and do the right thing." She sets the bottle of concealer on the sink. "I'll be right back."

Mom returns carrying a shell with sage burning in it. "We need to smudge you down before you leave."

As she waves the smoke around me, I close my eyes, instantly feeling a bit better about everything. I wave some toward myself. "Thank you," I say as she motions the sage smoke around herself, too.

"There's a pouch of tobacco on the kitchen table. You need to put some out before you leave. Talk to the Creator. Thank him for today, for everything you have, and ask him to give you the courage to make things right." Mom picks back up the bottle of concealer. "Now let's finish taking care of that ugly black eye of yours."

When I enter the gym, there are bright lights on stands and things that look like umbrellas. My teammates are streaming out of the locker room, one by one, decked out like we're about to play a game. I nod at the photographer, in awe of his cameras and equipment, reminded of Wes.

"Tre Brun?" asks a tall brunette woman in a fitted blue dress and heels.

"Yeah," I say, shaking her hand.

"I'm Blair Howe. We've spoken on the phone. Mind if we do our interview while our photographer gets some shots of your teammates?"

We go take a seat on the bleachers. Blair asks me if it's okay if she records me on a voice memo on her iPhone for accuracy. "I'm so delighted about this article. It's going to be unique, that's for sure. This is my first time writing a Native American basketball story. You don't see many. I was blown away by the footage your friend sent from his documentary."

"My friend?"

"Wes Stately. He emailed our office with a short trailer of his documentary and a very enthusiastic message about why we should feature you. The story of your following in the steps of your big brother, playing in honor of him, and trying to lead the first all Native American team to win the state tournament. We were intrigued, to say the least."

I'm the biggest asshole that's ever lived! Wes made this all happen. Because he's always believed in me. Always been there for me. Damn, I messed up so bad. I have to find a way to let him know how much he means to me, and how fucking sorry I am. For the next several minutes, I answer Blair's questions, and she compliments what she calls my "full and articulate answers." The interviews I've done with Wes were the perfect practice. Afterward, I say thanks and run over to join my team.

The photographer with Blair says, "We're going to try a few different looks, so the guys at *Slam* who make the big decisions have options." When he mentions "the guys at *Slam*," I feel like I'm dreaming. Everything is surreal. "All right, let's do the typical tough-guy one first. Look into the camera like you're staring down your worst enemy." The light bulb flashes. "That came a little too easy to you guys. You're naturals. Now let's try one of everybody smiling."

We mix it up, taking a variety of pictures and then individual photos.

"Now it's all you, Tre." The photographer digs into his bag for a handheld camera. "Do whatever you want. Dribble, shoot, make some layups and dunks."

I catch the ball and dribble out beyond half-court. I close my eyes, and suddenly, I'm twelve years old again, dribbling on a dirt court, daydreaming about being in *Slam* magazine.

I take a couple of dribbles to get a rhythm, and then a smile splashes onto my face as I picture what type of dunk I'm about to throw down.

Later, sitting in my car outside of the gym, I shoot a text to Wes.

> I'm sorry

Will he respond? What's he going to say? Is he still mad? Does he regret landing me the *Slam* magazine piece? Are we ever going to be the friends we were again? The air blowing in my car finally turns from arctic frost to heat. I put my chilly hands up to the vents. Picking my phone up, I rattle off more texts.

> Thanks for reaching out to Slam

> Thanks for helping me make one of my dreams come true

> Thanks for always being there for me

> For being my day one

> I love you bro

I set my phone into the cup holder and reach to put my car into drive. My text notification goes off, and I can't grab it fast enough.

> You're a dick

> I know. I'm the fucking worst

> You're welcome btw

> I owe you, Wes. Seriously!!!

> What else is new?

> Lol FR

> Stop by, I wanna show you something

On the way, I stop at The Other Store to pick up a peace offering—an appetizer sampler basket full of fries, onion rings, cheese sticks, chicken nuggets, jalapeño poppers. It's what me and Wes always used to order for our late-night hang sessions. That and his favorite, Sour Patch Kids, and a mango-flavored Rockstar energy drink.

Standing at his front door, I let out a deep breath. This is going to be awkward as hell.

Fuck it. Deal with it, Tre.

I knock lightly before opening the door. Machine Gun Kelly is blaring from the basement, so I go downstairs. Wes is sitting at his laptop. He nods but doesn't turn down the music. I set down the energy drink and snacks next to Wes. He's jamming to the beat, clicking maniacally at video editing software.

I grab a seat on the beat-up couch and set down the rest of our snacks. And wait.

Finally, the music fades out.

"Check this out," Wes says, cracking open his can. I jump right up and walk over, resting a hand on the back of his chair and leaning in to study his screen. "Dope, right?" He takes a sip. Music fades in—"Remember the Name" by Fort Minor.

The screen changes from black to a shot of Jaxon, pulling up for a jumper. The shot swishes through. It's followed by a clip of me shooting a jumper from the same spot.

The video moves back and forth between nearly identical clips.

Jaxon crosses someone over so bad, they stumble, and he splashes one on them. The next clip looks like a replay, but it's me instead. Our body movements, mannerisms, and movements are eerily identical. I get chills. The music drops until it's silent. We see a shot of Jaxon and his team holding up the district championship trophy. The screen goes black.

I fight back tears but fail. I never want the video to end. It's the

264

closest thing I've ever seen to me and my brother playing together, the closest I've felt to him since he died.

"You're up," Wes says, snapping me back to reality.

"Huh?"

He offers me a few Sour Patch Kids. "Well, now I need that next shot, of you holding the district championship trophy. Can't finish my video until then. No pressure, though."

Still looking at his dark screen, I say, "I'm really sorry."

"I know."

"Khiana still hates me, huh?"

"She's not your biggest fan right now. Give her space, and then find the right way to say you're sorry."

"I'll think of something. But we're good?"

For too long, he seems more interested in his keyboard than in answering. "Yeah, man, we're good. As long as you go and write a happy ending to my *stupid* documentary."

We laugh. And the laughter brings my best friend back to me. It washes away a bit of the mess I made. "Thanks again, man. I can't believe you got fucking *Slam* magazine to come here."

He's clearly low-key proud of himself. "What can I say? I got skills."

CHAPTER 32

FEBRUARY 7

THE HIGH SCHOOL gym is still cold this early in the morning, especially when it's zero degrees outside. I'm leaving my hoodie and beanie on for sure. I blow into my cupped hands, hoping to warm them. The gym is dim. Only a couple of the lights are on. I take a single dribble. The bounce of the orange leather against the cold hardwood floor echoes throughout the empty gym. I dribble up the court, jogging to get my blood flowing. Dad is sitting on the front-row bleacher at half-court, sipping coffee out of a thermos that has the Red Lake Warriors logo emblazoned on the side.

Dad takes a gulp of coffee. "Once you're warmed up, we'll get in our shooting drills, then our dribbling drills, then we'll end it with some sprints and free throws."

I give a thumbs-up and keep dribbling up and down the court, making little fake jab steps, spin moves, and crossover dribbles as I go, imagining defenders.

After I break a sweat, I walk toward Dad and toss him the ball.

He catches it and stands. He dribbles it a couple of times, comes onto the court, and takes a midrange jumper from the baseline. Nothing but net.

"Still got it. Still got it." Dad leans his head back, arms outstretched, fighting back a smile like he just hit a game winner. Then he stares at the district championship banners hanging from the rafters, three of which he helped put up there.

I track down the ball and go to my spot; we have this shooting drill memorized now. Dad jogs under the rim to rebound. We shoot ten from several places on the court. We start at the elbow of the free-throw line. I take my first shot. Swish. "Still got it," I say, mimicking my dad.

Dad shoots a sharp bounce pass at me. "Focus."

I hit my next nine before switching to the other side.

"How you feeling? Nervous?" Dad asks. I spin the ball in my hands and wait to shoot.

Dad glances over at me. The rare, gentle expression on his face tells me it's okay to be honest.

"About?" I ask, knowing he must be asking about our next game. My very first play-off game. I shrug and take a shot that bricks hard off the back iron.

"The play-offs. Lot tougher than the regular season. Teams spend so much more time scouting, they practice more specifically for their next matchup, and the games move way faster. Players play harder, meaner, tougher. In the play-offs, everyone has everything to lose and everything to gain."

I miss another shot. Dad grabs the rebound, dribbles it behind his back, and makes a layup, then passes it back.

"And the crowd noise. Damn." Dad shakes his head like he's reliving his own play-off battles. "If you thought it was loud during the regular season, it's a whole other thing once it's a play-off game. It's deafening."

I stand still, absentmindedly dribbling the ball. "I've been to play-off games before. It's pretty loud."

"It's different when you're on the court and the noise is coming at you from every direction. I know my first play-off game took me by surprise. I was . . ." And here we go. I don't shoot. I hold the ball against my hip. And wait. For another story about how my dad had his back up against the wall and still played a legendary Michael Jordan type game. Dad stops talking, then laughs to himself, so hard that he coughs his smoker's cough. "You'd be a horrible poker player."

"Huh?"

"Never mind. Shoot it. You're in a rhythm."

I put the shot up. Nothing but net.

He says, "That was a hell of a first season you had. Went from not making the team to averaging almost thirty points, eight assists, and seven rebounds a game. And one of the best regular season records any Red Lake team has ever posted."

I move to the top of the key. Dad passes me the ball. I hit another shot.

"Forget about the stats, the record—they're just numbers. You did something that moved people beyond the court. You did something special for more people than you realize."

Dad grabs the ball. I hold an open palm up in the air, calling for the ball. But he just keeps holding it, staring at it. "But, before the play-offs come, I just wanted to take a moment to appreciate this, right here." Dad motions an index finger back and forth between us. "I looked forward to every game of yours this season. And you never disappointed. Every night you did something new, something I didn't even know you could do. Every time I saw you smile on the court, every time a teammate gave you a high five, every time the crowd cheered for you, it felt like something inside of me was getting better. It was . . . I don't want to say a distraction, that's not the right word. But it took my thoughts off losing your brother."

Dad passes the ball to me. When I catch it, his eyes are teary. I want to give him space, to let him think I don't notice. I make a show of considering the banners hanging from the rafters. The banners are black, with red trim and lettering. Each one says from top to bottom, *Red Lake Warriors, District 29 Champions*, with the year it was won and the players on that team.

Dad walks alongside me and looks up. I say, "You got three district champion banners up there." I point to those from Dad's era. "And there are the two that Jaxon got for us. Hopefully by the end of next week, I'll have one up there with you guys."

Dad leans into me; our shoulders brush. For a second, I expect his short ass to lean his head on my shoulder. He swipes the ball away and smiles. "Don't worry about hanging another banner. Matter of fact, don't worry about trying to match me or your brother. I'm grateful for what you already gave me, your family, your school, your team, and the whole rez this season. It was exciting. It was fun. It was . . . healing. So, go out there when the play-offs start, and play your game, live in the moment, be proud of yourself, and let the cards fall where they may."

Dad gives me an awkward side hug. "We better get back to training. You bricked quite a few already."

CHAPTER 33

FEBRUARY 13

STEPPING OFF THE bus at Bemidji State University for our first play-off game, we're greeted with cheers, whistles, and hollers. We walk along a line of fans that stretches all the way down the building. Everyone is bundled up in winter coats, winter hats, and gloves while waiting to get into the gym. Kids hold up homemade Red Lake Warrior signs. A couple even have signs covered in red-and-black glitter with my name and jersey number.

Wes is walking along the line, capturing it on camera. Khiana is alongside him. It's the first time I've seen her since our argument. I've tapped laughing emojis on a few of her goofy IG stories, but she's never replied. I don't think she wants anything to do with me right now. That's fair. I wouldn't either if I was her.

As the team continues to the entrance, I pause to talk to Wes.

"Good luck out there," he says with a handshake and one-armed hug. "You got this."

"Thanks, bro." I sling my gym bag back over my shoulder. "Hey, Khiana."

Big black sunglasses take up half of her face. "Hey, Tre."

That's all I get.

"Let's go, Tre!" a fan yells, snapping me back to reality.

Someone else calls, "State, baby. All the way." I retreat, chasing after my teammates.

As we enter the arena, Coach Whitefeather warns, "Don't be feeling too special now. You haven't won a goddamn thing yet."

It's wild how much nicer the locker room is here compared to ours at home. Instead of cold linoleum floors, it's covered in brand-new green-and-white carpeting. And instead of a wall of metal lockers and a long brick bench, we have our own chairs. Each space is divided by little wooden walls for privacy, and there are even hangers for our clothes and cubbies for our things.

This must be kind of what an NBA locker room is like.

As I throw my basketball jersey on, I feel the weight of the moment. This is it. There's room for error in the regular season. You can lose a game. In the play-offs, one loss and you're done. Win or go home. Any game could be your last.

Kevin slaps my back. "Christ, we're only playing Baudette. We beat them by forty points both times we played them."

Coach Whitefeather walks us through our game plan. He clearly knows that there is almost no way on earth we will lose tonight. He isn't fired up or yelling. For once, he seems super chill. He grabs a chair and sits among us like he's just another hooper.

"I don't want you guys fucking around because it's Baudette. Go out there and stomp the fuck out of them. Step on their throats until they can't breathe. Let's blow 'em out and let our seniors get play-off action in front of this crowd. Bring it in."

We gather together, and Kevin hollers, "Warriors on three. One, two, three."

"Warriors!" we yell in unison. For the first time, Coach White-feather yells it, too.

Outside the locker room door, a couple of security guards are waiting to escort us to the court. The corridor to the gym is filled with pictures of Bemidji State sports history. Hockey, basketball, tennis, baseball, wrestling. The photos go from grainy black and white to the present day by the time we hit the gym entrance.

As we jog out onto the court, the lights are crazy bright. The court is shiny. Bigger than any we've played on before. It's surreal as hell, like I'm in a movie.

When we run out, our fans pump up the noise. I cannot believe the size of the crowd—so many people, and the seats go back so far that I can barely see the last dozen rows. It's elbow to elbow, not a single empty seat.

Kevin wins the tip and hits the ball in my direction. I throw a hard bounce pass between two defenders, and Dallas catches it for a layup. Our crowd gets mad hyped. I smile, then try to hide it.

If Coach sees me grin over one basket, he'll never let me forget it.

As expected, our fast-paced run-and-gun offense is way too much for Baudette. In the flash of a Steph Curry crossover, we are up 10–0. Their coach calls a time-out, and our fans—basically the entire crowd—cheer loud as hell. Dallas and Mason wave to the crowd to stand, to get even louder. The rest of the game is a joke, like we're playing against an eighth-grade team. We score when we want to score, grab almost every rebound, and stop them from running their offense. The buzzer blares, the crowd roars, and we are waving on our way back to the locker. The scoreboard reads 127–49.

"Holy shit." I can't believe that happened.

Mason slaps me on the back. "Good shit out there."

Meek Mill blares from Mason's Bluetooth speaker, filling the locker room with a party-like atmosphere. Mason raps along, and everyone dances as we change into our street clothes.

"Hey," Coach Whitefeather says, his voice knifing through the music.

As Mason turns down the music, Coach paces. "Don't be too proud about beating one of the worst teams in the state. We got Clearbrook waiting for us in the district championship. They beat you once this season and almost beat you the other game, too. Don't forget that while you're dancing around." Smiles fade, and everyone goes still. Coach Whitefeather puts on his leather jacket and pulls a black winter hat down to his eyebrows. I just realized—he looks a lot like an Indian Snoop Dogg.

The second the door closes, Mason turns the music up louder than before and shouts, "Fuck Clearbrook!" He jumps back into the music, flowing word for word with Meek.

Parked on the edge of a cliff overlooking the lake, Dallas hands me a beer and cracks one open for himself. The moon fills the sky and lights up snow blowing across the frozen lake. A gust of wind howls and nudges Dallas's truck like the Incredible Hulk is trying to push it over.

"Nervous, bro," he says. "Never felt like this before. This is my third year of play-off basketball, but I never felt scared, till now."

"How come?"

"This is my last chance to win state. Any game from here on out could be my last."

"We'll win, man."

"I always think that. Always felt that. I was sure we had it last year. You never know, man. One wrong bounce, one call against you, one mistake. Ain't much of a difference between being champs or getting sent home. Coach was right. Clearbrook beat us once—hell, they almost beat us twice." Dallas chugs the rest of his beer, belches, and tosses the can out the window before grabbing another.

"That was the regular season, though," I say. "We'll play harder and sharper than we did before. We got this."

Dallas has always seemed wild and carefree, but not now. "It's not that, man. This is it for me, bro. What am I going to do after this?"

"What do you mean?"

"Being a Warrior is the last time I'll ever be special. I'll never top this. After this season, I'll be working at the casino or bagging groceries at The Trading Post. No one's going to want to take pictures with me or ask for my autograph. I'll just be another ghost of Red Lake Warriors past. But that's okay as long as we get to state. It would mean the world to our rez forever, man." He's getting choked up. "We've been losing to the white man for five hundred years. The battles, the stolen land, the broken treaties, the way their cops hunt us down. We can finally have a victory. One they'll never be able to take away from us. And the kids here will know that anything is possible. And all of us on this team, no matter what, we will go down as heroes, as legends. They'll talk about us one hundred years from now. We have to win. We have to."

CHAPTER 34

FEBRUARY 20

WE STAND IN a straight line, still wearing our warm-up jackets and pants. Sweat gleams on our faces as we stare at the American flag. The IRL blond Barbie, wearing a Clearbrook letterman jacket, finishes singing the national anthem, and her voice is replaced by the beating of a powwow drum. Eyabay, a drum group from our rez, starts playing our tribe's flag song. They're sitting in a circle, ball caps on backward, pounding— *boom, boom, boom, boom.*

I remember warmer days, summer powwows. The beat flows, connecting me with my ancestors. Suddenly, I'm not scared. I feel calm. Strong.

We win the tip, and I dribble down the court. Without thinking, I gun up a deep three. It swishes in. Our crowd goes berserk.

Clearbrook comes down, unfazed by the noise. Cool and calm. Their point guard signals a play that they run to perfection, finding their small forward as he cuts to the basket for an easy layup. After exchanging baskets to start the game, everything becomes a frantic blur.

The harder we run, the harder they run. The tougher our full-court press, the harder and smarter they work. It's an even match, basket for basket. We go into halftime tied.

47–47.

We grab towels and water bottles, and take a seat.

"Those little white boys out there hate you. They learned it from their parents. Ain't nothing they've ever wanted more than to take out a bunch of Indians who finally think something of themselves. You guys wanna win this thing or what?"

A couple of players nod. A couple quietly say, "Yeah."

"What's that? I can't hear you!"

Kevin says, "Yeah!" Dallas, Mason, Mike, and others echo him.

"*Oh*, you are still alive. Tre, unleash ma'iingan on them. I wanted to save it for deeper in the play-offs, but we've played them enough that they have a feel for us. This will confuse the hell out of them. Let's go out there and win!"

Running our new set of plays works to perfection, and we carve out a six-point lead. I hit a couple of three-pointers, but they quickly switch up and start guarding me as soon as I cross half-court. I adjust, driving to the rim and dishing up my teammates for easy dunks and layups. After a 15–4 run, their coach finally calls a time-out.

"That's it, boys!" Coach says. "That's what I was talking about. Don't let up now. Keep pushing the tempo."

When we get back out there, they've collected themselves. They run their offense over and over until they eventually get good looks. We go cold from the field. I brick a couple jumpers, fuck up a reverse layup; even Dallas and Kevin miss shots they almost always hit.

The buzzer signals the end of the third. The score is 77–71.

We have a slight lead, but my stomach feels queasy. I sit on the bench and try to listen as Coach barks orders over the airline-jet roar of the crowd.

We trade baskets, back and forth, for the rest of the fourth quarter.

With one minute to go, the score is 99–97. We are holding on dearly to a two-point lead, but we can put the game away with one more basket. I'm dribbling, searching for my best option. Kevin posts up his defender and calls for the ball. I pass to him, but one of their guards comes out of nowhere and steals it and throws a pass ahead to his teammate for a layup.

Damn it.

Everyone in the gym is now yelling, cheering, booing. The score: 99–99.

I dribble past half-court and yell out a play. Dallas points to his ears and shakes his head. I dribble with one hand and put a fist into the air to signal instead.

My defender hits the ball when I'm not looking. The ball hits my knee, bounces off his chest and back into my hands.

Fuck it. I'm taking this one. I wave my teammates out of the way, then hit my defender with a crossover. I get by him and pull up for a jumper. The shot looks good. It rattles in. Then out. Clearbrook's center grabs the rebound.

Clearbrook takes their sweet time, passing and screening. They are winding down the clock, in hopes of taking the last shot of the game.

We are all over them, pressuring everything they do.

Our fans start chanting, "De-fense. De-fense," and stomping their feet in rhythm.

The clock reads twenty seconds and ticking.

Their point guard throws a pass from the top of the key to the wing. Mike gets a fingertip on it, knocking it toward half-court. Players from both teams rush to the ball. In a red-and-black blur, Dallas dives onto the court. Sitting on his butt, he throws the ball over his head toward our basket to no one. What in the fuck?

Robert streaks right into the path of the ball and makes an effortless-looking finger roll to put us up by two, 101–99. The sea of red-and-black T-shirts erupts, chanting, "Red Lake Warriors!"

Clearbrook's point guard catches the inbound pass and glances at his coach, who signals a play. I stay on him. Ten seconds. Their fans start a countdown to help their team stay aware of the clock. "Seven. Six." We cross half-court.

"Shoot it," someone with a Red Lake accent yells, trying to trick him.

No luck. "I'm taking you right to the basket."

"Try it." I'm low to the ground, arms outstretched, staying light on the balls of my feet, ready for him to go either direction.

"Pick," Dallas yells. One of their players steps up in my way.

Their point guard starts to dribble hard to his right. Dallas flashes out, pretending to switch on him, giving me the split second I need. "Four. Three."

Their point guard takes a hard dribble to the right and is about to cross over to his left, except I read it and steal the ball from him. I take off down the court knowing we've won. The buzzer blares, and it's the sweetest sound I've ever heard.

CHAPTER 35

FEBRUARY 21

MY HEAD IS throbbing as I lie in my bed with an ice pack on my forehead, scrolling through social media on my phone and hoping no one posted anything from the party last night. I can hear my parents talking louder than normal. They sound like they might be mad. I wish I wouldn't have stayed out so late. At least I got home before sunrise this time. But I should have never gone to that party. I could have said no. I should have been home, resting, hydrating, eating dinner with my parents. But nooooo. Now I feel like trash. And I'm pretty sure my dad is mad that I didn't get up in time to go do our Sunday shootaround. But this is it. I'm going to make a change. I need to be the one to say something. I've spent the last hour typing and deleting basically the same text to Dallas. But each time I feel brave enough and almost hit send, I panic. Delete. Delete. I set my phone down and wonder if I even want to or need to go this far. I wonder how my teammates would feel about the new guy asking something like this of them. I sit up on the edge of my bed and pick my phone back up. I lean forward as I start to text again.

> I need your help with something

Then I imagine the look on Mason's face. That infamous stare-down. The certain shit-talking explosion. Delete.

Knock knock.

Mom slowly opens my door. "Hey, Tre. What are you up to?"

"Nothing much. Just trying to figure something out."

"Yeah? Want some help? You look distressed."

"I do?"

Mom can't help but laugh to herself. She opens my door the rest of the way and does a little shuffle until she's sitting beside me on my bed.

"This is you." Mom hunches forward, shoulders caving in, arms super tight to her sides. She sits back up. "Looking like that. I thought you were possessed when I peeked in here."

"Hote. Not that bad."

"Eh?" Mom makes her hand do a so-so shake. "But seriously. If you feel like sharing, I'm all ears."

"Okay. So, promise not to be mad. That's the only way I'm going to talk about this."

"I promise. Believe me. When I was your age, I was pretty wild."

"Okay, Mom. I definitely don't want the details on that. Soooo . . . last night, I lied to you and Dad when I said I was staying over at Wes's. I went and drank with some of my teammates to celebrate winning the district championship. Had a ton of fun. Don't get me wrong. But I've felt, like, awful all morning."

"That's what me and your dad heard from a few people. Word travels fast around here. But by the time we found out, you were already back home and crashed out in your bed."

"And you didn't say anything? I thought I'd be in serious trouble."

"As you should be. We're really frustrated and disappointed that you not only were out drinking, but especially that you lied to us, Tre. We've—" Mom pauses and looks up at the ceiling, takes a deep breath, and exhales. "But after thinking it over, we decided to talk with you instead of getting into a big old fight with you the week of the regional tournament."

I look at my hands. At the LeBron James poster on my wall. At the framed pictures of me and Jaxon. Damn. They knew and didn't say anything. I feel ridiculous, thinking I was all sneaky. "I'm sorry."

Mom rubs my back. "You should be. We don't appreciate being lied to. We were kids once, too. We know how it goes. Especially around here. But we care so much about your safety, your whereabouts, your future, your life." Mom's lips tighten, and I know she's thinking about Jaxon. I know just how to stop her from sinking into that sad place.

"So, here's what I was thinking about when you walked in. When I looked like the girl in *The Exorcist*. Here's what I need your help with."

Mom's eyes light up and a slow smile appears. "Yeah?"

"I felt how much drinking messed with my game. With everything. I think it would be best if I got the entire team to commit to not drinking, not smoking weed, not partying, absolutely nothing that we could get in trouble for or that would slow us down. I'm just—"

"Afraid. Nervous. Feeling like the seniors won't want to listen to the new guy?"

"Exactly. How did you know?"

"Told you moms know all."

"So, what do you think? What should I do?"

"First of all, I just want to tell you that I think you're incredibly brave for even considering it. It's way easier to stay one of the cool kids, and not speak up or speak out when something isn't right. What would you think if we had a team meeting over here, tomorrow after school? I'll order some pies from the Pizza Hut down in Bemidji. Your dad and I will step out, and you can chat with your team."

"You think that would work? You know Mason, he kind of does whatever he wants. And Mike goes along with whatever Mason does."

"All you can do is try. How about you commit to doing the sober, no-party thing first?"

"Thanks, Mom. I appreciate you."

She reaches over, arms wide open, and squeezes me tight. "I love you, Tre. You make me proud every day."

I feel my anxieties and fears seep out with each second. "Same, Mom."

"Okay. Well, your dad and I are going to go grocery shopping. There's leftovers in the fridge if you're hungry. We won't be gone long."

"All right. Thanks." I wait for Mom to leave before grabbing my phone. I finally say fuck it and shoot Dallas a text. Any text. Once I get it rolling, I'll figure it out.

Monday after practice, Mom and Dad helped me rearrange the living room. We pushed the table against the dining room wall, arranged the kitchen table chairs to face the TV, and brought in some plastic chairs from the garage. Then they set up the kitchen counters with pizza, paper plates, two-liter sodas, and plastic cups. It almost looks like a kid's birthday party, not a sophomore geek turned basketball star overnight trying to tell a group of seniors what to do. In the middle of the living room, I count the empty seats. Looks like the perfect space for the whole team. I imagine giving my little speech one more time.

All night last night and all day at school, and then throughout basketball practice, I've been thinking nonstop about what I want to say, how I want to say it, and everything Mason might say. And I'm still a little shook.

A car comes down our driveway. My hands feel clammy.

Mom and Dad join me from the hall. Mom says, "You're doing

the right thing, Tre. Don't worry too much. The worst they can say is no."

"But then they don't get any pizza," Dad adds. Mom slaps his arm. Dad replies, "What? That was a pricey amount of pizza."

Mom shoots him a sideways look. "We'll be in our bedroom, with the door shut, and watching a movie to make sure you have space. But you know where we'll be if you need us."

"I got it. Thanks, Mom. Dad."

There's a knock on the door, but before I can answer it, someone lets themselves in.

Dallas's voice calls out, "Boozhoo."

Phew. Glad he's the first one here.

"Aye. What's up?" Dallas says, bounding up. "Smells like pizza."

"Yeah. My parents thought we should buy dinner."

"Hell yeah. I better stash some before Kevin gets here."

"Thanks for being on board."

"For sure."

Cars and trucks start to roll in. Kevin walks in. Robert. All of our bench players. Mike. Everyone helps themselves to slices of pizza and soda. There's chewing, sipping, and lots of laughing. I start to worry that Mason isn't coming. And then another car pulls up. I glance out the window. It's him. He knocks, and I go down the stairs and open the door.

"What's up?"

"Come on in."

Mason looks at the mess of basketball shoes all over the entryway and takes his off.

"We got pizza, soda—help yourself."

"Nah, I'm good. Ate already." Mason grabs the last chair in the corner of the room, sinks into it, and folds his arms.

I move to the middle of the living room and clear my throat. "So, I want to thank you all for coming over." I take a breath. "I know everyone is wondering what the fuck we're doing at Tre's house on a Monday night. But I had this idea. I know this is going to sound corny, but whatever. It's the truth. Since I can remember, I've been watching you guys hoop. You became heroes to me. It felt like watching rock stars when I went to your games. Then this year, we became teammates. At first it was surreal. I couldn't believe I was wearing the same jersey. And now that we've gone this far together, you've become more than teammates. You're like brothers to me."

Dallas gives a *you're doing great* nod. Kevin smiles and softly pounds his heart a couple times. Everyone is cool. Except for Mason, who is still slumped in his chair, arms still folded.

"I wish my brother, Jaxon, was with us. You guys would have for sure beat Bemidji and gone to state last year. And I'm sure this year you'd be ready to do the same. But he's not here. And you guys are stuck with me."

Mason shuffles in his chair and sits up, leans forward with his hands clasped. He clears his throat. Everyone stops eating. "You're not so bad, rookie. Been cool playing with you this year. Didn't expect you to step up the way you did. Jaxon's looking down on us, watching. I know he's proud of you."

"Thanks, Mason. That means a lot to me." My eyes mist up.

Come on, Tre. You got this. It's like shooting clutch free throws. Relax.
Breathe. Focus.

"So, here's what I brought you all here to ask. And if you want to tell me to fuck off, or that I'm a hypocrite, that's okay. I think we should all commit, right here and now, as one group, to not drinking another sip, not smoking any weed, not attending any parties until our season ends. Whether that's this Thursday night, or after the state tournament."

There. I said it. I glance at Kevin. Robert. Mike. They look stunned, confused.

Mason says, "You were drinking last weekend."

"I know. I was. And then I felt like shit. I wasn't at my best. And that's what made me think that this was the thing to do. I know how much getting to state means to you guys. I've heard my uncles, my dad, Jaxon, anyone who ever played, anyone who ever watched, they all talk about how they almost got to state. Almost beat Bemidji. I don't want to tell *almost* stories when I'm old. And I know you guys don't either." Mason nods, and, encouraged, I go on. "I know how much it hurt last season when you guys almost beat Bemidji and almost went to state. I know you were playing for more than yourselves, for more than the rez; you were playing that game for my brother, for Jaxon. And it fucking hurt me, too, even in the stands. I was crushed when you guys lost."

Dallas stands and walks to me. He throws an arm around my shoulder. "I'm with Tre. No one loves a cold one and a party more than me. But getting to state means more. Winning for Jaxon means more. Just for the next couple of weeks. And give this thing the best shot we can give it."

"Fuck yeah. I'm in," Mike says.

"Hell yeah. Same," Robert says.

Everyone nods in agreement.

"Let's go win this whole fucking thing!" Mason yells.

Everyone starts hollering, "Let's go to state!" and "Let's do it for Jaxon!"

"You fuckers save me any of that pizza?" Mason asks, and everyone laughs.

CHAPTER 36

FEBRUARY 25

MASON GIVES ME the meanest bear hug of my life. Kevin, Dallas, and the rest of the team rush up, and we squish together. Our fans cheer.

Mason sets me free and then daps me up. "You were on fire, bro. Straight fire!"

"Holy shit," Dallas says. "That was awesome. You were out of your mind at the end. What did you hit, six, seven shots in a row?"

The scoreboard reads 94–87.

"Who's next?" I ask. But I say it with a bark, and my teammates dap me up again and join in with shouts of, "It don't matter," and "They don't want none of this."

It's like I'm waking up from a dream.

Minutes ago, we were down by five points. But we never showed any fear. We kept hooping. I hit a fadeaway midrange, right in their tallest player's grill. Mason loved it and started talking trash to Bagley. The rest of my team got fired up. We got some stops, and every time down they got me the ball.

And the world changed around me. The stands filled with fans became a blur. The roar became a low, dull noise. Like light rain on a summer night. And the game slowed down. It felt like someone had given me a cheat code. Every shot I took swished through the net. And with each basket, I only got more in the zone. Missing never entered my mind.

"Come on," Dallas says. "Let's get out of here. I'm starving."

We wave to our friends, family, and fans, and they offer one last round of applause.

We jog back to the locker room high-fiving, laughing, smiles glued to our faces.

Kevin asks, "Bemidji plays Moorhead later tonight out west, right?"

"Yeah. Moorhead has a squad this year. But Bemidji beat them once by about a dozen, so who knows," Robert says.

"Don't matter. It don't matter. Tre?" Mason points at me. "Tre is going to light up either of those teams. But if I had my way, I'd say bring on Bemidji. I want that revenge. I ain't scared of them little bitches. Going to give them that first L from the Red Lake Warriors if they run into us."

CHAPTER 37

FEBRUARY 26

"HOW YOU FEELING, son?" Dad asks before taking a sip of coffee.

"I'm good," I say, pouring Fruity Pebbles and milk into a bowl. I don't have an appetite, but I've got to eat something. Even sugar.

"That was a hell of a game you played against Bagley. Picture of you throwing down a dunk right on the front page of the Bemidji newspaper today. Was maybe the most impressive play-off game I've ever seen. You had thirty-one points, eight rebounds, and seven assists. I used to put up points like that. So did Jaxon. But neither of us were getting those kinds of rebounds and assists. You've become a special player."

"Thanks, Dad." I smile at my bowl. "All of those Sundays of

working on my shooting and handles with you definitely played a part." And it brought us closer.

Dad sets a plate of toast and two boiled eggs in front of me. "Protein."

"Thanks," I say through a mouthful of cereal.

"Bagley was twenty-one and one on the season, their only loss to Bemidji. You guys could beat Bemidji tonight. You almost beat them before. You were still getting used to playing varsity, and you fouled out. You're a whole different player now."

I start to eat at double speed. I need to get to school soon. We have a pep rally this morning before they send us off to the regional championship game.

Dad is throwing junk mail in the garbage can and setting letters on the table. He pauses, looking at one extra careful. "Tre, you got a letter from the University of Minnesota."

I stop chewing; my spoon drops and clangs into my bowl. "From the Gophers?"

Dad holds it up like it's a trophy with a proud smile on his face. He sets it down in front of me. It could be a recruitment letter just for me, or it could be a generic letter sent to prospective students to encourage applications.

Dad sits next to me. He's giddy, like he's more a friend than my grumpy dad.

"Well, Tre, are you going to open it?"

Mom walks in, brushing her hair. "Open what?"

"Tre got a letter from the U of M."

The pressure is too much.

"Where are you going?" my parents ask in unison.

"If you don't mind, I want to open it alone."

Before they can answer, I'm down the hall but not alone. I open the door to Jaxon's room, then shut it quietly behind me. I haven't been in here since he died. It looks the same. LeBron James posters cover the walls, along with newspaper clippings of his highest-scoring games and district championship wins. His recruitment letters are taped up. His basketball still rests on his neatly made bed. I sit down with my letter and roll his basketball next to me, alongside my hip.

A cardboard box peeking out of his closet catches my attention. I get up and drag the box over to the bed. Opening it, I reconnect with our childhood. I dig through the box of DC Comics action figures. A black Superboy shirt with the Superman logo. Under the shirt and figures is a small stack of comics. I pull them out and thumb through issues of *The Flash*, *Aquaman*, *Batman*, then the very last one, the *Death of Superman* graphic novel. A collection of the comics that told the storyline of an alien from outer space named Doomsday. He was violent, filled with rage, and virtually invincible. He beat the hell out of the entire Justice League. When he began to destroy Metropolis, Superman tried to stop him.

They fought to the death. Superman lost. Superman died.

Afterward, other Supermen showed up and tried to take his place. My favorite was Superboy, a clone of Superman. He wasn't full grown or quite as strong. But damn, he wanted like hell to fill those shoes—er, boots.

I set the comics and figures back in the box, holding Jaxon's

Superboy shirt in my hand. I raise it up and wonder if it will fit. Jaxon hadn't worn this since right before high school.

I pull my shirt off and put on Jaxon's.

It fits perfectly. "You don't mind, do you, bro?" I ask before falling back onto the bed and resting my head against a pillow. Might sound silly, but I feel closer to him, wearing his shirt. Like our bond is stronger. "What kind of letter do you think this is?"

I can almost hear him say, "Just fucking open it already."

And the thought makes me laugh—I'm happy, but it's bittersweet.

Open the envelope. Unfold the paper inside. Skim the page. Look for key words. Near the bottom, I find what I was hoping to see. *We want to express our interest in you as a student athlete for our basketball program.*

"Jaxon, it's a recruitment letter. From the Gophers."

Tears stream down my face. I want to thank Jaxon for all the basketball drills he showed me. All the games of one-on-one where he kicked my ass but I kept getting better. For him telling me I could be as good as him, or better. For him believing in me. I'd give anything for him to be here right now.

CHAPTER 38

FEBRUARY 26

AT THE PEP rally, our tribal chairman is waving his arms and hollering into the microphone like a professional wrestler. My guy is hyped! The gym is packed like a basketball game would be, with a blend of students and fans from our rez, all wearing red-and-black T-shirts. It's decorated with red and black balloons, streamers, and homemade Red Lake Warriors signs. Kids from the elementary and middle school are waving red and black pom-poms. Classmates are holding up cell phones, capturing pics and videos.

"We closed the tribal council and all tribal functions to follow our boys to the regional championship. The casino is closing, and we don't close that even for Christmas. We're providing charter buses. They'll be leaving from The Trading Post at two in the afternoon for anyone who needs a ride. This is a special team. Boys, no matter what happens, I want you to know that you've made your entire reservation proud. Good luck. Go, Warriors!"

Outside the gym, we sign autographs and take selfies with fans as we get ready to board a charter bus instead of our normal school bus.

"Damn, bro," Dallas says, marker in hand as he signs the back of a kid's shirt. "They have TVs in there, coolers full of snacks and Gatorades, and reclining seats."

Wes is holding his phone high above his head, moving in slow circles to capture it all.

Khiana is with him, guiding him with her hand along his back so he doesn't bump into anyone.

I kneel to take a pic with a couple of little kids. One of them asks me to throw down a windmill dunk, like Jaxon used to. I promise him I'll try.

Someone pats me on the back. I turn, expecting to see another fan wanting to take a selfie or get an autograph, but it's our athletic director, Mr. Thomas. "Tre, may I have a word?"

"Yeah, of course," I say, but I'm nervous as hell, wondering if there was some rumor or report he needs to clarify.

He tilts his head and we walk down the sidewalk, out of earshot of everyone.

"What's up?" I ask.

"I'm proud of you. Taking control of the team. That pact you all made to make sure you all stay on the straight and narrow from here on out. That was super impressive, especially for a sophomore."

I feel a sigh leave my body and my shoulders drop.

"How'd you know about that?"

Mr. Thomas smiles and shrugs. "You've got a bright future ahead of you, in anything you pursue." He shakes my hand and gives me a knowing nod.

"Thanks, Mr. Thomas. I appreciate it."

"Good luck out there tonight. If anyone can do the impossible and beat Bemidji, I know it's you," Mr. Thomas says, before walking to his car and driving off.

"I hope so," I say to myself.

A couple of kids who must be twins yell my name and come running over. They're holding *Warriors District Champions* T-shirts and have big, missing-tooth smiles. I kneel down and sign autographs for them.

Wes and Khiana walk over.

"Getting some good footage?" I ask.

"Yeah, man. That huge turnout for the pep rally is going to look great in the documentary. Can't wait to edit. Nice shirt. Superboy, right?"

"Yeah, thanks. It was Jaxon's." Before it can get awkward, like any time anyone brings up anything to do with Jaxon, I turn to Khiana and say, "This guy had me crying the other day with one of his videos." It feels good to laugh with them.

Wes adds, "It would be dope to shoot an interview at Bemidji State. You think?"

"I'm in. Text me later and we'll find a time and place to link up. When are you two leaving?"

"Right now, since they let school out early. We're also going shopping for prom." Wes catches himself short, regret on his face.

"Dope. You'll have to send me pics of what you find." I try to sound as happy as I can for them. One, because I am, and two, because I don't want them to feel weird.

Kevin throws his overstuffed gym bag into the luggage compartment of the charter bus. "Speaking of prom, I need to show you this one girl online, gorgeous as hell. I guess she has the hots for you. She's my girlfriend's best friend. If you don't have a date, maybe you could ask her out and then we could double date. My parents are getting us a limo. You should roll with," Kevin chimes in.

"Yeah, maybe. I'll let you know," I say.

"Such a ladies' man," Khiana teases in a goofy, over-the-top way.

"I'll see you guys down there," I say, and give them a group hug.

Kevin wins the tip-off, and the ball is in my hands. I dribble up the court and call out JD.

The Bemidji players yell out, "JD," right after me.

I start the play like usual, with a pass to Dallas on the wing, but they intercept the pass and get a layup. Shit.

I dribble the ball up court and fight to be heard over the roar of the crowd as I yell out another play. Bemidji again yells the name of the play and adjusts their defense. They move around screens, knowing what's coming. They overplay the passing lanes, confident that they have help waiting behind them. It's impossible for me to get the ball to a teammate. In a panic, I drive to the basket, but their defense collapses on me and I cough up the ball.

They hit a quick three-pointer.

From the stands, someone yells, "Tre Brun, you should have stayed on the rez!"

I call out another play, and again, they shout it to each other and adjust. Their point guard catches me blanking out, trying to figure out what to do. He steals the balls and gets a layup.

Their crowd chants, "Overrated. Overrated."

One of their fans is holding up a sign that reads, *54–0 before. 55–0 after.*

The rest of the first half is more of the same. We turn the ball over a lot, and when we aren't throwing the ball away, we have to scratch and claw for every basket.

With the first half winding down, their point guard hits a three, right in my face.

We're losing, 40–54, with fifteen seconds left in the half.

We're outmatched. I'm not as good as I thought. We're going to lose.

I catch the inbound pass and dribble up the court. Crossing half-court, the crowd chants the countdown. "Ten. Nine. Eight." No matter what offense I call, Bemidji will know right where to go. "Seven. Six." All eyes are on me. Everyone's waiting for the play.

Out of nowhere, I call out, "Superboy!" It's not a play, but Bemidji doesn't know that.

My teammates are confused, but so is the defense.

I blow past my defender and drive hard to the basket. Defenders rush to help, but it's too late. As I rise, two defenders jump with me. I cock the ball back behind me and throw down a vicious tomahawk dunk. The buzzer blares as the Red Lake crowd explodes.

I land, pound my fist twice against my chest for my people, my crowd.

"Superboy?" Dallas asks as we run back downcourt. I give him the MJ shrug.

As dope as that last play was, we are still getting our asses kicked, 42–54 at the end of the half.

In the locker room, we're guzzling water as Coach pauses, a hand on his chin.

Nervous as all hell, I say, "I have an idea."

Coach freezes. "What is it, Tre?"

"Since they obviously know our plays, how about we forget about our plays?" Everyone shoots me a WTF look. "No. I know it sounds crazy, but what if we go back out there and forget about this being the championship game, forget about the crowd. Let's pretend we're hooping back home. Think about it, guys. If this was our best five against their best five, no coaches, no crowd, playing for fun, do you think we'd be losing?"

"Fuck no," Mason says, wiping his sweaty bald head.

"Hell no," Dallas agrees.

"Hote—we'd probably be getting tore up even worse," Kevin offers in an exaggerated rez accent. "Aye."

Mason grins and tosses his towel at Kevin. "Man, shut the fuck up."

"You all know we would rip them to shreds in a street ball

game. We are playing white-boy basketball right now, and they are better at it than us. If it's cool with you, Coach, can we go out there and play rez ball like we would back home?"

"They won't know what hit 'em," Coach says. "But mix it up by calling out made-up play names. Like you did with that Superboy shit."

"Fuck yeah," Mason says. "Never seen anyone do something like that."

We stand up, fighting back smiles like little kids who know they shouldn't bust a gut laughing or they'll get in trouble. We're about to have the most fun we've had all year.

"We're one half away from finally beating Bemidji and going to the state tournament. Let's do this shit. Rez ball on three," Kevin says as we all gather in a circle. This better work. "One. Two. Three. Rez ball!"

I wipe the bottom of my shoes and step hard on the court a couple of times. Usually helps me feel like they grip better.

"Rez ball, eh?" Mason holds his hand out, and we shake.

I catch the inbound pass to start the half. Holding up a fist, I shout, "Rez ball!"

Everyone is either cutting or setting screens. Freestyling. Feeling the game.

We quickly pass the ball around. No one stalls the offense by holding the ball too long or dribbling. I'm no longer a target. Moving without the ball, I cut to the basket. Robert finds me open. I go for a layup but the defense collapses on me, so I throw a no-look, behind-the-back pass to Kevin, who throws down a two-handed slam.

We pick up their players full court until we trap a guard in the corner. He jumps to throw a Hail Mary pass. Robert steals the ball, barely crosses half-court, and chucks up a three.

Swish!

We get another steal, and this time Dallas pulls up for a three-pointer on a fast break. It misses, but I time it perfectly and slam it down.

Their coach calls a time-out. Our crowd in red-and-black T-shirts jumps up and down.

One of the singers from the drum group war-whoops and pounds on his hand drum. We exchange high fives and smiles as we jog to our bench.

"Keep it up, boys. They're scared now. They know we smell blood in the water. That coach is probably over there asking them, 'What in tarnation is *rez ball*?'"

It's a corny impression of a white guy. And damn, for the first time all season, we are laughing during a game. I didn't know varsity basketball could be so much fun.

The frantic pace has left our opponents confused and nervous. Throwing the ball away, taking bad shots, struggling to stop us as our guys shoot three-pointers on fast breaks or from well beyond NBA range. By the end of the third, we are on top, 71–62.

I'm in the zone, so once the fourth quarter starts, I splash back-to-back three-pointers from deep. We are now up 77–62, with five minutes to go.

Their point guard calls out a play and drives right. I swipe the ball from him, knocking it down the court. We both race after it, but I catch it in stride with one hand, moving the ball into a forward dribble. He's still alongside as I go toward the rim.

Fuck him. Fuck Bemidji. I take off only a step within the free-throw line. He jumps with me and takes a desperate swing at the ball. He bumps into me, but it doesn't matter. I'm weightless. I'm invincible. The whistle blows.

Bam! I slam the ball through the rim. Hard.

"And one!" I yell. Since he fouled me, I get to shoot a free throw.

Their side of the gym, all the white people in Bemidji Lumberjack shirts, go from standing to sitting down real quick. From cheering and booing to dead silent. They're no longer mocking us or holding up those ridiculous racist signs.

The Death Star is exploding, in pieces in the night sky.

That one was for you, Jaxon.

I swish my free throw and point at my parents as I run back on defense.

Bemidji never gets closer than that. They never quit fighting, but they can't recover.

The buzzer sounds. Game over. Our drums beat. We won.

Mason throws his arms around me. "We're going to state!"

His hug, it means the world. I'm a hero. As good as Jaxon.

Our team crashes into one big group hug. We jump up and down. Is this real?

An announcer comes over the PA. "And now, to present this year's region eight championship trophy to the Red Lake Warriors . . ."

Dallas says, "We did it, Tre. We fucking did it!"

Holy shit. We really did do it.

In the stands, my mom is crying, her hands pressed together like in prayer. Dad is beaming. They wave. The people of my rez hug each other, high-fiving, cheering, smiling. We won together, all of us.

A guy in a suit walks toward our team with a microphone in one hand and a trophy in the other. Wes has positioned himself down near the bench, camera ready. He gives me a thumbs-up. I scan the stands—my classmates, my bus driver, my teachers, our athletic director. Everyone I've ever known is here. Everyone I've ever known is sharing this moment.

The guy in the suit calls, "Let's give it up one more time for this year's regional champions!"

We get the trophy and squeeze in close so we can each get a hand on it. We hold it up toward our fans. Our people. "Red-Lake-Warriors." *Clap-clap. Clap-clap-clap.*

I say the words out loud. "We're the first Native team in Minnesota to make it to state."

"Legends, bro," Dallas says. "We're legends."

CHAPTER 39

MARCH 4

THE LAST FEW days have been like a birthday and Christmas and Halloween all at once. School was filled with joy everywhere we went. The walls were covered in homemade Regional Champion Red Lake Warriors posters. Our school sold T-shirts, hoodies, and banners that read *Red Lake Warriors Region 8 Champions*. They ran out within an hour. Everywhere we went, people were wearing them. Our state championship pep rally send-off was *epic*.

Now I'm wowed by the view from my hotel room in downtown Minneapolis. Light beams shine out skyscraper windows. Slow-moving traffic fills the streets. People stroll along the sidewalks. The electronic billboard on Target Center shines the brightest, switching between a promotion for the Minnesota Timberwolves and the Minnesota state tournament. *SportsCenter* has been playing on repeat, but no one is really listening. Mason, Dallas, Kevin, Mike, and Robert are hanging out, staring blankly at the TV like they're under a spell.

This is the quietest these guys have ever been. Not one inappropriate joke, not one gross party story, no trash talking. We made it all the way to state, only to have to face Jacob Griffin and his Crestview Christian Academy team. The player that *Slam* magazine called the best Minnesota hooper of all time. On a team that has gone undefeated all season long.

In one hour, we are going to make our way down to the Target Center, to try to do the impossible, again. But hey, at least we get to play on the same court where the Timberwolves and Lynx play. The same place all the biggest bands and rappers perform.

Mason clears his throat and grabs the remote control. "Fucking sick of *SportsCenter*. We've seen the same highlights fifty times. See what else is on." He clicks through a few channels, skipping sitcom reruns, a nature show, coverage of the stock market, then he yells, "Holy shit, you guys. Look!"

It's the Minneapolis news channel. We all get closer to the TV. No one says a word. We watch highlights of our last game against Bemidji before it cuts to the news anchors. One is a guy with a neatly trimmed beard and slicked-back hair, the other is a woman with the whitest teeth I've ever seen. She says, "And tonight's matchup pits two of the top teams in the state against each other. The Red Lake Warriors versus the Crestview Christian Academy Hawks. Not only are these two of the best teams, they also feature arguably the two best high school players in Minnesota. Check out these highlights. This is Crestview Academy's Jacob Griffin. He is a seven-footer who moves like a guard. I've seen him play in person, and let me tell you, this kid looks NBA ready. He was one of the top recruits in the country and will play at Duke next fall."

The guy reporter adds, "He's a unicorn. It's rare to see a player that tall be able to handle the ball and shoot threes like Steph Curry. He's going to be a terror on the court."

The girl reporter nods. "Not to be outdone, the Red Lake Warriors have their own superstar. His name is Tre Brun. He is six foot four and can leap out of the building. He is only a sophomore, but his game says otherwise. Check out these highlights."

The TV cuts to clips of me throwing down a windmill dunk. My teammates jump up and down and shout, "Damn!" We go quiet to watch as I throw a no-look pass to Kevin for a dunk. Everyone daps him up and joyfully pushes him around. The next set of clips is me hitting deep three-pointers.

Dallas puts his arm around me. Mason and the rest of the guys stand up and give me fist pounds and hugs. "This is dope as fuck," Mason says.

The woman on TV concludes, "It is going be a barn burner in Target Center tonight. You still have time to get down there to watch it in person or stay in the comfort of your home, as we'll be broadcasting it right here on channel four."

The news shifts to a recent murder, and Mason turns the TV off. Mason says, "That's all you, Kevin. You ready to shut down that tall bastard?"

"You know it," Kevin replies, cocky as usual.

Dallas is scrolling on his phone. "Damn. Check this out, bro." He holds up his screen to show us. "This is my cousin's video they just posted. They're watching the state game before ours."

Robert says, "Holy shit. That's Target Center right now? We don't play for two hours."

Dallas hands me his phone. The video shows a wide scroll from the lower level of the place. It's already packed. The stands are filled with our fans. Red-and-black shirts and Red Lake Warriors signs fill the whole lower level.

Mike shakes his head, clearly wowed. "My dad said that Natives have come from all over to watch us. From White Earth, Fond du Lac, Cass Lake, Mille Lacs. Said he saw a lot of familiar Natives from his time on the powwow trail."

I move back to the window, press my face against the glass. This must be what Superman feels like. We are on the thirty-fifth floor. Almost feels like I'm flying.

My phone vibrates. It's a text from Wes.

> Good luck out there bro. I love you. You're going to kill it. I know it.

Wes follows up his text with a video similar to the one that Dallas's cousin sent. The lower level of Target Center, jam-packed with familiar faces. I replay it a couple of times looking for family and friends. I spot teachers, classmates, and former players, then I see my uncles, Liver and Ricky, close to the court.

They're going to be loud as hell. I spot Mom and Dad, wearing their *Playing for Jaxon* T-shirts. I wish I could get one last hug before I go play.

My phone blows up with texts, one after another. It won't stop dinging, so I put it on silent mode. There are too many notifications and texts to check. But I do a quick scroll and find a text from Khiana.

> You know I don't care for stupid sportsball. But this looks like a fucking concert in here. Kill it tonight rock star. I know we had some tiffs, but you are one of the coolest, strongest, best people I've ever met. I love you. You're going to kill it. I know it.

> Thank you, Khiana! I appreciate it. Thanks for coming to "stupid sportsball"

I spot one from Nate.

> Aye bro, no matter what happens out there, I'm proud of you and excited to watch you play where the WOLVES play. Wild! But also, drop a 50 piece on these bitches

> LMAO I'll try

> Fuck that fam. It's like Master Yoda says Do or do not, there is no try.

Mason grabs the remote off the nightstand and turns off the TV. He stands. "Don't get all shook now, boys. And don't think that just because we made school history by winning the regional championship, we're done. We still got three more wins to go until we are truly the state champions."

"For real. I'm not ready to play my last game yet." Dallas looks at me like his basketball fate is in my hands. I guess it is.

"How you feeling, Tre?" Kevin asks. "You look like you just seen a ghost."

I was starting to zone out. But we laugh about it, and the tension eases to a simmer.

"Aye, if it makes you feel any better, at least for once we're all on the same level. None of us have ever played in a state game at Target Center."

"So, you'll let up on the *rookie this, rookie that* talk?" I ask.

"Not until we win state." Mason winks. "You guys want to go down early? Might be good to let our eyes adjust to the lights in there. I came to a Wolves game once with my pops. We had some good-ass seats, too. Don't remember much about the game. I was too young. But I remember those lights hurt my eyes."

I've never seen him so happy.

"Come on," he says. "Grab your gym bags. And don't forget your state tournament player lanyards or you'll have to pay to get in. Now let's go win one more game."

CHAPTER 40

MARCH 4

WHEN WE STEP outside our hotel, a cold wind hits us. We pull on and zip up our matching hoodies. They have our logo on the left chest, and on the back, they read *Red Lake Warriors Region 8 Champions*. I shiver waiting for the walk light to turn green.

Target Center is right across the busy four-lane street. Dallas pats my arm and points to the digital billboard. It's another promotion for our state tournament game. But this ad features Jacob Griffin, Crestview's best player, on one side. On the other side—hey, that's me, holding the ball, ready to make a move. Dallas grabs his phone and takes a few pictures. "I'll send those to you, slowpoke."

"Miigwech," I say.

"Come on, it's green," Mason says.

Across the street, a line of familiar faces stretches all the way down one block and curves around the other side. Almost everyone in line is wearing our District Champions hoodie. Some wear Pendleton jackets, and others sport an assortment of Red Lake Warriors gear. Homemade Warriors signs are everywhere.

A kid with his hair in braids starts jumping up and down screaming, "It's the Warriors!" Everyone turns at once and begins cheering and chanting like we're already in the gym. The guy who works at our post office is wearing a red bandanna, a frayed jean jacket, and has a cigarette dangling from his ear. He tells us he's on mad Indian time and just barely made it here. Dallas tells him the lower level is sold out, but there are plenty of seats in the upper deck. He gives each of us a handshake and a half hug and wishes us luck. We stop and take selfies, sign autographs, and everyone tells us, "One win at a time" and "You've got this."

At the entrance, we flash our players' lanyards and are ushered to our locker room by two security guards and a lady in a fitted skirt with a phone in her hand.

As soon as we walk inside, the dreamlike quality of the night intensifies. Unreal. Impossible. The carpet looks crisp, brand-new, and has the Timberwolves logo that takes up most of the space in the locker room. Everything is shiny clean with fifteen individual locker stalls with wood dividers. Along the walls are framed pictures of Kevin Garnett, Christian Laettner, Karl-Anthony Towns, and other team legends. Mason cracks open a fridge, and when he sees it's full of Gatorade, he takes a bottle for himself. Pretty sure we aren't supposed to do that, but I'm not going to say anything. The current Timberwolves players' names are on their respective lockers. We all pick out a spot, set our bags down, and get dressed.

The Timberwolves locker room. An NBA locker room. I forget about switching into my basketball gear and warm-ups. Could I be here someday? Am I good enough to make the NBA?

I'm imagining traveling the country, becoming famous, being rich, playing on TV every other night, having a million followers on social media, being in commercials, dating amazing women, hitting a game-winning NBA finals shot.

The smell of sage snaps me out of it. Coach comes out from a back office with sage burning in a shell. We stand as he walks by us, one by one. We wave the smoke closer, carrying it up and over the back of our heads.

After Coach is done smudging us, he turns on a TV that is mounted on the wall and cues up Crestview's game tapes.

"Got these today from a guy I know who lives down this way. Asked him to get us footage of these guys. Let's study a few of their main plays."

The team is riveted. Feels like we're ready for war. Coach walks us through the video. It's mainly a pick-and-roll, with their seven-foot center setting the screen, which either leads to an easy layup for their point guard or an alley-oop to their center, depending on how the defense reacts. There are occasional kickouts to shooters waiting on the wing or corner. "Basic as it gets, boys. But also, nearly impossible to stop. They've destroyed everyone they've played this year. Haven't lost a single game. But every team has done the same exact thing against them. They double-team the center, every time. That's what makes it easy for the rest of the team to hit open shots and get layups." Coach tries to draw up whatever he is trying to show us on a provided iPad that is supposed to connect to the big-screen TV in the locker room. He drops it and grabs his clipboard he's used all year. "Fucking technology. Bring it in, boys."

Coach tells Kevin it's up to him to slow down their star center. He tells us to not double-team him like everyone else, but to fake like we are coming to double; he calls it *a flash*. A quick step like we are coming to help, then retreating to who we were originally defending. "When I yell *migizi*, it means to commit to the double. We need to occasionally mix it up to keep them guessing. This is it, boys. Our school's first state tournament. The best chance our rez has ever had at winning a state championship. Play smart. Play hard. Play together."

I close my eyes, clasp my hands together like in prayer, and lean forward. I take a deep breath and imagine me and Jaxon, back home. Smiling, laughing, talking way later than we should have. I whisper, "Jaxon, if you're out there, I hope I've made you proud. Give me your bravery tonight, your strength tonight. And I promise not to let you down. I'm giving my all for you."

Kevin pats my back. Dallas sets his hands on mine, to steady them. I had no idea they were shaking that bad. He says, "It's all good, bro. We're just going to go play the game we love. It might feel scary, playing at Target Center, in front of this many people, on TV, with so much at stake. But don't let that trip you out. At the end of the day, we're just hooping. Same way we do on the rez during summer."

We look up at one of the TVs mounted to the wall. One of the other state tournament games is finishing up. It was a blowout, and there's only a minute to go.

Coach clears his throat and turns off the TV. "One last thing, boys. This court is way bigger than the courts you are used to. So, get back after a miss; don't worry about chasing players all over the court like we usually do. Pick them up after they cross half-court. We need to conserve our energy as much as we can in the first half. Second half we will go hard. Bring it in," Coach says.

We all stand up and form a circle, hands touching in the middle.

Mason says, "This is for our rez, for our family and friends, for Coach, and especially for Jaxon. Let's go out there and kick fucking ass."

CHAPTER 41

MARCH 4

A REFEREE HOLDS THE basketball at half-court, in between Kevin and the seven-foot-tall all-state player, Jacob Griffin. I've never been this nervous before. It's a million times scarier being on the Timberwolves floor. The lights *are* blinding. The court shines with a watery sheen. I lean into one of the Crestview players, readying myself to grab for the basketball. Jacob jumps up and easily tips it to their point guard, who sets up their offense. They run a play, get an open jump shot, but it bricks. Dallas grabs the rebound and passes it to me. We run one of our plays, but they're glued to us. Robert finally gets an opening off a screen and takes a shot. Another miss. The next couple of minutes are nothing but bricks and turnovers for both teams.

The crowd is on edge. Every time we get a rebound, our side

cheers. Every shot we take, every drive to the basket, there is a collective gasp, like everyone longs to get this party started. We just need to splash a three or throw down a dunk and our crowd will come alive.

A Crestview player throws a bad pass that flies out of bounds. Coach calls a time-out. We're breathing hard and fast, hands on our knees, and we've only played a couple of minutes.

"You guys got to calm down. Get ahold of your nerves. Take a seat, sip some water. Deep breaths."

We do as Coach says, and he crouches in front of us. "You guys remember when the season started, and I said to never look outside of the four lines of the basketball court? To keep your focus within those lines? Well, now I'm telling you to do the opposite: look into the stands." Coach stands up, gesturing. Waving, pointing, smiling at people he knows. "Look at your parents, your grandparents, your teachers, your classmates, your friends, our Elders, our community. They're here to cheer you on, to show you love. We aren't separate—we're all connected. We are a tribe. You are them, and they are you. So, let's go out there, stop playing scared, and show these white boys what the fuck we are all about."

Jacob Griffin picks me up out of the time-out. He had been guarding Kevin since the game started since they both play center. I juke left to shake him off. Dallas hits me with a pass. I'm at the top of the key, surveying the floor. I yell, "Iso!" I wave everyone to get out of the way. My teammates go into the four corners, leaving me and Jacob most of the court.

Jacob waves me in. "Come on. Show me that weak-ass crossover I saw on the news."

Our crowd notices the trash talking and my smirk, and they rise to their feet.

Nate's voice cuts through the cheers. "Cross his bony ass up, Tre."

Jacob gets into a low defensive stance, his long arms outstretched.

I cross over from my left to my right, and he's still right on me. He is fast for a seven-footer. I hit him with a stutter step, and it throws him off just enough. I drive by him, but he's right back on me. He'll probably block a layup. So, I go hard, with two strong steps that force down into the hardwood. I rise, grip the ball in one hand, and cock it back. Jacob jumps with me, his long arms blocking my view. I twist my body midair.

Bam!

I land. I'm a lightning bolt. I scream to our crowd, more unleashed than I have ever been in my life. They scream every bit as loud in reply.

The Crestview players look shook as they take in me still flexing at Target Center, which is jam-packed, mainly with Natives. Then their coach yells a play at them, and the spell breaks. They set up their offense. Their point guard dumps it down to Jacob, who is posting up Kevin. Jacob dribbles twice to his left, spins right into a fadeaway. Kevin's hands only reach up to Jacob's elbows. Jacob's shot swishes and he does a fist pump like now he's ready to cook.

Dallas inbounds the ball to me. I dribble up the court and call out, "44–5." It's a play that is a pick-and-roll for me and Kevin on the right wing. Jacob is back on Kevin. If they switch on the pick-and-roll, Kevin will have an advantage against their short point guard and will be able to get an easy layup. When I get close to the wing, I wave in Kevin. He sets a pick on the point guard who is defending me, fights over the screen, and sticks close. When he realizes our plan failed, Kevin moves out of the way. Their point guard falls back so I fake a drive to the basket, take a quick step in reverse, and shoot a three-pointer. *Splash!*

Our crowd is still standing, roaring for my shot, when Jacob takes the inbound pass, races up the court, and takes a fast-break three-pointer that hits nothing but net.

Fuck. Basketball is like comic books. This is the moment when the normally stronger, normally invincible superhero should worry. When the superhero has thrown their strongest attacks at the big bad, only to see the villain doesn't have a scratch on him.

We trade baskets. I get mine or dish up a teammate for easy layups because I'm drawing double teams. But Jacob Griffin comes back down and scores effortlessly. Again and again. I'm dribbling near half-court and steal a glance at the scoreboard. We are losing by two points, 47–49, with seven seconds on the clock. I wave in Dallas. He races over and sets a pick on my defender, but as I try to drive, both defenders collapse on me. I throw a behind-the-back bounce pass to Dallas, who is waiting, hands ready. He shoots a smooth three-point shot . . . his rotation looks perfect . . . the arc is high. The buzzer blares. The shot swishes through. Our crowd roars. I grab Dallas in a half hug. I say, "Good shit, bro. Good shit!"

"I knew you were going to find me," Dallas says. "I was ready."

More than ten thousand Native people jump up and down,

clap, hoot and holler, whistle, and yell. Target Center feels like it's shaking.

We jog to the locker room.

The starters hunch in our chairs, towels draped over us as we sip water. Coach takes a seat in front of us.

"Proud of you boys. I don't know if I have told you that enough, or ever. But I am. I've been coaching since before you were born, and I've never been more proud of a team. You guys have the talent, but over the years, a lot of my teams had talent and didn't get this far. You guys have guts, you have heart, and you care about each other. That's winning. In a way, we've already won."

Toweling sweat from our eyes, we nod in appreciation.

Mason clears his throat. "Thanks, Coach. Proud of you, too. You're the best. We're lucky to have you."

Coach gives Mason a confused look. "You need to borrow some money or something?" The joke breaks the tension.

Mason says, "Christ. See, this is why I never say nice things."

Ready for the second half, I stand to stretch my legs.

"You guys doing okay?" Coach asks. He gets up, grabs his clipboard, then comes back over. "That center they got, I've never seen anything like him before. He looks like an NBA player already. Sucks that we have to meet him in our very first state game. But I've got a plan to slow him down. He's beating you single-handed. Let's make *his team* beat us."

Coach starts talking fast and frantic. He's drawing up what he wants us to do different on defense. He points out the angles that

Jacob Griffin has been taking, and then shows us where the help defense is at. "Kevin, I know you're outsized, and outmatched, but keep grinding, keep fighting. Your teammates are going to be there to help."

At the beginning of the second half, it's our ball. Fans are still taking their seats from their halftime. The gym is quieter. We hear clapping and people yelling out, "Go, Red Lake!"

Dallas inbounds the ball to me, but Jacob intercepts the pass and rushes down the court. I try to catch up to him, but he's as fast as I am. He throws down a windmill dunk, then winks at me. I bring the ball up the court, call out a play, and pass the ball over to Robert, who shoots a three, but it misses. Kevin tries to battle Jacob for the ball, but it looks like a kid battling Godzilla. Jacob brings the ball up the court like he's a point guard. He pulls up from NBA range, and the ball swishes in. We brick our next couple of shots, and meanwhile, Jacob cannot miss. He hits two more three-pointers. Coach calls a time-out.

The Crestview starters are jumping around in celebration, waving to their fans. Their bench and their small crowd of supporters, clumped together in the corner of the arena, chant at us, "Overrated, overrated, overrated!"

My entire life, I've watched Red Lake lose games just like this. Hanging in for a while against a great team, and then the floodgates open up. A couple of bad shots or turnovers, a couple of good shots from the other team, and the lead balloons. The game is over before the final buzzer. We're down ten, 50–60. We might be done for.

As I walk to our bench, someone lifts my chin up. Mason, his expression reminding me of Jaxon's. "Tre. Don't get down, bro. We're still in this. When you get back out there, match his bitch ass shot for shot. We can't stop him, but they can't stop you either. You're just as good as that dude. Shit, better. And you know me, out of all people, wouldn't bullshit you."

During the time-out, Coach tells us to go into a box and one, meaning four of us will play in designated zones, and Kevin will stay on Jacob. "Just trying to mix it up. We have to keep trying things until we figure this guy out."

Dallas inbounds the ball to me. I'm several feet beyond the three-point line so my defender isn't quite up on me. This is my range. I fire up a shot that swishes in. Dallas intercepts a pass and gets me the ball. Racing ahead, it's me and two Crestview players crossing half-court. They speed in front of me, assuming on a fast break that I'd take the ball to the basket. But I stop on a dime. One of the defenders runs at me, more aggressive, with a hand up. But it's too late. I shoot a three. *Swish!*

Crestview calls a time-out.

Now we're only down by four, 56–60.

The momentum is ours.

Nate's voice cuts through the cheers. "Tre! You're on fire! Keep lighting them the fuck up." Our fans are on their feet. Yelling, high-fiving.

As we walk to the bench, Dallas waves his arms for them to get louder. They do. Their energy fuels me. Makes me invincible.

"That's what's up, Tre." Mason gives me a super-tight hug. "That's what's up. I told you! You're in the zone now, bro." My other teammates dap me up, high-five me, hug me. I need to stay in this mental space.

Coach is talking. The defensive scheme he's drawing on his clipboard, I have it memorized. *Stay in the zone, Tre. Stay in the zone.*

I don't hear the buzzer signaling the end of our time-out. My teammates get out of their seats, and Crestview is back on the floor. I wipe my forehead with a towel and drop it.

Crestview inbounds the ball to Jacob. He brings it up the court and holds his hand in a fist, signaling a play. Kevin is on him, waving his arms around, moving his feet, doing his best to slow down Jacob. Jacob passes to a teammate on the wing. Robert swipes at the ball, knocking it loose. Dallas dives on the floor and taps it to Kevin. I sprint up the floor. Jacob is already rushing back on defense to protect the basket.

Kevin doesn't even take a dribble. He looks for me. We make eye contact for a second and he throws a hard, fast pass up ahead, anticipating where I'll be so I don't have to lose speed to catch the ball. Did Kevin throw it too far ahead? I push myself faster, burning energy. Each play matters. My fingertips touch the ball, and I'm able to twist it into a dribble motion. Jacob keeps up. We sprint toward the basket. I get a step past the free-throw line and rise with the ball gripped tight in my right hand, my left elbow out. Jacob leaps, too. His arms stretch forever like Mr. Fantastic. He swats at the ball. But I'm higher. The ball is out of his reach. His hand slaps my forearm. He crashes into me, changing my momentum, shifting my angle. I adjust. Twisting and contorting my body, I throw down a nasty dunk right in his grill.

Bam!

A whistle. A referee calls a foul on Jacob.

"And one!" I scream to the ceiling.

Our fans are a blur of noise and motion. I point to my parents and pound a fist over my heart. I hit my free throw. 59–60. We're back in it now.

Crestview's coach yells at them to take care of the ball. They're playing wild defense.

"Red-Lake. War-riors!" The chant echoes like an ancient ritual.

For the next few minutes, we exchange baskets like heavyweight boxers exchanging blows. We hit one. They hit one. When the third quarter ends, the game is tied up, 72–72.

Starting the fourth, I tap Kevin's chest. "Aye, I'm going to guard Jacob," I say.

Kevin shakes his head. "No. You'll use all your energy. Save it for the offensive end."

"I can stop him," I say.

"Okay. I trust you. Good luck, bro," Kevin says.

Crestview inbounds the ball to Jacob. But this time he's mine. I pick him up, full court. Every direction he goes, I'm already there. Low to the ground, shuffling my feet, stealing his angles. I'm making him work for every inch.

When we cross half-court, he yells out, "Isolation!" and waves off his teammates.

Dribbling, he tells me, "Mismatch right here."

"It *is* a mismatch. But not in your favor." I swipe at the ball.

Jacob starts a crossover dribble. But I've been watching him. I already know what he's about to do because right before, he brings the ball out high and wide. I watch the ball go up on his right side. Right when it's about to bounce, I knock it away. Dallas gives chase. Kevin is up the court already. Dallas corrals the loose ball, passing it to Kevin, who throws down a nasty two-handed jam. Kevin screams when he lands and pounds his chest. Our fans eat it up.

I stay on Jacob. Full court. In his face. Forcing him to pass. Making it impossible for him to get to his spots. And it's working. He gives the ball up to a teammate who turns the ball over. We get another fast-break bucket.

We're up. 76–72. Four minutes to go.

We might win this thing after all.

As I bring the ball up the court, Crestview's coach yells at Jacob to guard me.

Jacob leaves Kevin and meets me at half-court. He's reaching for the ball, trying to steal it. I dribble between my legs, behind my back. I call out, "44–2!" and throw the ball to Dallas on the wing. I run near the rim. Kevin sets a pick, then Robert sets one. They free me up enough. Jacob is at least a foot or two behind me. Dallas hits me with a perfect pass at the free-throw line. The lane looks open. I go up for a layup. Jacob catches up and jumps to block my shot. He slams into me, but I don't hear a whistle. I lose control in the air, throw the shot up.

My left foot lands on someone's foot and I feel a pop, a crunch. The pain blacks me out for a second. My ankle turns so far that, though my leg is straight down, I catch a glimpse of the sole of my shoe.

I scream and fall to the floor. My hands wrap around my ankle as tight as I can squeeze it. The pain. *The pain.* It spreads through my body. Takes over.

Dallas rushes over and kneels next to me. "Tre? Tre? Are you okay?"

Before I can answer, a couple of physical therapists are instructing me to lie down, to take a deep breath. They're assuring me that I'm all right. They're lying.

"You probably sprained your ankle. Possibly broke it. We won't know until you get an X-ray," one of them finally admits.

"Come on, let's get you off the floor and put some ice on that." They help me sit up, lift me up slowly. "Don't put any pressure on it. Step with your right foot. We've got you." The crowd applauds when I stand, but it's a somber noise. Like a celebration of life at a funeral.

The therapists help me limp to our bench. Mom is crying, praying. Dad looks like someone just punched him in the gut. Hurts to see them grieving again.

Coach comes over. "You're going to be okay, Tre. I've done that a few times myself. Hurts like hell, doesn't it?" I squeeze my ankle, shut my eyes. He adds, "They're going to go and grab you some ice.

You'll want to get that foot up on a chair, keep it elevated. That'll help keep it from swelling as bad. Once you take that shoe off, it's going to blow up. But you'll be okay. That was a hell of a run. You got two more seasons ahead of you. Can't believe they didn't call a foul on that shit." Coach walks over to the scorers' table.

A trainer hands me an ice pack. Dallas sets a hand on my shoulder. Mason puts his arm around me. Kevin, he's just there. There are no words for any of us.

The buzzer blares, and the refs wave both teams onto the court.

My Warriors run a play, pass the ball around, then force up a bad shot. Crestview is fired up; they smell blood in the water. Their passes are sharp, crisp. They run a play to perfection until they get a layup. Crestview goes on a six-point run.

Over the PA, the announcer barks, "Crestview scores! Crestview scores! Crestview scores!" It's like he's tossing dirt on our graves.

It's 76–78. Three minutes left in the game, we're only down two. But it feels like a sinking ship. Our crowd is quiet, occasionally bitching at the referees.

Crestview swings the ball around, taking their time on offense. They control the game. They just need to kill time. Warriors rush after each pass, trying their hardest to get a steal, to get a stop. After a series of passes and screens, Crestview gets a layup.

76–80, two minutes left.

Kevin goes at Jacob. He drives hard to the basket, pump fakes a couple of times, then gets rejected.

Crestview gets a fast-break layup. 76–82.

Ninety seconds.

I have to do something. Captain America never stops. Batman doesn't quit. Superman would die trying. Jaxon. Jaxon would play if he were injured. I pull the laces loose on my left shoe, then tie them back as tight as I can like a tourniquet. I try to stand, but almost collapse. I limp over to Coach.

"Sub me in."

"You can't play with an injury like that. You could mess up your ankle forever. You got a bright future ahead."

"So did Jaxon." Yeah, I went there. I had to. "This is the best chance we've ever had at winning state. We might never be this close again. Please. Sub me in. There's only ninety seconds left. I won't be out there long."

Coach shakes his head and points to the scorers' table.

As I do my best not to limp, not to wince, the referee waves me in.

Our crowd stands, silent. A couple people shout, "Let's go, Tre."

I sub in. It's our ball. "Keep running point guard, Mason," I say, knowing there's no way I can move as much as that position would require.

I inbound it to Mason and limp quickly to the corner, only able to put weight on my right foot, almost hopping instead of running. My left foot barely touches the court; any time it presses to the floor the pain grabs ahold of me.

Mason passes it inside to Kevin, who is posted up. Kevin fakes left, spins right, and tries to drive. His legs get twisted with Jacob, and he loses control of the ball. Mason dives on the court into a cluster of Crestview players.

Mason gets the ball and looks at me. I'm behind the three-point line, helpless. From the floor, Mason throws a sharp, one-handed baseball pass my way. On instinct, I catch and shoot a three-pointer. *Swish!*

Our crowd explodes with hope. The building vibrates.

"*Let's go!*" Dallas yells, throwing up his arms.

79–82. We're still down by three with forty-three seconds left on the clock.

I hobble down the court, guarding a Crestview forward who hasn't shown me any offensive skills yet. Crestview's coach yells at his players to go at me.

They pass it to the guy I'm guarding. We're on the wing, about twenty feet from the basket. I give him space. If he drives at me, I'm toast. Especially if he goes to my left.

Coach yells, "Thirty seconds."

I'm hoping this guy can't shoot from deep. He hasn't taken a three yet. Holding the ball, he checks the clock. Unless I guard him closely, he can stay there, using up the clock.

From behind me, Dallas yells, "Twenty seconds left. I got your back, Tre. Go after him."

I limp toward my opponent to force the action. The Crestview forward drives to his right, my left. I move too slow, and he blows by me. Dallas leaves his guy, jumps in the way, stands his ground, and gets knocked over.

There's a whistle. The gym goes silent.

A referee points in the direction of our hoop. "Charging foul!"

79–82, fifteen seconds remain.

"Take it," I tell Mason. "Just make sure we get a three." I hobble up the court.

Mason dribbles the ball out near half-court. Surveying the floor. Using his experience as a lifelong point guard. Our crowd chants the countdown. "Ten. Nine."

Mason calls out a play, and we move into place. Mason passes the ball to Dallas on the wing and sprints to the rim. Kevin sets a pick for him. I set a second screen and stop his defender dead. Mason runs to the top of the key. Dallas passes it to him, and Mason lets it fly.

"Seven. Six."

The ball rattles around the rim, popping up, down, spinning. It slips out.

Kevin battles with Jacob for position. Nudging, pushing, leaning. Kevin gets up before Jacob, but Kevin can only get one hand on the ball and bat it backward. Dallas jumps up in between two Crestview players, grabs the ball, and throws it to me while he's still in midair.

"Four. Three."

The ball is in my hands. It's like a dream. The seams and grooves of the ball run parallel just above my fingertips. Jacob sprints toward me. He leaps into the air. Arm outstretched.

I tuck my elbow, bend my knees, and jump to shoot.

I'm reminded of what it was like before my growth spurt when I played against Jaxon. He was way taller than me. It was impossible to shoot over him. He'd always block my shot. Until I adjusted and learned how to launch a higher arc to get it up and over him.

Jacob crashes into me, and I'm on the floor. A referee blows a whistle.

I wince as I hit the court. The ball is spinning, high in the air.

Come on. Come on. Please.

The ball descends, spinning, sinking.

Swish!

Yes! Dallas, Mason, and the guys run over, help me up to my feet.

Mason throws his arms around me. "Clutch, bro. That was clutch as fuck."

A referee announces, "Shooting foul on Griffin. Basket is good. One free throw for Brun."

Dallas gives me a double fist bump. "You got this."

82–82. Two seconds left on the clock.

I limp to the free-throw line. If I make this, no overtime. I can give us a one-point win.

Players line up along the paint. A hush falls over our crowd. The Crestview fans are in the corner near the basket. They whistle, stomp, wave their arms. Some people pretend to choke themselves. "Miss it!" they scream. "Miss it!"

The referee hands me the ball. "One shot." He holds up one finger, puts his whistle in his mouth, and backs out of sight.

Dad shouts, "Just like you're at home, Tre! Sunday-morning free throws. Shoot it like you're at home."

Dribble. Dribble. Dribble.

Deep breath in. Spin the ball in my hands.

Exhale. Bend my elbow. Focus. Imagine the shot going in.

I shoot.

Nothing but net.

I point over at Dad.

83–82. Two seconds left.

Crestview calls their last time-out.

We huddle. Coach says, "They're going to need to pass it the length of the court. Everyone get all the way back. Dallas, Kevin, you two get near Griffin. Except Tre, you get in front of the guy inbounding. Wave those long arms, make it hard for him to see. It's going to be a high, long pass. No fouls. Whatever you guys do, no fouls. All we need is this one stop."

We return to the court. Behind me, a couple of the Crestview guys are getting ready to set screens. A referee hands the ball to the Crestview player. I wave my arms, so my hands are in the way. My ankle is worse. Tighter.

The Crestview player cocks his arm and throws a football-style pass high into the air. The clock doesn't start until someone touches it.

One Crestview player sets a screen for Jacob. Another gets tangled up with Dallas. Jacob runs toward the ball. He catches it and, in the air, turns back toward the rim. He lets go of a fadeaway jumper that's way beyond the three-point line. It's too tough a shot. Impossible. We got this. Oh, please let us have this. The ball spins toward the rim as the buzzer sounds.

Swish.

With a huge smile, Jacob throws his arms into the air and runs down the court. His team chases after him, celebrating.

I fall to my knees. Fuck. No.

After all that.

I can't breathe.

Mason is hiding his face with his jersey. Dallas is lying on the floor. Kevin's head is hanging. I let them down. I'll never get to play with my heroes again. They'll never wear a Warrior jersey again. They didn't win state. We didn't win state.

I fight to stand and hobble to my teammates. "Mason. I'm sorry. I could have—"

"Red-Lake. War-riors! Red-Lake. War-riors!" Our fans, our family, our community—they don't let up. They keep chanting. They keep cheering.

Dallas gives me a hug and then shakes my hand, grinning through his tears. "Almost, bro. Fucking almost. That was fun, though, wasn't it?"

When I can finally talk, I tell Mason, "I'm sorry. I wanted to win so fucking bad. I wanted to win it with you guys. Finish what my brother started. But I failed, I—"

Mason isn't hearing it. "It's okay, little bro. That was a hell of a ride. Was a pleasure playing with you. Wish we could have won it all, but damn, look at this." He gestures at our fans, at the Timberwolves' home court, at the TV cameras. "We'll have this memory forever. Nobody can take it away from us. This is special. We are fucking special."

CHAPTER 42

MAY 25

KHIANA IS CARRYING a box to her mom's car.

"Need help?" I ask.

"I've got it," she says, wiping some sweat from her brow. "What's up?"

"I wanted to stop by before you left. Felt weird to not to say goodbye in person. And I wanted to say sorry." I gaze at the lake, fishing for the right words. "For everything."

"Yeah. You were kind of a dick there for a while."

"I really was. I. Am. Sorry. I suck at the whole platonic *friendable* thing."

Khiana reaches out. "Apology accepted."

"What are you, running for chairwoman or something?"

"Shut up." Our smiles heal the last of the hurt.

"That was a hell of a game you played in the state tournament. I don't know that much about basketball, but you were killing it out there."

The memories hit me like a gut punch. "Thanks. Wish we would have won."

"Hey. You have a couple more shots at it," Khiana replies. "You'll get them next time. How's that ankle?"

I force a smile. "It's okay. Little sore. But it's not swollen or bruised anymore. So, you're off to Los Angeles, huh?"

Khiana shrugs. "Yup. My mom is road-tripping with me. Who knows, maybe I'll make it big out there. Maybe I'll fail and come back. But I'm going to give it a go."

"Have you talked to Wes lately?" Even though he knows I eventually was chill about them, it's still a little awkward. He really never talks to me about Khiana.

"No, just a text here and there. Once I committed to moving, we chilled on spending time together. We're good, though. Who knows? Maybe he'll follow me out there someday."

I make a note to myself to check in on Wes. He's all heart, and Khiana might've broken his more than she realizes.

"I hope he does."

"Same. Give me a hug, you big dummy."

"Aye, it's Tre Brun," a Native dude with gray braids in an AIM shirt says. "Let this man up to the front." The other customers good-naturedly shuffle aside.

"Oh, no. That's okay, man. I can wait back here."

"You don't get too many years like this in your life. Come on up. Tough luck in the state tourney. Proud of you boys for getting there, though. Next year."

"Thanks, man," I say. "It was a good run."

Me, Nate, and Wes walk to the front of the line. "Next year is right," Nate says to me. "I'm going to be catching bodies every game."

"Yeah, I know. I know." I talk like I'm tired as hell of hearing it. But honestly, I can't wait to hoop alongside my boy next year. Nate killed it this last season on JV. Should've gotten more attention for it. I'm going to start talking him up more.

A few minutes later, a mall security guard opens the door. We all rush to the bookstore, to the magazine rack.

"Aye, look," Nate says. "Your little crush is working. If you were ever going to talk to her, today's the day. What's her name again?"

"Sam. Her name is Sam."

"Damn, you still remember that?" Nate asks.

"Shush."

Sam has a confused look on her face at the sight of the flood of customers coming in right when the store opens.

I wave. Because I stay awkward.

She waves back. Her undercut has freshly shaved lines in the side.

My eyes shift around at gossip and news magazines. I see Jennifer Lawrence, Brad Pitt, Kylie Jenner, Drake. And that's when I see it. LeBron James.

Slam magazine.

I open it up, thumbing through the pages. Wait, that's me, flying through the air, the ball cuffed as I went in for the windmill dunk.

A guy in a POW ball cap says, "Holy fuck, that's ace!"

"Hey, will you sign a copy for me?" someone asks.

"Yeah, will you sign mine, too?" chimes in another voice.

I grab a handful of copies. In no time, they're sold out.

"Aye, do you have any more of these?" an Elder asks Sam.

"Umm . . . no. That's all that came in. I opened the box of new magazine deliveries this morning."

I place my stack on the counter, staring at LeBron.

Ringing me up, Sam asks, "What's the big deal with this magazine anyway? Why's everyone buying multiples?"

Wes points to me. "He's in it with the rest of the Red Lake Warriors basketball team."

"Wow, really?" she asks, wide-eyed. "Now I wish I had an extra. I want a signed copy. No one from around here is ever in a magazine."

"You can have one of mine," I say.

"No. I couldn't."

"Nah, it's cool. I insist."

"Will you sign it for me?"

"Sure," I say with a sheepish grin.

Sam hands me a Sharpie. "I think this is the first time I've ever seen you buy something other than a comic book."

Damn. She remembered that? It's been months since the last time I was in the store.

Nate elbows me as I autograph her copy. "He wants to know if you'd like to go out with him sometime."

Holding up a hand, I say, "I've got this." Which sounded spot-on, but then my mind goes blank. "Uh, would you like to go out with me sometime?"

Sam blushes. "Sure. That sounds like fun. Add me on social. My handle is the same on everything and it's easy to remember. It's @GreeneggsandSam17171717."

I punch it into my phone and hear her phone ding. My face feels flushed. "Cool."

"Tre, will you sign my copy?" asks a little boy with long black hair.

"Mine too," adds a girl about his age.

I sign every copy handed to me and then we bounce.

There isn't a cloud in the sky and the sun is shining. Perfect weather for outdoor basketball.

We spend time warming up, shooting jump shots, dribbling around, driving in for lazy layups. Every so often, someone will pretend like they're in a game and bust out a little crossover or spin move at half the average game speed. Every so often, it's like I catch a glimpse of Jaxon, hooping with us. He might be buried across the street, but it's here on the ball court that his memory lives on.

"Twenty-one, then." Nate throws the ball to me. The shot swishes in.

It's not state. It's a game of twenty-one with my two best friends.

I miss my first free throw and Nate grabs the board. Dribbling, he says, "About to take a dude who's in *Slam* magazine right to school."

"Psshh . . ." I wave at him to bring it on.

We disappear into the music and poetry of the game. A fadeaway jumper here, a flashy crossover there, a blinding spin move, a double pump reverse layup. Nothing but highlight reels and fun. Because we're playing rez ball.

AUTHOR'S NOTE

THE FIRST TIME I put on a Red Lake Warriors basketball uniform, I wasn't playing the same game that I had been playing on the dirt court with a hoop nailed to a pine tree in my parents' yard. I was going to war. It took place in gymnasiums packed mainly with people from my reservation. They were passionate, feverish fans, to say the least.

The game I had been playing for fun had changed, and now had an intense, us-against-the-world mentality. We played against almost exclusively all-white teams from communities that had historically not been on the best of terms with our people. That divide, that history, made every game feel almost life or death.

Not only were the games intense, but my life off the court changed dramatically. I had always felt like an outsider. I was never cool or popular. I was the quiet, shy kid. Sometimes I even got singled out for being a teacher's pet or being light-skinned or being a nerd. My freshman year I played on the JV team. The varsity team that season was the first ever in our school's history to make it to the state tournament. They went on to play in what is still referred to by many as the most exciting game in Minnesota state tournament history, coming back fast from a nineteen-point deficit in a matter of minutes to force overtime. The next season they returned almost the same exact team. Plus, me.

I had never played a meaningful game of basketball. Before the season even started, our team was ranked number one in the state, with the expectation that we would likely win the state championship. In my second varsity game, I grabbed nineteen rebounds, cementing my starting spot on the team and changing my life. From that game on, I was signing autographs, being asked to take pictures with fans, and being invited to parties. I went from being unable to get a date to a school dance to being considered one of the "cool kids" at school.

Even my own dad treated me differently. I knew somewhere deep down he loved me, but once I put on that Warriors jersey, it was like he saw me for the first time. I became someone his friends admired. I was what he had aspired to be.

We won the majority of our games, often dominating teams. We appeared in *USA Today* and on ESPN, played in a nationally televised game, and were featured in *Slam* magazine. It felt like being a rock star. It was exciting, surreal, and seemed like the experience would never end. For the three seasons I played, we came damn close but never did win the state championship.

Rez Ball is filled with a lot of experiences of my time as a Warrior. Some of them are amalgamations of stories and situations, mashed together and fictionalized for the sake of the story.

Thoughts that ran through my mind during a game, the passionate basketball fan base on my reservation, the characters, and scenes showing moments on the court and at after-parties were inspired by my sophomore year of high school.

Speaking of which, I exercised my artistic license to turn back the clock on the structure of the Minnesota state play-offs. At one point, every school in the state had to battle one another for a shot at the state championship. Small farm towns had to play against bigger city schools, with the city schools winning most of the time. Today that's been reenvisioned and divided into classes based on school size.

As I was writing *Rez Ball*, it grew to be more than a basketball story. I found layers beyond the court. I felt compelled to share the social, racial, and economic differences between Bemidji and my reservation. Those nuances are as much a part of this story as the games on the court.

From a storytelling perspective, it made the most sense for those two communities to face each other on the court for some of the biggest games.

That said, there are a lot of open-minded, loving, caring people in Bemidji, as well as in the surrounding white farm towns. During high school, I had non-Native friends in almost every white school near ours. My high school girlfriend was from one of those communities. Her family and friends welcomed me with open arms. So, there are nuances to the relationships between my rez and the non-Native towns around them.

However, there is a lot of hatred and racism as well. I once received a death threat while in high school, warning me to stay on the reservation. I've been harassed by a white state trooper in Bemidji who told me he knew all about people from Red Lake and insisted I had drugs on me. I've had security follow me and my Native friends around stores like we were going to steal something.

One of my intentions with this story was to share the added pressure of being a Native high school athlete. For me, it felt like my team winning state would have somehow changed things for the better for my rez. The local narrative at the time became this pie-in-the-sky notion saying that if we could somehow win state, our community would have more hope than before and that younger kids would be inspired. It was a lot to live up to as a teenager.

Meanwhile, many student athletes from my reservation struggle to maintain their grades and their focus on sports while dealing with the loss of a loved one. It's not unusual for us to lose someone close to us before or during high school.

So, again, *Rez Ball* was my attempt at showing the divide and the unique challenges kids from my rez face while trying to keep up with nearby white student athletes.

To Native athletes: This is just the start. For the longest time, we had one or two Indigenous athletes to look up to. Now there are so many incredible Native athletes who have played college ball, as well as those who made the leap to the pros.

It is harder for us. We do have more challenges and struggles to overcome. But it is possible. At the same time, sports are only one aspect of who we are. Learn as much as you can in school; make the most of your education. Being disciplined in school and in sports can take you where you want to go in your life.

To the youth of Red Lake: Keep your heads up; keep your dreams alive. Have fun. Be grateful for what we do have, but don't be afraid to go after more.

You have always been my purpose for writing, my reason to keep going. I always want you all to know that you can do anything you want to.

I went to the same school. I'm from the same place. I thought I had zero business being an author. I scratched, clawed, and fought for every lesson learned and every step taken. I did it. I wanted to show you that you could, too. But also, I couldn't have done it without you.

Miigwech and much love.

OJIBWE GLOSSARY

Boozhoo (boo-jhew): greetings!; hello!

Miigwech (mee-gwech): thank you

Niij (nee-j): my fellow

Ma'iingan (muh-een-gun): timber wolf / gray wolf

Migizi (mi-gi-zee): bald eagle

ACKNOWLEDGMENTS

My heart is filled with an unbelievable amount of gratitude to everyone who had a part in making my debut novel. The support of so many friends, family members, people from my reservation, and established authors all helped carry me over the last ten years. I'll never be able to fully express the depth of my gratitude.

About a decade ago I decided to become an author, with no clue where to begin. Even back then, my family supported and championed my creative endeavors. Miigwech to my mother, Victoria, for letting me cowrite our bedtime stories and always nurturing my creative side. My sister, Serena, you have always loved and promoted everything I ever wrote. I have felt like a rock star since the Myspace days thanks to your posts. Thanks to my siblings Liz, Tara, and Matt for loving me unconditionally and cheering me on. To my amazing nieces, nephews, cousins, aunts, and uncles, I love you. This book couldn't have happened without all of you.

My patient and supportive partner, Gina. Whenever the bat signal hits the sky, you always have my energy drink and utility belt ready to go. Thanks for being the best teammate I could ask for. You the real MVP. Love you.

Thank you to my lifelong friends Dalton Walker and Dustin Harris. Your support has meant everything. I'm so glad we survived those Rainy River days.

To my loving and supportive agent, Terrie Wolf, you were the first in the industry to give me a shot. I'll never forget our first phone call. You told me you saw something special in me, in my writing, and in my message. You believed the world needed to read my work. You fought for me and never gave up. Thank you for helping me fulfill my dreams.

The support and camaraderie of so many authors made me feel like I had a seat at the table. Rachael Allen, thank you for your mentorship. You taught me how to write. You taught me how to get through the most challenging stages of writing a book. There would be no *Rez Ball* without your undying support and friendship.

Kosoko Jackson, Cam Montgomery, Rebecca Roanhorse, Traci Sorell, Stacy Wells, AJ Eversole, Jen Ferguson, and countless other author friends, thank you for always being there. Thanks for assisting with edits and for the support along the way. Rest in peace, Louise Gornall. You were the rumored Pink Power Ranger, one of my favorite authors, and always lifted me up and helped me out with writing critiques.

Special thank-you to Natasha Donovan for creating the beautiful cover artwork for *Rez Ball*, and to the entire creative team that assisted with bringing the artwork and design together. I'm so appreciative. Thank you to the editors, copyeditors, and everyone else at Heartdrum and HarperCollins who had a helping hand in bringing *Rez Ball* to the world.

Special thank-you to Cynthia Leitich Smith for carving paths and lighting the way. You understood my vision for *Rez Ball* in a way that no one else possibly could have. Thank you for your tireless work, for your belief in my writing, and for teaching me so much. You helped me sharpen and polish this book until it became what I had intended it to be.

Rosemary Brosnan, thank you for your support, for the laughs, for sharing your knowledge, and for helping me get this book out into the world. I cannot wait to write the next one with you.

Lastly, miigwech to everyone who has ever suited up in a Red Lake Warrior jersey and to everyone who has traveled the snowy winter roads of northern Minnesota to cheer on the team. You're all my family. You're all my teammates. I hope you see a part of yourself in this book. Red Lake, this is for you!

A NOTE FROM
CYNTHIA LEITICH SMITH,
HEARTDRUM AUTHOR-CURATOR

DEAR READER,

What a season! Did you cheer along with the Red Lake fans? I sure did. I teared up, too, sharing Tre's grief for his big brother. It probably comes as no surprise that this novel, by author Byron Graves, is inspired by his own real-life experiences playing for the Warriors.

High school is different for everyone, even those in the same community. Maybe you've never suited up for an Ojibwe rez team, but you've had to deal with bigotry against Indigenous people. Maybe you've never lost an older sibling, but you understand what it means to mourn a loved one. Or maybe Tre's journey felt like an echo of your own.

The highest highs, the lowest lows, the toughest choices. We all feel overwhelmed at times. Our world spins like a basketball, for worse or better, and sometimes we struggle to hope and hold fast to the truth of our hearts. It can help to talk to a trusted friend, a family member, or an Elder. Or maybe there's a counselor, teacher, or coach you can confide in.

Curling up with a story like this one is good medicine, too. Have you read other books by and about Ojibwe people? Hopefully *Rez Ball* will inspire you to read more. The novel is published by Heartdrum, a Native-focused imprint of HarperCollins, which offers stories about young Native heroes by Indigenous authors and illustrators.

We wish you slam dunks—loyal friends, loving kin, the courage to go after your dreams, and the strength to persevere. We're rooting for you.

Mvto,

Cynthia Leitich Smith

IN 2014, We Need Diverse Books (WNDB) began as a simple hashtag on Twitter. The social media campaign soon grew into a 501(c)(3) nonprofit with a team that spans the globe. WNDB is supported by a network of writers, illustrators, agents, editors, teachers, librarians, and book lovers, all united under the same goal—to create a world where every child can see themselves in the pages of a book. You can learn more about WNDB programs at www.diversebooks.org.